# We Leave The Flowers
# Where They Are

**Trigger Warning:**
These stories are the real-life experiences of women in Montana, and often contain graphic descriptions. Please proceed with caution.

Cover photo by Gregory Hanrahan
www.greghanrahan.com/Instagram
@gregoryhanrahancreative

"Familiar Flowers of North America," by Marylor Wilson, appears in her upcoming collection *Summer Lightning*, published by Drumlummon Press.

"Not The Women Frida Slept With," by Emily Withnall, first appeared in the *Indiana Review*.

A version of "Zoetrope: A Drinking Memoir" by Sharma Shields, first appeared in *The Inlander*.

ISBN: 978-0-578-52987-5

Layout & Design: word west
hello@wordwest.co
www.wordwest.co

Printed by Sweetgrass Books in Helena, Montana, USA.

## Familiar Flowers of North America
### Marylor Wilson

❈

In dark winter, a sun-blazed snapshot of two Wood's roses
pitched me onto a noon-hot trail:
its shroud of fevered bloom and rot,
the scorching scent of tightly woven forest life,
the roses' scarlet petals and inflamed yellow stamens.
Wood's roses are the untamed ancestors
of costly wedding bouquets and funeral sprays.
You could say they're vain
the way they thrust themselves at the camera.

When I was five, I feared nothing in the forest,
never too hot for me, or cold.
My eyes were for every flower and every bud.
I cruised those wild paths on hands and knees,
hidden in plain sight, like I-Spy.
Our family rule was, "**We leave the flowers where they are,**"
but it was okay to collect the little tokens:
cones, bones, feathers, berries,
a rock shaped like a bird
or a loaf of bread
or a wizard's hat.

The glint of mica lured me most.
I thought
its glitter
*could be God.*


*Jefferson Street*
*Missoula*
*2014*

## Number One
### Dolly Browder

When the phone rings in the middle of the night, I turn on a small light, and it wakes my husband. It is just after two in the morning. He turns over in the bed, accustomed to these late night calls. Sarah is in labor, and I must go to work. After years as a midwife, the rush of an impending birth jolts me awake, and I move quickly, a familiar routine, but still exciting every time.

I have three bags that are always packed. A midwife must be ready at a moment's notice. After every birth, these bags are sterilized, and repacked. Birth has a clock of its own. In the black bag: A blood pressure cuff, stethoscope, Doppler, gloves, 4 x 4 pads, reflex hammer, measuring tape, extension cord, three prong plug, flash light, and extra batteries. In the blue canvas bag: More gloves, alcohol pads, space blanket, two pairs of scissors, umbilical clamps, tweezers, suturing kit, scissors, needle nose clamp, lidocaine, a scale, a sling, liquid Vitamin K, a smaller stethoscope for the baby, lab requisition forms, olive oil, enema kit. In the green canvas bag: Two oxygen tanks with flow meters, 12 x 18 inch blue pads, three oxygen masks for adults, three oxygen masks for newborns, tubing, newborn resuscitation masks in three sizes, and two heating pads.

I rush to my car in the middle of the night. It is May of 1988. I have been a midwife for eleven years, and have delivered over three hundred babies. I drive into the darkness with my three bags. I am ready.

Sarah and Michael Cobb own a cattle ranch outside of Augusta, but they have relocated to Missoula during the final month of her pregnancy. It is a cool morning, and I enter the house quietly, without knocking. I carry my bags toward the sound in the back of the house. Sarah is moaning, but stops when I enter.

"Hi," she says, giving me a big smile. "So glad to see you."

The contractions are strong, and coming close, and our greeting is interrupted as she squirms on the bed, in the throes of a powerful pain. Mike rubs her back with large, calloused hands. Sarah is a strong, tall woman, a life spent working on a cattle ranch.

After an hour, Sarah's contractions grow stronger. She moves into a warm bath, and as she begins to push, the baby's heart rate slows.

"Hands and knees may help," I suggest. After a slight improvement, the fetal heart rate slows again. As the heartbeat of the baby grows weaker, the faster my own heart pounds. I lean close and speak gently. "I think we need to go to the hospital, Sarah."

Sarah responds without hesitation. "Okay."

Mike is frantic. "Should we call an ambulance?"

"The car is faster," I announce. "You drive, and I'll help Sarah." I turn on the oxygen tank and place the mask over Sarah's face. Again, I listen to the baby's heart. Sarah has stopped pushing, and the heartbeat is encouraging.

The black Suburban pitches back and forth as Mike races to the hospital. The car stops in the emergency entrance, as Mike and I move quickly to help Sarah inside.

In the birthing room, a man stands by himself, in a ramrod stance, arms crossed over his chest. This is Dr. Marks, a new family physician, and tonight he is on call. He watches as the nurses help Sarah onto the bed. I watch as he listens to Sarah's heart, but ignores the sounds of the baby.

"Excuse me," I say. Dr. Marks looks up at me, disdain on his face. "It's the baby who isn't doing well. Please listen to the baby."

"Who are you?" His tone is condescending, harsh.

"Sarah's midwife."

Dr. Marks moves the fetal monitor, and the sound of a slow fetal heartbeat fills the room. He looks me straight in the eye as he makes his declaration. "She needs a cesarean."

***

Exhausted from the long night, I return home to a quiet house, and fall asleep as soon as my head hits the pillow.

Two hours later, the familiar ringing erupts beside my bed.

"Hello?"

"Dolly, this is Dr. Marks." Groggy, I am confused as to why he would be calling me, after barely acknowledging my existence hours earlier.

"Yes?"

"The police will be contacting you soon," he says, in his harsh voice.

I sit up in bed. I swallow hard. "What for?"

"I reported you," he says. "I let them know you are practicing illegally."

I struggle for a response, but he hangs up before I have the chance.

Wide-awake, tears begin to course down my face. Jail? I leap from my bed, and peer through the curtains, certain I will see police cars. None. Shaking, frightened, I call my husband at work. He calms me, instructs me to call John Whiston immediately. Thankfully, we are friends with a good lawyer.

On the phone with John, I catch my reflection in a small mirror in the kitchen. Redness has spread across my face, and dark circles rim my eyes. I do not recognize this woman. John does his best to ease my fears, but after I hang up, I immediately go back to the window, searching for signs of the police. I return to that window for the next two days, checking, watching, waiting.

John calls to inform me that Dr. Marks has gone further, and contacted the Montana Board of Medical Examiners. They have cited me for practicing medicine without a license.

A week later, John and I review the cease and desist order that arrives by mail. After I leave John's office, I return home, devastated. A friend

finds me in bed, in the fetal position, racked with sobs.

"You'll be fine," she promises, gently rubbing my back. "Many people in this town support you."

"It's not enough," I protest. "They are more powerful than us."

She climbs into bed with me, and holds me tight, just like a baby, small and vulnerable.

***

It feels like we are preparing for a war. All six feet, ten inches of John Whiston prepare me for what is to come. He pushes the cease and desist letter across the desk.

"What happens if I don't sign this?"

His face is grim. "The medical board will indict you."

Dread runs through me. I think of all the other midwives in Montana, my sisters. "I'm not signing," I say, and crumple up the letter into my fist.

"The order requires you to go to court and defend your case, or agree to quit practicing."

"Let's go to court," I say, clear-headed, determined.

On November 30th, I attend the hearing at District Court. John has informed me how to dress on the witness stand. Nothing flashy in color or design, and I chose a white sweater and black slacks. Judges like women with long hair, but I had just cut mine short.

John has coached me to take my time when I am being questioned, and I made notes, but they are crushed in my hands. As I climb the stairs of the Missoula courthouse, my heart pounds, and I follow John into the largest courtroom, chosen for my civil trial. When I enter, every seat is taken, and as I walk through the rows, I realize the crowd is filled with mothers and fathers and children, all of whom I assisted in birth. As I pass, a nursing mother offers encouragement. "Stay strong, my dear," she says, and I am filled with hope as I sit at the defendant's table.

I turn to examine the room, and see some familiar faces, forced to stand in the back, leaning against the walls. We are all in this together.

"Breathe," I say quietly to myself. "Breathe." This is how I help laboring mothers relax.

The bailiff enters from a side door, and we all rise for Judge Henson. He is a short man with a big stride, a pudgy face and balding head. As he sits down, I feel a slight breeze as the bailiff closes the door, and suddenly I am scared. It seems like a tiger has entered the room, and he raises his right hand and motions for us to sit. I cannot focus on the crumpled notes in my hand, am caught in the daydream of a tiger. I will not run. I will face it, stand as tall as I can, and will not look it in the eyes.

The plaintiff's lawyer is a petite woman, in a smart navy blue suit, and I can't help notice her long hair, pulled into a tight bun. She begins her opening statement. "We are here to confirm that Dolly Browder is practicing medicine without a license. We will show that her practice includes diagnosing during maternity care and we contend that she must stop practicing as an untrained, unlicensed layperson."

3

John rises from our table, and addresses the judge. "It is our belief that Dolly Browder is practicing midwifery, which is different from practicing medicine during a low-risk pregnancy and natural childbirth. She does not diagnose but enables an uncomplicated pregnancy to continue to a natural birth. Pregnancy and birth are not illnesses."

Testimony begins, and I endure Dr. Marks while he disparages me, and all my sister midwives. "All home birth midwives need to be stopped."

The next witness is an obstetrician, a woman who I have tangled with in the past, during births at our local hospital. She shouted at me, she pointed at the door and demanded that I leave, while my home birth mother cowered in the hospital bed.

The fear returns, but I suddenly notice a mural behind the bench. It's an unexpected solace, an enormous painting of two blindfolded women, draped in soft white clothing, each balancing the scales of justice. I think of my predecessors, all of the midwives throughout history. I try not to think about the ones that were burned at the stake. I hope for a much better outcome.

The obstetrician is adamant. "I can say with professional certainty that home birth is extremely dangerous to the baby's well-being and life-threatening to the mother. The only place to give birth is in the hospital, under the care of an obstetrician."

John stands again to cross-examine her. "Would you agree that childbirth is not an illness?"

She takes her time, and carefully considers her response. "It is not an illness by common understanding. But a pregnant woman's condition can change to a dangerous illness at any time."

When John calls me to the stand, I stare out at the audience. I notice a little girl, and realize she is my daughter's best friend. She sits next to her mother, who smiles at me, and lifts up her knitting in a kind of salute. The little girl waves a coloring book. I can do this.

John stands before me, and nods, another reassurance before he begins. "In your practice as a midwife, do you diagnose medical conditions?"

I take a deep breath. "No, I practice midwifery, not medicine. All the women I help are healthy and don't need medical intervention. If they have a problem, I refer them to a physician or to a hospital." My clenched hands relax; my breathing slows.

Forty-five minutes later, the tiger returns, and I fall apart during cross-examination. I doubt my knowledge and my experience, while being drilled on prenatal laboratory results. I stumble over an obscure term. I return to the defense table, crushed. I can barely look at John.

"Sorry," I murmur.

I absorb what has just happened, I feel an urge to run. I close my

4

eyes and remember a birth from my past, a woman from Germany who was having her first baby. I remember Greta leaping up, just as labor was progressing, and watching as she began to jog through the house during each contraction. She took off down the hall at a good clip, and I followed her at first, until she ran for nearly two hours. She did not tire. Finally, I stopped her, and she faced the labor, and stopped running away from it. I think of her now, and it gives me strength.

***

After the first day, the judge declares that his calendar is full for the rest of the year. The trial will resume in January.

I return home, and for the next five weeks, my life has changed. Waiting has put my family on edge, and doubt creeps in when I leave my house. In a small conference room at the Holiday Inn, I attend a lecture on fetal heart monitoring. Even though I sit in the back row, and try to be inconspicuous, two women turn in their chairs and whisper to each other. When I ask a question, the speaker ignores me. During a break, I approach a table for tea, and a woman glares at me, a truly evil eye. I just stare back at her, until she quickly looks away.

My daughter returns from school one day, and describes the bus ride home. "Elsa and Brinn told me I can't sit with them." My heart breaks, as she continues. "Elsa pointed to another seat and said I had to go there."

"What did you do?"

"I moved," she responds, matter-of-factly. "Elsa tries to be the boss, but she's not."

Elsa and Brinn are both daughters of doctors in our town. Battle lines are being drawn.

I am still obligated to be the best mother I can, and I fulfill my promise to chaperone a dance at my daughter's school. I am burnt out, eyes sunken inside of dark circles, my posture slumped, exhausted. Of course, I am faced by other parents, including doctors and nurses in the community. I smile, but only out of duty. I cannot talk to them, but I will not express my fear or react to their condescending smirks. I am facing the enemy, but they will not defeat me. They are just imaginary tigers.

One afternoon, I respond to a knock on my front door. On our porch is a woman named Jackie, who has attended many of our peer midwife workshops. She hands me a twenty dollar bill. I am stunned. I know she is not a wealthy woman, but she is adamant that I take the money. She is well aware of the cost of my defense.

"Thank you," I say. "This is so generous."

As she hugs me, I feel her good intentions course through me, and I realize I am supported, and that I must continue to fight.

***

The second day of testimony resumes on January 4th. I listen as a

5

series of family physicians, nurses, and hospital administrators testify against me. I can handle it. John calls several of my former patients to the stand, and I feel nothing but love as they tell the stories of how I brought their babies into the world. We return the next day for more of the same, and the civil court case ends that afternoon. Before I leave the court, I stare at the painting of the women, and quietly pray that their scales be tipped in my favor.

On January 19, 1989, we return to hear the judge's decision. The courtroom is packed with community members and the media.

The judge enters and sits at his bench. He stares directly at me as he makes his announcement. "After reviewing both sides, I find Dolly Browder guilty of practicing medicine without a license. I hereby order her to cease practicing immediately."

As he speaks, I barely hear or understand him. All I can think of are the twenty pregnant women who have planned births with me during the next few months.

***

Midwives are practical, efficient. We organize. That same month, we go to the state legislature to plead our case. There are many of us, and we are joined by lawyers, supporters, and our lobbyist.

News of the court's decision has been picked up by local radio, TV and newspapers. CNN comes to my house for an interview. At every legislative committee meeting, they know who we are. In our faces, they can see our determination. The legislation passes both chambers with 75% approval.

The governor signs the bill in April of 1989. Midwives in Montana are exempted from the Medical Practice Act. In 1991, the legislature establishes the Alternative Health Care Board, to create regulations and licensure qualifications. Montana becomes one of the first states to offer a license for home birth midwives.

As of 2019, thirty-two other states have joined us.

My name is Dolly Browder.

I am License Number One.

*Guts*
Elke Govertsen

❄

I'm indoorsy.

I square up my body when I announce this. I own it. I have given up, gone soft. All of my friends continue to search for what I denounce, and I no longer care about their nice biceps. I no longer care about my previous life of layers, mittens, little rubbers spikes on shoes to weather the weather. I do not miss the countless hours on trails and slopes, the scrambles, the thousands of dollars spent on skis, boots, running shoes. I had that gear. I had that history. That was enough.

I'm indoorsy. I stay warm, I stay gentle, I stay home.

I have my reasons. I have been gutted.

At age 25, on a humanitarian trip to South America, I still had guts. I also had naiveté and a massive savior complex, a bad combination in a tiny village in Peru. My entire group was affected by the poor sanitation, and I watched them fall apart, violently ill. Except for me. I remained cocky. I was sure that my body was built to withstand travel, adventure, the outdoors.

A month after returning home, I woke up in the ICU, choking on an intubation tube.

My body was not built by me.

\*\*\*

A mouth full of pennies, I choke on copper.

I have no idea the cost.

My head clears and I realize there are no pennies. The metallic taste of medicine and the beeping and the stinging smell tell me I am definitely in a hospital. The choking is real. A thick tube is in my mouth, pushing air into my body, and pulling it back out. I imagine fireplace bellows, opening and closing. Being awake while intubated is terrible. Flailing and fighting and coughing to get it out so you can breathe, but the bitch is breathing for you, and the timing completely falls apart. Inhale. No. Wrong way. Exhale. It doesn't work. I am drowning. Try to cough, but my entire body has rearranged itself, wrapped around that damn tube, and it won't let go.

Unable to turn my head, I can't see details of where I am or if I am alone. I match my breathing with the machine, but the machine does not know I am afraid. I adjust, pace my breath, slow, tricking the machine into thinking I am unconcerned about this. Tricking the machine into believing I know exactly what is happening.

I am not alone. A single nurse floats in the furthest corner of my

peripheral vision. She intently examines a screen, and she knows I am awake. She leaves the computer, and approaches, tells me I will feel so much better when the tube comes out. I know she is right. Nurses are always right. I trust her, but she has not told me the whole truth. She has not warned me about the pain.

"Ready?" She asks me this, and I can only blink, mouth full. She pulls swiftly and up, and my own spit whips my face. The tube catches on each ridge of my trachea. The tube wants me to remember that it kept me alive. The two-second yank is so terrible that I feel the shock in my knees, elbows, fingernails.

My gasping quiets, my mind thinks of things other than breathing. I am suddenly aware of the hurt. A deep, unfamiliar pain burrowed in my belly. Electric, it radiates from my gut, paths to other, smaller centers of pain. A thin, clear tube above my clavicle feeds into my body. Another tube, much larger, drains from my right side. I am made of tubes.

Every muscle aches. A giant, white gauze rectangle is taped over my belly and I have no clue what is underneath. I am awake enough to know it is all very, very bad.

***

When I wake, the people around me—the nurses, the doctors, my family—tell me the story of what happened. This is a story about me that I did not take part in. The only story I own is what I remember before I ended up here. I remember driving myself to NowCare. I remember the shock of the staff; they could not believe a dying person drove themselves to a walk-in clinic. I remember being rushed to the ER, fully delirious, seeing squirrels everywhere in the operating room, my fever so high. Delirious, I remember sparks exploding under my right rib cage. I remember a doctor with a squeaky voice, just before he removed my rupturing gallbladder. I remember my belly fizzing, as I dreamed of a shaken soda bottle, as they pumped in air for the scope. I remember the next day, as the surgeon returned to check on my progress, took one look at my huge, distended belly and rushed me back into surgery.

I remember this: "Can I see my family?"

He leaned in close, forehead to forehead. "There is no time."

I have memories but no information, I am terrified. The enormity sinks in, gushes, floods, drowns me.

I have a choice. I cannot control my body, but I can control how to leave it. So simple.

I don't think of my family or my friends or my life or my hopes. I don't think of how madly in love I am with my boyfriend, or the grief of my devastated family.

I give up. Everything they say about dying is real. Only better. The white light did not blind me, instead I saw everything in a heightened way. I am so weak, all I have to do is lean slightly, and I fall. A wind inside of me, hollowed. I see angels. I know their exact number. Sixty two, but I don't have to count. My body doesn't hurt anywhere. I never want to leave this feeling.

Swoosh, rewind tape. Up. Back in my bed. Back in my gutted body. Back to tubes and drains and monitors and pain. So much pain. When my eyes open, I see intense green eyes, and a nurse with the peeling sticker of a four leaf clover on her nametag. Next to a fraying leprechaun, her name: Kris.

Her arms curl under my armpits until she props me up, and I sit, cut and weak. All of my tubes are in the wrong places. The machines beep around me, sirens.

"I know what you're doing, and I totally understand why. But I can't let a 25-year-old die on my watch." Kris speaks in a determined voice, leaning in so close I can smell her cinnamon gum.

She took my choice away. I hate her intensely.

She untangles herself from me to fix the tubes, punch buttons on the machines. "You flatlined," she announces. I want to go back, and I try so hard to find my sixty two angels. But it is no longer as simple as falling.

"Why am I here?"

"They didn't know your gallbladder was filled with typhoid." Kris gives it to me straight. "They took it out with scopes, to minimize scarring."

"What is this giant bandage covering?"

"The typhoid covered your guts and the infection was uncontained in your belly." Kris returns to the machines, examining the screens. "You had a second surgery. The doctor will explain it."

Kris allows my mom into the room. I slip into some lucid sleep. My mom's cool fingers trace figure 8's on my forehead, and this is another kind of delirium, the best kind. Infinity. Infinity. Each rotation is silent, and I wish for it to be endless, but when I open my eyes, she stops.

I can only whisper. "Don't stop or I will leave my body." I fall into a true, deep sleep.

When I wake, she still goes round and round, and it feels like she has rubbed an 8 shaped trench into my forehead. I must have slept a long, long time. She must have done twenty-thousand figure eights, holding me in my body. Infinity. Infinity.

I sleep for days. Sleeping is so much better than hurting.

Finally, I am awake enough for the doctor to explain what happened after they took me to the second surgery. The infection was everywhere. They stopped worrying about scarring and sliced me breastbone to pubic bone.

"Enormous amounts of puss," the doctor informed me, "so much." They flushed and flushed me. They moved my organs, some sat beside me, still connected while they were washed. I can feel the shapes of my organs inside of me, because they are all bruised. "In a few days we will remove the bandage and take a look together so I can explain more."

My surgeon's name is Tom, and he is a good doctor.

My infectious disease doctor is not. He rips my bandage off, and underneath the giant, bright, white pad is the mystery, the thing to know later. Eleven monstrously sized staples pinching me together, Frankensteined. So much discoloration, it seems someone has spilled ink across my stomach.

When I finally leave the ICU, transferred to a regular hospital room, I sob when I have to say goodbye to Kris Anderson.

In my new room, my mom sleeps on a rollaway bed, and my boyfriend on the windowsill. Raging fevers, escalating within seconds: 102. 103. 104. 105. When I moan, my mom and boyfriend strip off my blankets. Ice is packed all around me. When the fever breaks, my bed is soaked through. New sheets, new clothes. I can't move, and the little things are too much. New hospital gowns are stiffer and scratchier. A cleaning woman snags the oldest gowns from the laundry, and over the next few days, I collect a secret stash of the soft gowns. Perhaps she is one of my sixty two angels.

Over the next week, my first love appears, my friends come, and in their shocked faces, I finally understand the enormity of this. My boyfriend never leaves the windowsill. My mom rubs my head, even though it hurts.

I dread the physical therapist. She insists that I walk. First, one step, and then back to bed. Days later, I walk a full lap of the 5th floor, a marathon. Eventually, I can walk to the elevator. Hunched over, clutching a pillow to my gut to replace my cut stomach muscles. I travel down to the ICU to show Kris my progress. She cries. So do I. She tells me that most ICU patients move out before they wake up. Most of her patients don't remember her. I will never forget.

I invite her to my birthday party in November. It is February.

In November, she is there.

So am I.

*** 

Montana is a place of big adventures. At first blush, these all seem to take place in epic landscapes under Charlie Russel clouds painted in colors that look like they would give cavities. Many of the great Montana stories are stunning. More often than not, they are wet, cold, buggy, no sleep, injury-inducing journeys.

Instead of spelunking, I explore the dark scary crevices in myself. Instead of climbing, I descend into other types of bravery. I slow down, and I do not skip over the truths. Indoors, I find the grit I had always been looking for.

Lewis and Clark already did the work. They endured the storms, the savage river crossings. Reading their journals is enough for me.

Hear my call, indoorsy Montanans. We have permission. We have gathered our stories. We have earned this rest. Our guts are seen.

Montana has a stunning and shocking surface, but it has guts. Below, it is deeper and slower and thicker, and we are the storytellers. We make art with our past. We stay indoors, and make love, make food, make music. We make this place more than a playground.

Indoors, we tell our stories.

*Family / My Father*
Jenn Ewan

When Pa gently shook me awake, it was milky black in my room and I quickly changed from scared to excited. The hushed, middle-of-the-night rousing was rare. I could see the twinkle in his eye when he pulled my covers back and waited for me in the doorway. I knew what this was.

I pulled on my Wrangler jeans with worn-out knees up underneath my long, warm nightgown. I slipped my bare feet into a pair of dark purple, Care Bear moon boots stacked side-by-side near the front door, then squirmed into a winter jacket. Pa pulled on rubber boot covers that fit over his White's and fastened them like a pro after years of routine.

Using the glow of the porch light to guide us, Pa and I let the wooden screen door slam as we scurried over to his dark blue and white Ford pickup. He was proud of that truck, a late-1980s extended cab F-150. The truck tires crunched the gravel as we pulled out and headed south toward the calving shed. The birthplace of thousands of calves over the years was four miles from the white ranch-house that Pa's employer—the Climbing Arrow Ranch—provided for us, and eleven rural, washboard miles outside of the small town of Three Forks, Montana, in a place called The Madison.

Slowing down, Pa turned off the county road. The last 300 yards were rutted, frozen tracks and I giggled silently as I bounced up and down on the front seat. The truck's headlights were shrouded in a cone of mist and they exposed the gray and brown knotted boards on the weathered barn. Pa threw the stick into first gear and killed the engine, leaving the keys dangling in the ignition. I hopped out and followed him into the doorless entrance, navigating the soft, worn, uneven dirt floor in the dim light. My father need-ed to determine what stage of labor the heifer was in when we got there and what he needed to do to pull the calf out, so I sat patiently trying to act more grown-up than I was.

The heifer had been moved into one of the wooden stalls that lined both sides of the long shed. A young cowboy worked the shift and he needed help to get her into the calf-pulling chute. The calf was unwilling to emerge on her own. The mother was in pain and unhappy. Slobber and hay lay inter-twined and drooped at the corners of her mouth. Her eyes glistened wild and searching.

"It's time to go to the cookie room, Jenn," Pa said, with gentle force.

It was the only room in the shed with a door, a place to sit, and things to eat. I didn't hesitate. I grabbed the rickety, round, pot-marked metallic knob, stepped up onto the unswept plywood floor, shut the faded dark green door,

and turned to look out the small window encased within the door. The room smelled of dried cow shit, hay, leather, dirt, wood, and cookies. I inhaled and closed my eyes for just a moment.

My mom baked during calving season, sending treats out the door nearly every trip. The soft oatmeal, walnut, and chocolate-chip cookies sat inside an old ice cream tin that was never washed. The container was born before my parents were, the design worn off by years of gnarled hands prying the lid open in a head-lock next to the pearl snaps near their navels. From that small window, I watched them pull the calf.

The first time I was brought to the calving shed, Pa had warned me.

"A heifer can kill you if you get between her and her calf, 'specially when you have to pull her baby out; she gets very mad and she's fast. You have to get out of the way if she charges. You understand?"

I knew I was an easy target and this door was not pregnant-heifer-proof, so I stood away from the window until they had her securely in the chute.

I heard them hollering and whistling in short bursts, hands slapping against jeans. The gates moaned, clanged and finally closed. The new mother-to-be brayed loudly. The gears and levers of the paint-chipped chute engaged, hooves rattled against metal. I knew she was fighting hard now. I wondered if Pa had been kicked.

"Alright!" he yelled. I stepped in front of the window. I saw her swollen belly sandwiched between two metal grates in the shape of a vee, as the last lever was pushed upward with the heel of the young cowboy's hand. Her head and neck were stabilized independent of her belly between two singular metal bars.

Pa removed his coat and his button-up, long-sleeved shirt until he was down to his opaque, pit-stained tee shirt. He plunged his right arm into a bucket of sterile blue water, rubbing the blue with his left hand up to the edge of his right sleeve. Arm held upward and away from his body, Pa walked towards the rear of the heifer.

He checked her as she bawled and railed against the chute as much as it allowed. When he returned to the bucket, he sterilized both arms and grabbed the stainless steel pull-chain. Using both hands and his forearms as a widener, he entered the birth canal again, blindly wrapping the chain around the calf's hind legs. Her head dropped. Once secure, he removed his arms and set the pull hook, waiting for a contraction so he could extract her baby. I saw two tiny slime-covered hooves appear and I stifled a squeal, hoping it wasn't dead already. He braced and pulled again, the veins near his sideburns bulging. I could see knees and the tip of a matted tail. They both rested again. With one last heave, the calf's hips were visible and she slipped out on her own, so black the hair appeared bluish. Pa knelt, and jostled the calf while the mother's eyes searched for her offspring. He grabbed straw from the ground and began to clean her nostrils, to help her breathe. He motioned for me. I helped wipe off the birthing sack to stimulate the calf.

"Don't wipe it all off, kid, it's how the mama bonds with her baby," he said, smiling. He motioned with his head towards the cookie room. "Go back

12

in there while I move the calf to another stall and get the heifer outta the chute."

The babe bawled and the mother kicked. The heifer backed out and walked with purpose towards the stall when they released her from the chute. She immediately began licking her baby. He closed the gate and waved me out again. While he cleaned up, I found a lower rail on the slats of the stall, rested my forearms under my chin, my knees on the dirt floor, and I watched her lick her daughter dry. After several minutes, the calf stood up, wobbling, stumbling, and collapsing, until she was strong enough to search for an udder.

"Come on kiddo, let's leave 'em be; they get to stay in here tonight."

Pa looked happy. We grabbed a cookie from the tin before we left. He mussed my hair as we headed to the truck, the cookie resting between his lips. "Well, what'd ya' think?" I don't remember my response, but that was how our relationship always was—unspoken. We connected over moments like that.

In 1989, our family left the ranch and moved to Troy, Montana. I sobbed as I looked through the windshield of the moving truck when we pulled away from the house on Buffalo Jump Road. I woke up just before we arrived at our new home. Pine trees, thick with nettles and brush choked either side of the two-lane highway as we approached our new driveway. The mottled sky watched us overhead.

We settled into a temporary rental. Pa started work at a mine, underground as a diesel mechanic. He made considerably more money than he'd made on the ranch. While living on the ranch, on very special occasions when money allowed, we rented a VCR, hauling it home in a padded case with a shoulder strap along with the movies we'd chosen. Each of us got to pick one. We moved because my parents wanted to own a VCR; plus some land to go with it.

I was in fifth grade and I ached, missing my friends in Three Forks. When Mrs. Cain introduced me to my classmates, they just stared. No one introduced themselves. During the first couple of weeks at recess, the boys tried to talk to me, but the girls circled me in a pack.

"Oooooh, look at the new girl, thinking she's hot shit because the boys like her; think you're too good for us? What, aren't ya gonna say somethin', Jenny?"

I made my way to the swing set, bent my body over the black seat, and let my head and arms droop. The tips of my shoes scraped the wood chips as I swung. I refused to respond. I refused to cry in front of them. The boys stood two feet away.

My family eventually bought 20 acres of land and a log cabin, but my dad was going underground every day into darkness and stale air. My mom worked the graveyard shift at the Champion Mill in Libby. It would be months until I had my first real friend.

My Pa spent his entire life outside, first on a ranch near Big Timber, and then in Three Forks, barring a minor stint in the Army and the oil fields of

New Mexico. In Troy, he and his friends stopped regularly on the way home from the mine at Little Joe's, a rustic, wood-clad bar with a hand-painted sign and a covered front porch.

My parents' muffled arguments behind their bedroom door increased. Our family supper routine was all but gone, dependent on shift work. My mom still gardened, canned, cooked, and cleaned when she wasn't working. While we kids had been doing chores since we were young, my younger sister Josie and I took on more responsibility to help out.

A few years passed and my dad was often irritable and short, seemingly happiest when he was a little buzzed. The men from the mine came over to drink sometimes. My parents didn't go out together like they used to. He was reminiscent and sweet when he drank, and a pattern emerged.

"Girls, get in here," he'd holler playfully. My youngest sister Jamie, a toddler then, was usually in bed, and Josie and I would smile at one another just before we sat down. Pa's eyes smiled, a little glassy. He started off stuttering, "N-n-n-now you know how darn proud of you I am, don't ya?"

We nodded at him and giggled out loud and exchanged knowing glances at one another. He started again, leaned towards us a little. "No, darn it, I mean it. You girls...well, shit..." He paused for a bit, smiled to himself, and shook his head knowingly. "I mean it, you two make me and your Mom proud. You three I mean. You know what I mean. I know I don't tell you that all the time, but dammit, it's true."

Josie and I laughed out loud.

"What are ya' laughin' for, ya' goofballs? I mean it," he continued.

The first few times this happened we enjoyed it, but when the scenario replayed time and time again, I knew something was wrong.

I was nearly sixteen when I walked down the hall and heard him speaking to someone on the phone in a low, hushed tone, behind the door of my parents' bedroom. I looked behind me and crept nearer to listen. I couldn't make out any of the words, but the conversation was intimate; he knew the person on the other end. I acted as if I didn't know he was on the phone and barged into their room. He was seated on the edge of the neatly made bed with his back to me, and when the door opened, he spun around, eyes wide, mouth agape.

"I have to go," he said, and slammed the phone into the cradle.

"Whatta ya' need?" he asked me, irritated.

I stared at him briefly and stormed out. I didn't want to look at him.

Several nights later, I awakened in the middle of the night to the sound of my mom yelling into the phone. When I entered the kitchen, I saw her lit only by the light of the moon coming through the kitchen window, standing there in her fleece robe and socks, stretching the phone as far as it would go, as she paced between the wooden cabinets on the flowered linoleum floor.

"I can't do it anymore!" She screamed, and threw the phone.

It hit the floor with a plastic thud. The cream spiral chord dangled over the front of the cupboard as I heard her open the front door. My mom was not the type to yell, let alone swear. She adored my dad, but for some reason

14

my mom was losing it. When she ran outside, I attempted to follow her.

"Go back inside," she hissed.

"Mom, what....?" I asked, panicked.

"Now," she ordered and begged at the same time.

Wide awake, I made my way back towards the house in the dark, walked down the hall, closed my bedroom door, and crawled under my light teal comforter. I stared at the ceiling until I finally fell asleep.

In the months leading up to that night my dad seemed like a trapped animal to me. He was suffocating underground, and my mom was smothering him above ground.

In 1995, Pa left to live with Judy near Bozeman. My mom lost weight. I refused to speak to my father for a few months. He had bought a new Ford pickup when we moved to Troy. It was a single-cab, brown and cream, with silver handles, and it was also left behind. Defiantly, I dropped the rear end out of it, off-roading with a girlfriend. We got a ride home and I told my mom what had happened. She wasn't upset.

"Tell your dad," she said.

I was barely speaking to him by then, but I called his cell phone.

"Pa?" I asked, when I heard him pick up the phone.

"Yeah, I'm here," he said.

"The truck's dead," I dictated flatly. "I think I dropped the rear end out of it near Lake Creek Reservoir with Kerensa. We left it there. Just wanted to let you know." I hung up. No one punished me for killing the truck.

Even though I didn't see him as much as I'd like, I was proud of my Pa, imperfections exposed, a little hard of hearing, no calves to pull, a small belly, his nose buried in a book when he wasn't working or doing chores.

***

When I went through my own divorce in 2002, Pa drove from Bozeman and helped me move some of my things. After I thought he had left, I heard a knock on my front door. There Pa stood with his hands in the pockets of his Carhartt coat. He choked up as he made sure I was settled.

"Really, kiddo, how are ya'?"

*Digest*
Mara Panich

It's my fortieth birthday and I am ready to eat. My friends and I border on hedonism when it comes to food, and we've been cooking all day to create the feast laid before me. The table is brimming, edge-to-edge with dishes and casseroles filled with savory meats, cheese laden potatoes, and a rainbow of vegetables with bacon and garlic. My house is foggy with mouthwatering scents. We load our plates with dripping green cabbage rolls, filled with spicy sausage and stewed in rich tomato sauce, thick crusty bread dipped in golden Spanish olive oil, and hot Russian dumplings topped with cool tangy sour cream. Our cups have been flowing with dark red wine for hours. I admire my friends, laughing and digging in with ardor. I take a few slow bites and let the salty, savory flavors dissolve into pleasure in my mouth. I chew my next bite, but instead of enjoying the tang on my tongue, the pressure builds in my esophagus. It feels like choking, but I can breathe. No matter how often it happens—and it happens all the time—it still catches me off guard. My eyes brim with frustrated tears and anger. This is my life at mealtime.

***

I was born a giant. Two months premature, yellow-tinged, with a full head of hair, and a hole in my heart. I weighed over 7 pounds. The nurses rolled a special incubator into the NICU to fit me. I was double the size of the other babies in their tiny incubators and specially made beanie caps.

I came into the world as one of the biggest people in the room.

After the dismay of changing horrifying messes in diapers, the doctors discovered I was lactose intolerant. I was quickly switched to soy-based formula. Growing just as rapidly, I cried to be fed. My mother struggled to adhere to the doctors' strict rubric of the number of calories I was supposed to ingest. But she was used to pain and calorie counts, having struggled all of her own life with fad diets and eating plans. My calorie intake never went unregulated. They told her that if she could control me and my eating, protect me, that if I lived to be seven years old, I would likely live a long and normal life. I was a chubby and quiet baby, easily brought to emotion, but rarely a tantrum.

At eight years old, my mother declared we would adhere to the Weight Watchers plan. She didn't take me to meetings, but my food intake was constantly monitored. We walked nightly. We weighed and measured our food at every meal, weighed and measured ourselves weekly. If I reached for the spoon to add a second helping of mashed potatoes, went to the pantry to find a salty snack, I was intercepted. Always the same question: "Do you

really need that?" The yo-yo dieting caused my mother's body to shift and morph in size and shape throughout my childhood. Following the same pattern, I varied in size. My belly protruded with winter hibernation and my collarbones and ribs became visible in summer. Swimming to escape the sweltering July heat and riding bikes with other kids kept me constantly on the move.

Never an athletic person, I played some sports, particularly enjoyed swimming, and loved to dance and sing with my friends and cousin. But I was chubby. I was tall, for a girl of my age, at five feet, but my shoe size was an enormous 9. Each semester in elementary school, the nurse wheeled a scale to the hallway outside the door of our classroom. One by one, students were called out in alphabetical order to be weighed and measured. The school nurse diligently wrote our statistics in a file folder, next to our attendance records and other data that was supposedly important to tracking our health and well-being. It was supposed to be private, the scale kept in the hallway, to avoid comparisons and exposing this deep, dark secret of weight.

A boy from my class returned from the bathroom just as the nurse read me my weight. "One hundred and eight pounds." she said, a statement of fact which had no malice behind it. When I returned to the classroom, I heard the whispers. "She weighs OVER A HUNDRED POUNDS!" It was the news of the day. I was mortified. Horrified. My biggest anguish was now fodder for all. Prepubescent, budding breasts forming on my chest, the whispers and jeers made me internalize the idea that I was physically and emotionally fat.

I came of age in the time of heroin chic and grunge. School shopping was a particular version of hell. My mother and I headed to the crowded mall sales and department stores as I imagined all the hip outfits I would wear that year. The racks overflowed with narrow tank dresses that didn't fit my breasts, jeans too small for my thick thighs, and crop top t-shirts made purposefully in childlike sizing. I began with my arms loaded with trendy clothes in the biggest sizes I could find, hauling them to the dressing room. Mom stood outside the tiny closet, sighing with exasperation and empathetic nervousness. My exuberance quickly faded as shirts stretched awkwardly across my breast and dresses clung to the rolls of my belly. I slipped on a black velvet and lace baby-doll dress, cut short with a wide neck. I was giddy with the fact that it fit my breasts and the sleeves didn't constrict my arms. I stepped out of the dressing room to show my mom my treasure.

"You don't have the right body for that style," she muttered, and I retreated into the fitting room stall, kicking the discarded, ill-fitting clothes that covered the floor, weeping with rage and turmoil. After I had collected myself, we deposited all of the discarded hopes to the return rack and ventured to the edges of the women's section. Forced to leave the trendy Junior's department for the deep recesses of the store's fat-folk hinterland, she tried to be helpful. "Maybe we can diet together. If you lose fifteen pounds, I'll buy you that dress." I shuddered to hold myself back from screaming. In the dark corners of the plus size department, I uncovered a single dress that

was cut for an older woman, decorated with sunflower print. I could rock it, combined with combat boots. The rest of my school shopping was completed in the men's section, my choices more Kurt Cobain than Courtney Love. Extra baggy band t-shirts and loose-fit jeans were my uniform. I was almost never without a flannel button-down tied around my waist or wrapped like a security blanket.

I wasn't bullied much for my size. My overweight teenage body issues were a quiet inner struggle. The systemic norms that excluded me from the style of the day made me feel lumpy, clothing segregation drove me to think I was gargantuan, that my body must be hidden. The more I hid, the lumpier I felt, and the heavier I got.

I've always reveled in the idea of new beginnings. When I was young, I dreamed of my parents relocating from our small Indiana city to a new town where I could start over, in a community that hadn't known me since kindergarten. I wanted to reinvent myself.

At twenty-two years old, fresh out of college and still looking for re-invention, I lived temporarily with my parents in Indianapolis. Graduate school enticed me as a means of escape. I applied only to schools that were far away from home, looking west to the mountains and anonymous towns that weren't already familiar with my name. I loved my friends and family, but I disliked myself. One day, I came home to an acceptance letter to the University of Montana. A life away from the flatlands of the Midwest; this was my chance.

A week later, something else lay on my bed: a trifold brochure, the front featuring a happy, thin woman in a pretty summer dress. At first, I thought it was about graduate school, but then I looked closer. My mother had left me a flier about weight loss surgery from the local hospital. Inside were statistics and medical drawings and more pictures of happy, thin people. On the back, a sticker with dates and times of free informational sessions. I read it, with excitement, but also shame.

"I think you should go," my mother said, as she walked into the room to find me sitting at the edge of the bed. "You want to make a new life, and this could help. We're worried about your health." Within days, I found myself sitting in a sterile waiting room at the hospital with four middle aged women and two men. Our bodies squeezed into the cramped chairs, and everyone adjusted themselves in discomfort. A woman pulled at the bottom of her t-shirt like a bedcover for warmth. A tall bulk of a man stood next to his wife, constantly shifting from foot to foot, nervously assessing everyone else in the room. No one spoke. We were taken to a hospital classroom with long rows of tables, facing a large screen and a healthcare professional who waited to save us from our girth. The gaps between strangers allowed our discomfort to hover in the open space. We dutifully listened to the doctors and nurses describe how they would rearrange our internal organs to make a less efficient body. A video showed sad fat people transformed into happy thin beings. It was high pressure medical sales: without the surgery, we would all die, and soon. I left without making an appointment.

I arrived in Missoula young and still fat, looking to start anew. Reinvention was not as simple as I had imagined. I had gotten exactly what I wanted. I knew none of the young hippies that gathered in Caras Park on sunny summer evenings, had no friends to visit on porches and sip Moose Drool. Everyone in Missoula appeared young, fit, and happy. I struggled to make new friends, spending my days without leaving my dark, cool basement apartment. Classes started and I searched for a place to study. The Raven was a coffeehouse that was open late, with pool tables in the back, occasional live music, and a crew of regulars who smoked, caffeinated, and conversed outside the front door. It was a place to socialize, less subdued, more like a bar. I lugged my books across the bridge, and set up at a table to read and write. Soon, the baristas greeted me by name and made my double Americano before I had a chance to order it. The regulars reminded me of the hippies and organic intellectuals I knew back in Indiana. I still didn't have friends, but at least I could go to a place where I felt known, where I existed beyond myself.

I met a few friends and began a relationship with an assertive man who gave me support, love, and affection. Within months of our first date, we were living together. Underneath the smiles and new adventures, depression loomed. I was still unhappy. I continued to expand, and was plagued with health issues. Painful boils arose on my skin, appearing in the dark places of my body where skin touched skin. Under my breasts and in the inner crease of my thigh, bumps swelled red with the agonizing pressure of infection. I was diagnosed with diabetes, suddenly terrified by the reality of my own mortality. My blood pressure was elevated for the first time in my life. Graduate school overwhelmed me, and I considered dropping out and moving home. I considered disappearing. I completed all of the coursework for my graduate program but struggled to finish my thesis. During a meeting in my advisor's constricted campus office, she declared that my thesis wasn't strong enough. I would have to start over. Defeat and failure engulfed me, and I gave up.

I worked a couple of different retail and coffee shop jobs without any real direction. I spent a significant amount of time curled on the couch, remote in hand, watching reruns of *Gilmore Girls* and *Northern Exposure*. Commercials for fast food and sugary energy drinks enticed me to constantly snack as I lay prone on the couch. One day, a commercial grabbed me: a new kind of bariatric surgery, significantly less invasive than gastric bypass. I could be thin and happy like the people on the commercial, like the people in that flier, years ago. I worked as a clerk at the bookstore on campus and I could easily get the time off for surgery and the subsequent recovery. My boyfriend supported me, and my parents offered to pay for it. I wasn't the only one who attributed the size of my body to my health and happiness.

At 327 pounds, I clearly qualified for the elective surgery. I had convinced myself that this outpatient procedure, where they would place a small inflatable band around my stomach, was the answer to all of my problems. There was another information session in a room so similar to the first

that I felt as though I was time traveling. This time, I signed up. I thought about my body constantly, and how satisfying it would be to feel comfortable in my own skin. I was nervous and intimidated, but my mind was set.

The pain, when I came out of sedation, was excruciating. The nurses floated around the recovery room dispensing medications like stoic angels of relief. I went home that day and recovered in my bed, sipping salty broth and eating Jell-O for a week until I could move to thicker liquids. I shuffled around the house, unable to bend at the waist or lift anything heavier than five pounds. One month of soups, protein shakes, light cheese, and pudding. I dropped forty pounds by the time I returned to work. Co-workers, strangers, and friends showered me with compliments. I was proud, losing weight was a monumental accomplishment, visible from near and far.

Pounds shed off my frame like days on the calendar passing. Always tugging at my jeans to keep them from sliding off my hips, I had to replace them every other month. I did feel better, happier. The excitement of a lower number on the scale or a smaller pant size gave me continual rushes of joy and validation. I was a dog, salivating for treats given freely and frequently.

Soon, the numbers dropped at a slower rate. The energy I had gained from the initial weight loss waned. I began having gallbladder attacks and had another surgery to have it removed. My mood and my weight loss both plateaued. I cried in the doctor's office when he told me my BMI was still too high. I had lost one hundred and forty pounds, wore a size 10/12, but according to my BMI, I was still fat.

Sagging skin plagued me, and my flapping bat-wing arms were even flappier without the fat to fill them. My breasts hung low, two grapefruits swaying from my chest in a pair of athletic socks. I was still fat, according to that damn chart. I didn't need meds for diabetes anymore, and my slightly high blood pressure had evened out, but I lacked energy. I was iron deficient. Dark spots began to appear on my face from hormonal flare ups. Days passed where I could barely ingest more than water and protein shakes. When my body allowed, I ate with fervor. The numbers on the scale soon began to slowly rise, causing emotional pain, and the vomiting inflicted physical pain. My emotions were as varied as the Montana landscape: mountains and valleys, hills and plateaus, bluebird days, wildfires and blizzards. My attitude was determined by the number on the scale, and that number was rising. Eventually, I threw the scale away, but I didn't have the thousands of dollars to have the band removed from my stomach.

As my body shifted so significantly and frequently, I shopped thrift stores to save money. In the charity shops, I found a love for style that I had always admired, but never embraced for myself. The fat positive movement began to trickle into my social media and into the books I chose to read. I embraced my body as it wanted to be, loved the foods I craved and allowed myself to eat them without guilt. I struggled, but my husband, my friends, and strangers continued to comment on my beauty and style. Negative thoughts continued to plague me, but I countered them with positive actions. I hiked to enjoy the beauty of Missoula, not to negate the calories from nachos and

beer. I bought dresses that hugged my curves. I wore dark red lipstick at all times of day. I referred to myself as fat, not as an insult, but as a descriptor. I went out dancing with friends and enjoyed it as if I were a kid again.

***

At my birthday dinner, I quickly rise from the table, my chair scraping the floor. My discomfort is visible. I rush to the bathroom, steps away from the celebration. I switch the fan on, and close the door. A feeble attempt to mute the noise of my body rejecting the food that refuses to enter my stomach. I heave, gag, and vomit my undigested food into the toilet bowl. The spell passes. After a few minutes, I splash water on my face, take a few deep breaths, and return to the empathetic glances of my friends, if they look at me at all. They are all too familiar with my struggles.

I am a reluctant bulimic. I followed this path years ago while hating my body, my Self. My friends and my husband have grown accustomed to my quick exits from the dinner table. I have not.

I can only keep trying, keep hoping, to overcome a lifelong conflict between my body and the fuel it needs to operate. I will make peace with myself. No longer fighting, but embracing.

*Lost, Found*
Jessica Bruinsma

✻

I was five when I first heard the sad news. Sam, the son of a family friend, had died in a plane wreck in the mountains of Colorado piloting a small aircraft from Telluride to Aspen.

In second grade, there was more bad news. My sister's best friend Danielle died in a car accident. Not wearing a seat belt, she was ejected through the windshield when their white minivan was hit.

In fifth grade, the husband of my elementary principal and her two sons, my classmates, died in another plane crash. She was supposed to be on the plane too, but had come home early to work.

In middle school, my best friend's two year old brother died in a rollover car accident. Her mom was driving. The other two year-old in the car survived, burned beyond recognition.

In high school, my brother's best friend wrecked his car, inadvertently causing his father's death. Practicing passing on a two-lane highway, he swerved back into his lane to avoid an oncoming vehicle, overcorrecting and rolling the vehicle.

In high school again, a student I didn't know, and worse, had never heard of, committed suicide.

In college, two friends lost parents to cancer within a year. I drove twelve hours from Montana to Colorado to attend both funerals. At the reception for my friend's mother, I only remember the tree; its huge, dead, branches stretching, tightly gripping the roof of her dead mother.

The same year, a girl from my hometown high school died in a bathtub of a heroin overdose. She was in the class above me. Her mother found the body.

Six months later, another girl from my high school committed suicide. We had sang in show choir together. I remember her as beautiful, talented and overworked.

These were the deaths of my youth.

\*\*\*

I was obsessed with death, and my anxiety seemed to grow by the month as I worked through my undergraduate degree in Missoula. I ran long miles to escape it, rode my bike long miles to outrace it. Too tired to be anxiety ridden, exhausting myself was the cure among the mountains in Montana. My mind found quiet solace in the woods. Still, I vaguely wondered how my love of the outdoors and sports was morphing into a way to deal with worries of having mad cow disease, being too fat or having a stroke or heart

attack. When I went to the ER for extreme chest pain, the cute doctor assured me that the pressure in my chest was actually just constipation. It didn't matter. I knew for certain that a car accident or a plane crash were inevitable. My dream had always been to travel. I wanted to study abroad and put my years of German study to use. But when the time came, I backed out at the last minute, losing my $600 deposit and the rest of my dignity because I couldn't get on the plane. Instead, I moved back into the house I had so carefully packed up in preparation to leave. For the remainder of my junior year, I slept on a futon in the office of the living room since my room was rented out.

In my senior year, I tried to fight back by making myself do the things I was afraid of. Progress felt painful and questionable. I forced myself to get on planes because I wanted to see my family, often crying the entire flight. As I cried during a turbulent take-off to Nashville to visit my grandparents, a kindly, older, overweight Native American woman in full regalia asked me if it was my first time flying. Was I fourteen? Fifteen? When I told her I was twenty two, she didn't speak to me for the rest of the flight.

Only a few people knew how bad it was for me. Most people thought I was fine as I worked fun jobs after college, ski instructing and leading trips at summer camps. I didn't want drugs and I didn't want counseling. I just wanted to feel normal. Instead, I felt alone and embarrassed, scared of people finding out my thoughts, and thinking I was crazy. I felt crazy. I felt like I was ensnared in my own tree of death; gnarled, bare branches holding me hostage from the life I wanted to live.

In 2008, I made a decision. I would push through. I would get on a plane to Germany and fulfill my dream of studying abroad. Determined to figure this out on my own, I felt that if I could do this one thing, I could make the whole thing better.

## June 16th, 2008

I keep screaming for help, throwing my voice into a void of thick air that disappears into nothingness. Sitting on a flat rock on the edge of this cliff, a small creek flows past me on the left. Behind me, the waterfall from the cliff above bounces off the rocks, as flecks of water ricochet onto the back of my neck. Tucking my head into my shirt, I focus on using my breath to warm my wet, shivering body. I sit here, legs pulled into my chest, huddling deeper into myself. Voice gone, I can only open and close my mouth in disbelief. Leaning to the right, I throw up. Rain falls, and the dark, disbanded clouds of the afternoon blend and fade into the darkness of night. Looking out and down, I scoot slowly backwards, hands searching for softer, higher ground, away from these slippery, wet rocks of my precarious perch. My hands find a grassier area on the slope just above me, and I pull myself slowly onto the soft moss, angling to use the soft ground as a pillow. Lying on my right side, I cradle my injured arm, and curl up, waiting for daylight to come.

Soft light in a pale, blue sky of low lying clouds quietly brings morning to life on the mountain der Untersberg in Bavaria, Germany. The beginnings of daylight allow me to examine my surroundings. I am at the bottom of the ledge of the steep slope I fell down onto. Where can I go? Where should I go? I slowly ascend the rocky slope, dragging my injured foot behind me. My left arm hangs limp and useless by my side. I curse my carelessness when I slip on the soft ground, landing hard on an already bruised and scraped back. I can't afford a mistake like that. Moving at an upwards angle, I pick up a sturdy, smooth stick to use as a walking aid. Leaning heavily on the wood, I slowly traverse toward the top of the slope. At the top, a smooth limestone face opens up into a wide cave that travels the length of the face of the ledge. Inside, I take off my wet clothes. I lay them across rocks to dry, for fear of hypothermia.

I notice a large rock in the middle of the cave. One drop of water falls precisely into a shallow, dimpled hollow. How long has this water been falling there to carve out this groove? Drip. From the mouth of the cave, I look into the valley below and see billows of clouds soaring directly upwards. They twist and turn wildly, dancing up the mountainside. As I examine the cave, I see a white plastic bucket, carefully placed in the corner. Above it are the fixed bolts of a climbing route. People climb through here. Drip. I sit, moving the bucket into a comfortable place between my legs. I grab a rock, and slowly, deliberately, attempt to crack the locked canister. I don't know if I work for an hour or three. Finally, I break the plastic enough to fit my hand through a small and awkward hole. Plastic bites my hand as I work my arm down, feeling for the resources inside. I remove my prizes: a long rope, carabineers, toilet paper. Carefully unscrewing the top off so as to collapse the plastic, I maneuver an empty, plastic water bottle through the small bucket opening, holding the top between my forefinger and thumb. Staring down at the bottle, I feel slightly affronted that not only is there no water in it, there is also no vodka, as the label promises. I find no food in the bucket. Of the spoils, I see the water bottle is most precious. I am so thirsty now. Standing up, I lean heavily against the rough surface of the boulder, my scraped hands and knees burning as I place my mouth directly onto the divot, sucking out the small amount of accumulated water.

Leaning on my stick, I explore the perimeter of the cave. A lizard dashes by my foot. I tell him that if I get hungry enough, I will catch and eat him. Looking down towards the valley, I think about freshly picked blackberries being rinsed in a colander. Is it really that easy down there? At the front of the cave, I move towards a small piece of land jutting out from the hillside. I haven't heard any helicopters, but this is the place I will be the most visible. It reminds me of an island in the sky. I notice a cable line running along the ground, and it appears to run all the way down the mountain. Above, a smallish wooden crate hangs suspended in the air. It looks old and worn. I wonder when the pulley was last used. Years ago? There are many such

systems on this mountain, bringing goods up and down to huts like Storhaus, where I am living and working for the summer. I wonder what is happening at the hut right now. Did Robin let anyone know I was missing when I didn't come home last night?

I look at the cable and wonder if I could fashion my own pulley to slide down the mountain. How fast would I scream down the cable line before I was smashed to pieces upon impact at the bottom? I'm cold. I want to be home, in bed, pulling a warm blanket around me. I push the indulgent thought aside. There isn't room for that now. Besides the weather and my injuries, my biggest concern is water. The clouds that danced up the mountain earlier have since shrouded her in a crown of fog. The cable line above, visible only moments ago, vanishes from sight. I am thirsty, having drunk only the water from the rock since yesterday morning. As I look toward the small waterfall at the bottom of the slope, I know a descent in my condition is a treacherous move. It needs to wait until absolutely necessary. I see in this moment how close death and I are to each other. I see the line; a thread, all that is separating one from the other. I see how easy it is to die, and I realize I'm not scared. It is clear to me in this moment that we only go back into what we came from, into something much bigger and more powerful than all of us. In this realization, I'm overcome with a sense of peace and acceptance, but just as strongly, the feeling of a distinctive choice.

I position my water bottle to catch the water that falls. Drip. I don't want to die. I'm not done, and more than anything, I don't want to put my family and friends through the stress and heartache of me dying. I wonder how much daylight is left. Drip. It is a careful calculation, but when it misses the bottle, at least it remains in the divot. Sometimes it splashes out. As the evening starts to dim, I make a bed of rope and wonder if rolling the toilet paper around me will help with warmth. I try. It covers my legs and part of my arms. It moves and breaks as I shift. I lie on my back in a nook centered between the two rocks. Lifting my injured foot into the air, I shift my body to try and alleviate some of the pain. I want to sleep, but I can't. Instead, I lie there, imaging things that could keep me warm, like wine and chocolate. I don't even like red wine that much. But nothing could warm up this cave more as I lie in my damp, long sleeve t-shirt on a bed of rope. I will go as long as I can.


## June 18th, 2008


As light of a new dawn slowly brightens through the morning's cloud cover, I move onto my island in the hope that today I will be seen. On the ground, I wait to hear a helicopter. It is too painful to stand. When I think I hear an engine, I stand up, and wave my bright yellow neoprene shirt. The noise gets louder, and I strain my head in every direction to see the bird that can take me away from all this. As the whoompf, whoompf, whoompf of the helicopter fades, I can only fall back onto the ground, wishing, willing the life-saving noise to return. I can see helicopters in the distance.

All morning this continues. I hear a helicopter. I stand up. I wave frantically. I lie back down.

Lying, waiting, I hear a rustle of dirt and rock. I look over and see the cable line running along the ground starting to move. I take a quick inventory of disposable items, and reach for the sports bra hanging around my neck. I had taken it off yesterday to dry. Unable to pull it back over my head because of my shoulder, I had considered using it as a sling, but it didn't work. My arm felt the same regardless of whether it was resting in the sling or hanging useless and numb at my side. The bra could go. Maybe Search and Rescue will know where to look if someone finds the clothing and reports it. I scoot downslope to the cable. Maneuvering the bra beneath the running line, I let the cable run over the cloth as I carefully tie a knot. Pulling it tight, confident it will stay, I let go. As I watch, the cable line and my bra lift off the ground and into the sky, as the cable above lowers to meet it, and the pulley system becomes fully functioning. The pulley system runs throughout the morning, and then it stops, both cables suspended above me.

I return to waiting for helicopters, watching with a sinking heart as the same clouds from yesterday blow up from the valley. The white clouds whip upward through the air, violently dancing, frenzied, until they melt together in a cover of fog, mist and light rain. Socked in, there is no way a helicopter can get close enough to see me. And there is the danger of the cables. Moving up from below, the fog marks the time I have each day to be seen. To be found.

Disheartened, I decide to move back to the cave while the daylight remains. As I push myself up, I look down and notice blood. At first, I am surprised, and then I am annoyed. I thought bodies in emergency mode were supposed to turn off all but the most vital mechanisms to function. I consider the full moon and the pull of the tides, my body in ancient rhythm with the earth. Then I am annoyed again. This is super gross on top of everything else. The toilet paper is in shreds from being wrapped around me. Sighing, I move to the cave and go to my rocky nook to lie down. It's foggy, and although there is daylight left, I know I can't be seen. However, within minutes, I hear the unmistakable sound of helicopters. Unable to gauge the distance, I'm suspended in disbelief, noting the thick fog outside. Suddenly, the noise is on top of me, rumbling outside the cave entrance. I scramble to my feet, hobbling to the entrance of the cave, along the small path that runs parallel to the cliff. I can't see because of the clouds, but there is no mistaking the loud whoomph, whoomph, whoomph slowly climbing up the mountain somewhere above me. Then, just as suddenly as it was upon me, it's gone. I missed it. I remain outside, hoping they will return. They don't. The night is clear with a full moon. I lie in the wet grass outside the cave, watching the sky and trying to get comfortable. After the moon fades from view, I wander back into the cave to wait out the remaining hours of darkness.

Watching the sunrise over mountains on the distant horizon, the dawn's pinks, oranges and reds in a sky of deepening blue is the most beautiful sunrise I've ever seen. Finally, the sky is clear. As the morning grows warmer, and the sun moves higher, I lie on my back, absorbing the warmth. I've been so cold. By mid-morning, I know I'm getting sunburned. It feels good. I'm so thankful to get sunburned. I've never felt warmer. Now that the sun is out, so are the insects. They find their way into my cuts and wounds. I suddenly realize my thirst, having only four ounces of water in the past two days. I need to get down the hill to the waterfall, but my injuries and the steep grade make me nervous. A slip could be catastrophic, even sending me plunging off the cliff below. But I am dirty and bloody and definitely need water. I reason that to successfully survive a few more days, I need to be cleaner and hydrated. With the aid of my walking stick, I slowly descend the face. The moment I reach the flat spot, I bend down and drink. Nothing will taste as sweet again. I need to drink at least two liters, or as much as I can without getting sick. I sit in the hot sun and I drink, patiently filling up my water bottle and drinking until I can't. I remove my clothes and work to get the blood out. Laying out my shirt and pants on the rocks to dry, I wash my body as best I can, watching red water flow down and over the cliff next to me. Clean, I sit on the rocks, warming my body in the sun, taking small sips of water while I wait for my clothes to dry.

Suddenly, the whoomph of helicopters fills the air. They are right here and I know they are looking for me. I need to get back to the island immediately. Taking care to get dressed, and filling up my water bottle in case I am not seen, I carefully scramble up the slope as quickly as I can. At the top, I tie up the rear of my pants, ripped since my fall. I try to be practical and modest.

Forty-five minutes later, I am spotted by a police helicopter. I see it from a distance, bouncing through the sky, closer and closer, until the pilot and I are looking directly at one another. He waves. I wave back. He motions he is going to return. As he turns the helicopter around, I collapse in relief, feeling the way I've only seen people feel in the movies.

The same man who spotted me rescues me. Slowly, the helicopter maneuvers beneath the cable lines, and I watch as he rappels down. Upon reaching the ground, he unhooks himself and checks on me, asking about my injuries. I explain my shoulder and ankle are hurt. I hope my German is understandable. He reaches into his duffel bag and pulls out a Red Bull. He tells me that I need to drink it immediately. Some part of me chuckles; the duffel bag is full of Red Bull.

Lorenz introduces himself and connects us together with rope, harness and carabiner. The helicopter, which had moved away, returns, and lowers a rope to us. Once connected, we are immediately lifted up and off the mountain, swinging over the ledge and and by rock walls as we are pulled into the helicopter. We land in a field, where I again explain my injuries. Medical

personnel asks for my permission to put me to sleep in order to put my shoulder back into place before we reached the hospital. I say yes, flooded with relief that I can finally rest. A needle is inserted into my arm, my world going black as I am lowered into the helicopter bed.

## June 2019

Sitting at home, I watch the evening alpenglow settle on Columbia Mountain from my back porch. Mind drifting, I remember watching a wolverine scurry up a steep embankment just below Logan Pass last summer. It was the tenth anniversary of my accident. I was riding my bike up Going-to -the-Sun Road, appreciating being able to finally exist in the world without fear.

My mind drifts and recalls all of the surgeries, all of the recoveries; physical, mental, spiritual. I glance down at my new external prosthetic, a gift, a sweet surprise to finally be free of chronic pain.

I consider the struggle and point of the whole journey. One truth, made of two parts, resonates. My home is in the mountains, with their finicky tendencies, haughty natures and surprising graces. My home is also in people and the help we offer each other. I am not alone. I never was, and it took those four days on a mountain in Germany to help me realize it.

Montana's mountains have always kept me safe from the threats of the world, real or imagined. Resting in her rocky crooks, gazing at beautiful vistas, drinking from her rivers and exploring with people I love and who love me, I'm made whole.

In the end, the point is the people: who we help, who we hurt, who we love and who loves us. Then, the mountains keep our perspective. For me, love of one cannot exist without love of the other. Mountains, like people, hold our most sacred stories. I am still writing mine.

I can see the line, the thread. The branch of death retreats, releases me.

*Montana Bound*
Victoria Emmons

❊

I type in the word "Montana" and discover a tourism website. Big Sky Country, it says. I have seen more than half of the 50 states, but never Montana. The website promotes the state's greatest natural treasures; one can hunt, fish, hike, ski, kayak or white water raft.

Great. I am not a skier and I can't imagine pulling a slippery fish from an icy stream. I have never sat in a kayak in my life. I nearly drowned once while whitewater rafting in north Georgia. My father used to hunt moose and taught me how to use a rifle, but that was decades ago; guns are foreign to me now.

Will Montana welcome me? Will it welcome a 60-something Caucasian grandmother, a retired healthcare administrator? A sometimes poet, a bad golfer and a great volunteer Rotary Club member? What will Montana think of me?

***

It is late September 2015. Sweat dribbles down the side of my face as I pack box after box, each filled with 30 years of my California life. Strangers finger my garage sale offerings under my watchful eye.

"Will you take ten cents for this?" asks a gray-haired woman, a tattered blue poncho skimming her bare knees. She holds up an ashtray marked at $15.

"No, thanks," I reply with certainty. "That is sterling silver and turquoise."

She places the ashtray back on the overcrowded shelf of trinkets. After she leaves with her meager purchases, I pick up the ashtray and put it in my pocket. I have never smoked and abhor the habit, but the ashtray was a birthday gift to my late mother-in-law. It will follow me to Montana, I decide.

My daughter Kate lives in Missoula, the reason for my interest in this unknown territory. I say goodbye forever to my home in Pleasanton and drive to Sacramento to meet Kate, who will accompany me for a three-day drive north through crowded freeways and lonely, mountainous two-lane roads. Eventually U.S. Highway 93 deposits us into Missoula, tired and road-weary.

Moving to a different state resembles settling in a foreign country; I empathize with immigrants trying to make it in America. The Montana culture reveals itself to me in small ways. A day after I move into my new house situated in the hills, there is a knock on the front door. I shove boxes out of the way as I open the door just a crack to peer out. A man and a woman

holding a plate full of homemade brownies are smiling at me. They are my new neighbors, welcoming me to the community.

A few days later, the previous owners of my house arrive at the door with a potted plant in hand. Never has a home seller given me a welcome plant, so I am suddenly suspicious. People are not that nice unless they want something.

I assume the kindness of these Montana strangers is merely an accident. As I drive to the grocery store nearest to my neighborhood, people wave hello to me. Have I met these people? Why are they waving at me? Is there something wrong with my car?

Montana kindness seems to extend to every aspect of life in my new town. The post office workers smile at me and chat about things. The Fact & Fiction bookstore staff discuss the books they sell. The owner of Plonk, my new favorite downtown restaurant, acts as though we are old friends. Even the guys at Gary's Gas Station are pleasant as they fill the gas tank and clean my car windows. Nobody in California ever pumped gas for me and certainly never cleaned my windshield.

The week in November that my older sister Anita comes to visit from New York City, I am already working at my new job at the University of Montana. While I am on campus, my sister unpacks my fine china. Tall, slender and attractive with very little gray hair for her age, Anita is quite generous with my grandson, who is also her godchild.

"Let's get some early Christmas shopping done," Anita suggests.

On Saturday, we find ourselves at Target. We locate the toy department and try to decide what my two-year-old grandson might like.

"I want to get Alex something educational," Anita says. "He's so smart. He needs a toy that will challenge him."

As we look through the rows of Ninja characters and LEGO kits, a tall, middle-aged and bearded man wearing dirty jeans and an open, checkered shirt interrupts us.

"Where're you from?" he asks, peering out from underneath a weathered, blue baseball cap.

My sister and I were both born on U.S. Navy bases in California and raised mostly in sunny Florida with a few other places in the mix—Hawaii, Texas, Maryland, Newfoundland. Anita chose to live on the east coast and I landed in the west. After nearly 50 years in New York City's upper east side, my sister sounds refined. She bears no hint of a Woody Allen or Archie Bunker voice. As for me, most Californians don't have a distinguishable accent. Does our way of speaking grab the scruffy man's attention? Are we so different from Montanans?

"I'm from New York," Anita responds to the gentleman with the caution all city dwellers adopt for survival.

"I live in Missoula," I say, proud of my new home. We both smile in a friendly manner. The man snarls a little.

"But you're not from here," he corrects me.

"Well, no, I didn't grow up here," I confess. "But I live here now.

I moved here from the Bay Area—Northern California."

Wrong answer.

The man stands taller, pushing his shoulders back so their broadness is accentuated. He puts his hands on his hips, his fists crunching the dangling shirt tails. He stares at us both as though we are aliens.

"You need to go back to California," he says.

I swallow back a gulp.

"Thanks, but I like it here," I say with a tentative smile and shuffle my sister away from the toy aisle.

That one unfriendly encounter is outweighed by so many other terrific experiences in Montana. Every day, I gaze at Mount Jumbo from my living room window, soaking in the majesty of the impressive mountain and its fellow peaks in all their seasonal glory. Herds of deer crowd my neighborhood and streets. One day, a dozen of them cause a traffic jam as they shuffle across Higgins Avenue. It's the kind of traffic jam I don't mind.

*** 

Despite the awkward layout of the street patterns in Missoula, I learn to find my way home from just about anywhere in town without using GPS. I know which side streets to avoid in winter, the intersections with no stop signs in any direction, and the one where motorists are not allowed to turn either left or right. I can drive down an icy hill without sliding. I own snow tires for the first time in my life—and a snow jacket, too. My drawer is filled with winter scarves in a zillion different colors.

I grew up in warm, sunny climates; thus, my snow experience consisted primarily of what I saw on Christmas cards. During my first few months in Missoula, I learn the verb "winterize" and the checklist of actions needed to assure that my sprinkler system won't freeze, my heating system will work, and the snow will be removed from my driveway. To my delight, I discover that my Infiniti has a "snow" button to help navigate slippery roads. Unfortunately, I also discover there is no Infiniti dealer in my new hometown. Servicing my car will now require a three-hour drive to Spokane.

I learn that my plants have to be winterized, too. I need to bring indoors those that have thrived on the back patio during summer and fall. Others die off in winter. Everyone assures me my plants will bloom again in spring, but I have my doubts. All I had ever done in the past was cover flowering bushes with a sheet during cool nights; snow is an entirely new element.

To get to work, I have to trek across campus from the parking lot to the Journalism School. When snow starts to fall, the idea of walking on icy sidewalks makes me nervous. A colleague suggests I buy Yak Trax. After searching blindly for what these could possibly be, I locate some of the unique contraptions at Cabela's. Attaching the spiky things to my boots only makes me even more nervous, so I abandon them after a couple of attempts.

Months later, at a New York City shoe store, I find some Canadian boots with built-in ice tracks. Even the fancy boots do not prevent me from my first big spill on the ice, knocking my head so hard on the sidewalk that it requires a trip to the emergency room.

***

My first year in Montana, I learn the significance of John Steinbeck. His quote about loving Montana appears on bar and restaurant walls, coffee mugs, tee-shirts and growlers; if only Steinbeck knew what he'd started. I now understand why the author wrote those words of adoration.

Making close friends in Missoula is a slow process, despite the neighborly warmth. Many people introduce themselves proudly as 'fifth generation Montanan.' I know I will never be able to live up to that moniker. Fortunately, I am a member of a Rotary Club in California, so I attend the Missoula Rotary Club meetings where people welcome me, assuring my place in this niche Montana community.

I am a Montanan. Perhaps not a fourth or fifth generation, as so many locals describe themselves. I am a first generation Montana woman.

## *When I Say This To Your Face, I Won't Need A Veil*
Julie Janj

There's no way to accurately describe the feeling that comes over you, a mix of anger, fear, and exhilaration not unlike when you realize you've unexpectedly harmed yourself. You find a bathroom or a mop closet where you can change. Your backpack holds two filthy pairs of leather gloves, red eye makeup, a head covering, the niqab that goes over it, a knife bound in tape, and an empty syringe. You rub the red around your eyes, the only part of you that will be seen. You pull the head covering over your hair, tucking it into your collar. You put the niqab over your face, tying it so tightly behind your head that it causes a dull pain. You bring up the first layer of material and things become slightly visible, then the second layer and you can see through a slit just large enough for a narrow range of vision. You adjust it so the black ribbon between your eyes is perfectly centered. You pull on long gloves and smooth the veil flowing to your shoulders. Your uniform is complete. The crowd outside is typical for a bar show. Mostly smokers who come out between songs or during, as if they don't care what goes on inside. Their attention shifts from their conversation to you when you walk up, since you're dressed head to toe in black and the only context they have for your head covering is foreign. As the oil drum, pitchfork head, rakes, chains, and pig iron are arranged, they take out their phones and start to film. This is the generation that would foolishly die rather than not record content. You flip the switch on the megaphone and wait for the opening sound of metal on metal. You look at no one, despite the fact they don't know who you are. When the beating on the oil drum starts, you begin to scream into the hand-set, widening your eyes and staring unfixed into nothing. Everything slows down. You have no concept of how much time passes, or the movement of people on the periphery, you just know they're there. You stride down the sidewalk, directing your vitriol at no one and everyone. The things that come out of your mouth are not rehearsed, but range from monologues you mem-orized in high school drama to quotations to hate speech for the powers that be. When you come close to people, you see them move back uncomfort-ably, some afraid, some annoyed. You wonder which one could consider you a terrorist, the one with a knife or a gun. Some try to join in but you don't let them. You break a bottle on the stone windowsill where a stupid bitch is sitting, holding her phone toward your face. You resist the urge to grab her phone and smash it. You pick up a chain and swing it overhead, aware of the space it occupies but getting dangerously close to the crowd. You let it fly into a piece of sheet metal and double over, screaming like you're being

tortured. You're aware of the sounds the others are making with the metal, but it's not ending. You pick up an iron bar and smash it again and again into the drum. You resume your ranting, this time it devolves into a string of expletives regarding everyone and no one. You turn off the megaphone, placing it down on the sidewalk, which acts as a stoppage for the others. People stand silently for a minute, waiting to see if it will continue, then very honestly cheer or very obviously abstain. You don't speak with anyone, but pick up as many implements as you can carry and walk down the alley to the truck. You pull the niqab off your head, overheated. Someone has followed you and you recognize the woman whose phone you wanted to smash. She gushes at the others how much she liked that, but you ignore her. You sit in the front seat and remove your gloves, realizing just then that your wrist has been cut.

*Birthday*
Anonymous

It's been my experience that most young, American adults dream of turning 21. Of the freedoms associated with finally being a legal adult, I was no different. I had planned for years how my 21st birthday would play out. I would have a party at one of the bars in town, with all my closest friends in attendance. Games, maybe balloons.

I knew better. I knew this would be far from the birthday I had imagined.

I was two years into an abusive relationship, but held on to a thread of hope. I am going to refer to him as WPE, Worst Person Ever, because I cannot use his real name. Over twenty years later, I still live in fear.

We lived off the grid, several miles from town, or any neighbors. WPE had been a borderline alcoholic when I met him. I made excuses for him.

He didn't mean to give me a black eye. He was drunk and didn't know what he was doing.

On my birthday, he was six months sober. But still the Worst Person Ever. The only difference between drunk and sober was that he remembered things the next day.

The sixth of June, I woke up to several inches of snow on the ground. Happy birthday. We both worked for the same construction company, and headed to work. It was miserable, and I was cold and soaked through within a few hours. Thankfully, WPE was not a workhorse like me. He was raised a spoiled brat, and the weather was too much for him. He stopped our work early that day.

I didn't have much for family that lived close, so I expected mail, birthday cards from other zip codes. I asked him if we could stop by the post office, but he refused. Instead, he wanted to go to his grandmother's house, to take a shower, to warm up.

"Don't tell her it's your birthday," he warned. "She's the type of woman who would feel bad for you."

His grandmother fed us lunch, and fawned all over him, as usual. She was his biggest fan, and he reveled in it.

When we headed home, he immediately began berating me. Even though he was sober, he was sure that I wanted to drink to celebrate my birthday, sure I was angry that I couldn't. I assured him that it didn't matter, repeated it over and over. In his mind, it did.

I focused on the regular chores, splitting firewood, feeding the horses. He chose dinner, as usual, and I made deer steaks and potatoes. We ate in silence, except for his grunts and guttural noises. His nose had been broken

from decades of drunken brawls, and he had a hard time breathing. He made the same kind of noises at night, sleep apnea, and many nights I lay there and hoped he would stop gasping for air. Permanently.

After dinner, I started the generator, and we watched a movie. His choice, of course, something science fiction that I had no interest in. Every night, I rubbed his feet while he watched a movie. It was mandatory.

I thought the day was finally over. Exhausted, I came into the bedroom, only to find him laying naked. He demanded a blow job. "Do it, bitch."

This wasn't the first time I'd heard those words, but I had hoped today would be different.

"It's my birthday," I stammered. I don't know where the strength came from, what finally broke and freed the words I'd been holding onto.

He just stared at me. I knew the repercussions of denying him what he wanted. I did as he demanded, hot tears coursing down my cheeks. Every time this happened, I swore it would be the last. This was true of every minute of every day of the past two years, always something I swore would never happen again.

When I finished, I laid in our bed, perfectly still, completely silent, another routine, another demand. He could not fall asleep unless I remained motionless and quiet, and every night, I waited for twenty minutes for the gasping snores to begin. Always twenty minutes. I watched the pendulum clock on the wall, waiting to roll over, without being yelled at.

Tonight, I listened even closer. I couldn't stand being next to him.

I had to escape.

When 11:30 struck on the clock, I gave myself a few minutes before I quietly eased myself out of the bed. In the kitchen, I paced back and forth, crying, wondering what the hell I was doing with my life. I needed out, needed my family and friends. I needed to reclaim my life.

I crept back into the bedroom. In the dark, I knew exactly where everything was. I stood next to my snoring husband. I stared at him, hating him more than I had ever hated anything.

Tears flowed as I raised my hand.

The clock suddenly began to chime. Midnight. My birthday was over.

WPE snorted and rolled over in his sleep. His movement and the sound of the clock brought me out of my trance. I slowly released the hammer on the loaded pistol.

My birthday was over, but he received the gift. I spared him. I slept on the couch that night.

*Not The Women Frida Slept With*
Emily Withnall

Though my heart is free, my hands, if they stray, can be dangerous.
***

My girlfriend and I visit Phoenix together with the sole purpose of seeing Frida's art. The timeline in the gallery chronicles Frida's and Diego's separate artistic paths and their tumultuous relationship. It names Diego's many lovers, including Frida's sister, Cristina. It names two of Frida's male lovers, Nickolas Murray and Leon Trotsky. The captions beside the paintings and photographs in the gallery give more details, spooling out an intimate history with each image. In one black and white photograph, Frida is stretched out on a bed, fully clothed, smoking a cigarette. Another woman spoons her. The caption refers to the woman as a good friend of Frida's.

I didn't dare hold my girlfriend's hand in the gallery. We have had many talks about safety, about where and when it is safe to be visible. We live in Missoula, Montana, and despite its liberal bent, we cannot hold hands downtown. Phoenix was a new city to both of us and we weren't sure if it was safer. And so my hands dangled at my sides as I read about Frida's surgeries, her unquenchable thirst for mutual love and longing, and her good friends.

Adrienne Rich knew the pain of erasure and the enormity of lost female and lesbian history. In "Diving into the Wreck," she writes about reading the many varied myths about the wreck she wants to see. She writes about donning the constricting and unwieldy scuba suit to bear witness to the wreck. She writes of darkness and the solitude of her quest. My girlfriend and I bore witness and acted our own charade, dressed in our own awkward and invisible costumes, masquerading as "good friends"— but in a new century. We whispered when we discovered some intimate detail about Frida in the gallery and wanted to hold it up against our own longing, our own reflections of ourselves and each other.

The omissions in the captions reflected us more honestly than Frida's unwavering gaze. Like Rich's body-armor of black rubber, our limbs were constricted. We moved freely throughout the open rooms with high ceilings, and yet our hands and voices were bound. And as we gazed at Frida's art, read parts of her story, and mapped our own longing and pain onto the artifacts of her life, we were in turn being witnessed by others in the gallery. In her poem, Rich discovers that she is the wreck and its observer.

Perhaps some gallery-goers detected joy in our smiles or love in our eyes as my girlfriend and I glanced at each other across the space. Or perhaps our charade was as convincing as the photos' captions.

In one of Frida's paintings, "The Love Embrace of the Universe," she sits on Cihuacoatl's lap and is embraced by the goddess of earth and the goddess of sky. Waterfalls gush from the Cihuacoatl's stone nipples. A baby Diego sits on Frida's lap and he has a third eye on his forehead, like Shiva. Although two small tears emerge from each of her eyes, it is her heart that gives her away. Blood spirals out of her chest like a fireworks display—a detail that highlights the stillness of the images around her heart. The stories exist in the gaps and spaces between words. What an image says and does not say. There is a loneliness in not being able to demonstrate affection to someone you love. A wreck exists in the space between my hand and my girlfriend's. I am not sure whether we traveled to Phoenix for the wreck or the story of the wreck. I don't know how to begin to untangle the two.

In January of this year, two men were assaulted outside the Rhino Bar in Missoula. Minutes prior to being beaten with fists and boots, they were attacked with homophobic slurs. Like everywhere else in the country, hate crimes did not begin with the new presidency, but they have continued to ramp up, to intensify, to signal to those who live in the heart of fear that violence is an acceptable way to deal with fear. I met my girlfriend in January, too. It was an antidote to fear in so many ways, a choosing of love. Though I don't want to live in fear, I do. What happened at the Rhino, what happened at Pulse in Orlando, what happened at Stonewall—it has happened before and keeps happening. People say over and over, "We've come so far. It's not the way it used to be." This is true. Still, when it comes to LGBT equality, time feels like a Salvador Dali clock. There is no moving forward, just constant meltdown. And each incident is a warning. The men who committed assault outside the Rhino didn't just commit assault; they also issued a warning through their actions: this is what could happen if you live your life in the open.

In downtown Missoula, a ghost dog clenches my severed hand in its jaws so I don't surrender to the yearning of touch. The hand is bloody, but I am alive. It is hard to know if the ghost dog is our culture of fear, sent to keep me in check, or whether it is my protector. I am not sure how I will learn the difference.

I think again of Rich: I am here for the wreck, not the story of the wreck. I am here for the unapologetic eyebrows and the eyes glinting with pain and ferocity. I am here for the images of a woman who is simultaneously broken and unashamed. Still, I tell her: You could have known more joy if you'd relinquished your longing for him, if you'd reshaped it all into a longing for yourself. I imagine how the self-portraits might have multiplied then. I tell him: Asshole. You didn't know what you had. I tell

the woman in photos with her: I hope you both experienced a fragment of time in which you were nourished.

Through Frida's bus accident and her multiple surgeries, she kept painting. She painted her body cast. She painted a self-portrait of her body with a broken column within, nails piercing her skin, and tears emerging like lace from her eyes. She was unrelenting. What I struggle with most is the feeling that I have allowed fear to dictate how I live. I don't want to accept life on the fringe, or in the shadows. I don't want to hide my love for this woman who walks through the gallery with me. In a dream, I once came face-to-face with a grizzly. I ran, eyes bulging and mouth open in a silent scream. I was certain death was imminent, but what scared me the most was that my voice didn't work. I couldn't speak of the terror I was running from. In that dream, I faced a near death that does not seem unlike the small daily deaths that occur as I find new ways to hide who I am and to hide who I love. My phantom hand wiggles its fingers and stretches for my girlfriend.

At the end of her poem, Rich writes about how all of us are compelled to return to the wreck even when its story hurts or has displaced us. She suggests that by pointing to the myths that should bear our names but do not that we might withstand erasure. I want to believe it is possible to move faster than a melting clock. I want to believe the names that belong in the book of myths will one day appear. I am still attached to the story of the wreck. Without it, the wreck would not exist. When I whispered to Frida, I almost believed I could save her so many years past her death. I almost believed that my anger at the museum's blanching of her story could resuscitate her gender bending, pants-wearing bisexuality. I almost believed that my anger could preserve her status as an LGBT icon in mainstream history books. In the gallery, my girlfriend and I studied one of Frida's paintings featuring watermelon, coconuts, an owl, bananas, an open papaya, and a tiny bride peering over a watermelon slice, at the fruit across the table. The painting's title was "The Bride Frightened at Seeing Life Opened," and the caption said the motifs captured Frida's unquenchable longing for love. My girlfriend turned to me.

"Do you have an unquenchable longing for love?" she asked.

"I don't think so," I answered.

Now, I suspect my response was too hasty. I long for a time when genuine love can always be spoken. I look at my pale, freckled hands. My hands know the ache of reaching and retreating. At the exhibition in Phoenix, Cristina Kahlo and Leon Trotsky were in the book of myths, but not the women Frida slept with.

*Providence*
Hannah Bourke

❉

In the sterilized quiet of the intensive care unit of the psychiatric ward, the nurses watched over me. There was no door; they could see me from their desks. I sat up on the edge of the bed, bedsheets a mess. The little window at the head of the bed didn't look out over much, but it let some light in. The night before came washing over me like a surreal wave of shame.

\*\*\*

I walked across the Higgins Bridge in downtown Missoula, chilly in the February night. I lifted my leg over the edge of the railing, straddling the barrier. Spontaneous suicidal tendencies stirred frequently in me, especially after heavy drinking. It was like I realized I could make it all stop; it was all so easy. I had to die.

The two guys I was with, Maxon and Doug, pulled me back onto my feet. We stood there for a few seconds before I bolted across the road to the other side of the bridge. I teetered in a pair of little black ankle boots, sporting a chiffon red mini dress that I had borrowed from a friend, and a big black faux fur coat. I'd been wearing that outfit for 24 hours straight—aside from the prior night's vigorous undressing. I turned the corner at the end of the bridge and fled down a flight of stairs leading to the river bank.

I slowed down at the water's edge. Step by delirious step, I trekked into the raging waters of the icy Clark Fork River. The cold hit me instantly as I waded further out from the shore. The current destabilized my balance, making it a challenge to stay on my feet. I turned around when the water lapped up to my shoulders. The last thing I saw before I went down was Maxon stripping off his clothes on the shore.

My head dipped under water, the heavy coat wrapped around me, dragging me downstream. Breath was still in my lungs. I reached down through the black water to the river bed, holding onto a rock to keep me anchored under.

\*\*\*

A nurse interrupted my memory as she came in to take my vitals. She would have made the cutest grandma, a big bun of gray hair on top of her head. I didn't say much to her; it was hard to make small talk with anyone, let alone on my first day in the hospital. She brought me a box of 2% milk, an apple and a cheese sandwich. I ate it out of boredom as much as hunger.

I was eventually transferred to the main unit, where patients were able to walk around and watch tv and do other activities. A piano sat in a back room, beside rows of windows on the back wall of the building that looked

out over I-90 and the big sky horizon. The staff gave me purple scrubs to change into, and dreadful socks with sticky pads on their soles to keep patients from slipping on the linoleum floor.

My first experience with the doctor left a bad taste in my mouth. He was an older gray-haired gentleman with glasses. When we got to talking, he found it rather amusing how I had wound up in the river and ultimately in his office.

"Don't you think it's kind of funny?" he asked me. I did not find it funny; I was shaken and insulted. Images of that night raced through my mind. I left his office feeling hopeless and angry. Mostly at myself, although I tried in my mind to blame it on him.

Afterwards, I went to the back room and sat down at the piano and let my fingers tinker over the keys, playing the automatic melodies that always came to mind. When my fingers stopped moving, I found myself lost in thought once again.

*** 

Arms wrapped around my shoulders to pull me up from the river, turning my face to take a breath of thirty degree air in a state of silent shock. Maxon had pulled my body through the rushing water, weighed down by the coat that was dragging me like a sail. He staggered us to shore. The EMTs met him at the water's edge. I don't remember much; a wash of blue and red lights and cold metallic instruments, bodies in blue uniforms. It was like a Monet painting, the paradise and water lilies of his final years.

From the ambulance, they wheeled me into the emergency room at St. Patrick's Hospital. I don't remember the transport; to me it was as if I had suddenly teleported into a private padded room with a glass wall that overlooked the nurses station. I had been in restraints, but when I came to I was on the cold hard floor, wrapped in blankets and dressed in a patient gown. I inspected the white plastic identification band on my left wrist, partially covering the tattoo I got when I was eighteen.

*** 

By an act of fate, my next interaction with a doctor was with a different man. A quiet, focused man with a gentle presence. He put me at ease. He never made me feel like a ridiculous mess and he wanted to try me out on some medications I'd never taken before. He recommended Geodon and Gabapentin. When asked about my drinking history, I told him I knew I needed to stop but I didn't want to go to treatment.

He told me he thought it was a good idea. I told him I knew a woman who could be my sponsor in AA when I got out of the hospital. He nodded in gentle acceptance.

I asked the nurse staff if I could only see that doctor from then on, and they agreed. He would continue to see me every time I entered the psychiatric wing at that hospital. I came to think of him as a healing friend. I left the hospital in early March of 2013; I was twenty-two years old.

Something about the end of winter pulls me into myself. Deprived of sunlight and sobriety, I would just lose it. Almost always, my internal attacks came on the cusp of winter and spring.

One year later, I awoke in a hospital bed again. They told me I had been briefly comatose. I was angry I was awake at all. Visitors came whirling in and out, mainly Maxon and nurses, phantoms of the hospital space and time.

I don't remember much. Again, it's all like the final Monet paintings; everything begins to blend together into one. I was back at the Providence Center, back to detoxing while remaining subdued by whatever meds they doled out to me during my time there. Back to stale bed sheets and gross slipper socks with pads of rubber on the soles. Half-length toothbrushes and ordering meals from a tiny white hospital index card menu.

My old friend, the doctor, said he was sorry to see me there again. He assured me that it was going to get better. I barely believed him, but it was enough to hold onto. At this point, I was genuinely afraid of myself.

I went to the group meetings on the psyche floor. Some were interesting, but some put me to sleep because of the medication. I didn't want to die; I knew I had to stop drinking, and that scared me, too. I didn't really know how to live. Being told I was in a coma after what I had done was enough to get me to sit up straight and pay attention at meetings.

\*\*\*

My next trip to the Providence Center was unlike those before. I was so in love with the universe. I wanted to hug everyone and make friends. I'd ask them to teach me words in other languages. I was writing and drawing obsessively, filling up so many notebooks with the ranting thoughts of my manic mind.

I documented each thought with the exact time and date the thought occurred. I came up with a personal reference for the meaning of each number and how it supported the thought.

"Godspe!" I'd exclaim, but only when witnessing an act of synchronicity or magic. My mind perceived almost every minute as a momentous occasion. "Every moment is momentous," I'd write in my notebooks.

I started wearing a purple wig I had bought at Albertsons months earlier. I was still going to school, but I was unraveling there as well. My thoughts were so unfocused that I could not read or follow along in class. My brain was beginning to synthesize the Russian and English languages; I began writing made up phonetic Russian-English hybrid language all over everything. My arms, my walls, my notebooks. It was like a code only I could crack. I had symbols I was drawing all over everything too, like a signature. I started calling myself Fen.

I drove myself from Missoula to Vashon Island to meet my family for Labor Day. It took me over twenty-four hours to complete the nine hour drive, because everything was enchanting. I kept collecting trash on the side of the highway to make art. My mother tried to take me to the hospital in Seattle, but I refused to go.

"I'll only see my doctor in Missoula. He is nice," I stated. My mom relented and drove my manic self to Missoula and I checked back in.

I still wanted to hug everyone, so it took forever to go anywhere. My doctor, the healing friend, had never seen me like this before.

"Why Fen?" he asked, sitting in his chair in the windowless office.

"Because it sounds like Fun," I told him. "And its short for Fenix."

He put me on Latuda, which I dubbed the "latitude of my attitude," and Lithium. They barely had any effect on me.

At night, I'd wait for the moon to rise out the back windows looking over I-90. I'd sit staring up at her, devoted to basking in her presence. I'd had a vision of the moon at the peak of my mania, when I was on the side of the highway just over the Washington border. Every night since, I'd look up to the moon and wait for her to show her true beauty to me again. She didn't change again for almost a year. I never minded; basking in her glow was pleasure enough.

The night nurse was a lovely woman with long white hair that she wore with the top half tied back with a silver barrette. She had a Russian name, so I immediately wanted to be her friend.

"What does your name mean?" I asked her one night, as I sat at the window waiting for the moon to rise.

"It translates to Starry Hope. What is your fascination with Russian? Are you Russian, my dear?" She asked, her soft accent curious.

"I'm not Russian, but I am studying the language at the University of Montana. I think it's beautiful." I said the last part in Russian, a big grin on my face. We chatted for a while and she went about her responsibilities. I doodled and wrote down my thoughts, checking the clock to document the time for each.

\*\*\*

I'd drink tea and hide my trash away in a shoe box in my room. I suspected the nurses hadn't found it yet. It was mostly the wrappers from the tea bags, each dried tea bag rolled and placed beside it. They had dates and times written on them in black pen. Everything had dates and numbers, cataloging my frame of mind with the world's time.

I wished I'd had more supplies to create with. I longed for the days just before entering the hospital. I'd wander around the streets of Missoula, taking photographs at dawn with my 35mm—I never went anywhere without it during that period of my life. I continued to wear the purple wig and yell "Godspe!" when it felt right. I catalogued my trash even then, although to a somewhat lesser degree of neurotic compulsion.

I wanted to save every part of me for art; everything had potential. Everything was a part of me. My head would spin with ideas of how to orchestrate my creative visions. My thoughts would spin much faster than the rest of me, and I'd get distracted by something else and start another project. A never-ending spiral.

It was fun eating dinner and watching movies with the other patients this time. I didn't have a depressed thought anywhere in my head. I wasn't

worried about what was going to happen, what people thought of me, how I was going to fix this mess, or all the thoughts I'd had every other time I'd been there. I felt completely free and in love. One of the nurses joked that when I was feeling better I should come back and apply for a job. "You're half the treatment staff as it is," she laughed. I smiled, thinking it sweet of her to say that, but she hadn't yet seen my beloved box of garbage.

Everywhere I went, I talked to people. My energy lifted people's spirits and we all became very close. When I was released, they signed my notebooks like you would a yearbook on the last day of school.

I almost didn't get out that day, since they found the shoebox full of archived trash. There were some bizarre items in the box, meticulously recorded and placed gently in there. Feminine products, in my mind, were in the name of art.

"What the hell have you been doing?" my discharge nurse asked me. "This makes me think you're not ready to get out of here."

The truth was that I wasn't ready to get out of there. It would take months for me to come back down to Earth after sailing the rings of Saturn for so long, but I wanted to get out of that hospital. "I promise I can do it. Look, you can throw it away. I'll watch," I told him frantically. It pained me to watch him dump my beloved items into the trash bin. They released me later that day, in September of 2015.

***

I had Facetimed my mom the morning before I checked back into the hospital. She was horrified; I could hardly speak and was laying on my back, gurgling with my eyes partially closed. She hung up and called my neighbor, Jimmy, in a panic.

The next thing I knew, both Jimmy and his friend were knocking on my door saying they needed to take me to the hospital. They loaded me into the backseat of my silver Passat. Jimmy drove to the emergency room despite my wails in protest. "You don't know what it's like!"

The nurses took my blood and found five different drugs, including high levels of benzodiazepines and a high BAC. That set off a red flag from their perspective; my previous attempt used those methods, leaving me comatose.

"I wasn't trying to kill myself," I told them. I stayed there for several hours before the van came to wheel me across town to the Providence Center.

That was my darkest stay of all. I felt like I'd lost everything. I'd lost my mind, my sobriety, my schooling, my job. I could get it all back once I got well, but in my mind at that point in time, there was no light at the end of the tunnel.

I was weighed down by a blanket of darkness. I hardly left my room. I wore the purple scrub pajamas they gave me upon intake, and even the scratchy yellow socks with the padded soles. I wrote very little; I mostly tried to sleep away the time.

It seems to be a rule that what goes up must come down. Down I crashed, dust settling in the air around impact. I felt abandoned. How could it all be so clearly beautiful and accessible, only to be taken away by some

44

twist of cruel fate? I wallowed in doom for many months, struggling to find meaning or beauty in anything.

I laid in the hospital bed, unable to sleep. My roommate at the time, Larissa, was snoring in the bed next to me. She was a girl about my age who tried to kill herself, too. I agonized over how it all went so wrong. My thoughts hurt, the act of smiling hurt. My healing friend, the doctor, was rarely there. I longed for the energy I had when I was Fen; to be inspired by the world and optimistic for my future.

I was none of those things. I wanted to disappear. I got out of bed and walked over to the shower, hanging my purple scrubs on the door nub outside. We couldn't have actual hooks in there; pain makes people do desperate things. This was more soul pain than physical pain, I felt completely lost and hopeless. I turned the shower on and stood under the water for a long time. Fen would have sung and danced and marveled at the water's light reflecting on the wall. I stared down at my feet as the water disappeared into the drain.

I barely spoke to anyone besides Larissa. We talked about how we had fantasized about killing ourselves. She told me the only reason she didn't do it was because of her cat. I told her that I used to want to die, but I hadn't actually wanted to this time. I just lost control and took too much.

I shuffled myself, half awake and half dead inside, from group to group. Chair to chair, toilet to bed. I waited out my time. It had only been three months since I was last there as Fen. They let me out a few days later.

***

Four years later, it's still hard to make sense of everything sometimes. It's hard to find the will to go on, especially when you're in the thick of crisis after crisis. It is such a gift to be on the other side of so much struggle, and I have found peace within myself. I'm learning to love myself, how to cook, how to eat healthily and sleep regularly, how to get up and actually feel good about my day. All I had to do was reach out for help and let the universe carry me through the process of healing.

I started practicing kundalini yoga, meditation and Reiki. I moved back in with my family, where I've been for the past two years. I still get off balance; I still am who I am. It takes what it takes to get us to see the light. For the first time in my life, I feel like I have a life to look forward to.

*Passing Seasons*
Jessica Fuller

Footprints in the snow: mine, the birds under the feeder, the skittish field mice, the gentle deer and majestic elk. All creatures invisible to my present view. The patterned soles of winter boots, scrimshaw impressions, hooved grooves, and paw prints leave remnants frozen temporarily in time. Fleeting reminders of the steps taken yesterday or the day before.

Captivated by the freshly fallen snow, I follow the prints out onto the prairie where time stands still. I recognize my daughter and son-in-law's boot prints. Their blue heeler, Juno, left pawprints that weave along the path. As I walk, I discover bits of chewed Ponderosa pinecones. Juno has most likely left them behind after begging for them to be thrown.

Glimmering snow-covered mountains envelop this glacier carved valley. The stark white peaks accentuate the stillness and chill in the air. Sparkling diamonds of transformed moisture carpet the slumbering earth. A lone bald eagle flies from the familiar half dead Ponderosa Pine, preferring solitude to my approaching company.

There are no smells today; the air is cold and still. I zip up my insulated coat tightly under my chin and stuff my gloved hands into pockets, desperately seeking warmth. My hand-knitted hat and crocheted scarf help to keep out the frigid air. The snow crunches under each step; soon it will be too deep to walk on without snowshoes. My labored breath mingles with the cold to create thick clouds of vapor. Determined to complete my walk to the Big Tree and back, I press on.

I long for the earth's rotation toward the sun. Winter's magic will lose her grip and the earth will awaken with joyful new growth. Vibrant green grasses and wildflowers will profusely carpet the ground beneath my feet and all around me. I will tread softly upon this prairie and admire the glory of fresh new life. But for now, my reward will have to be the anticipation of the changing season and the cup of hot tea awaiting my return home.

My goal complete, I breathe in herbs steeped in warmth. I am comfortable and relaxed in the worn brown leather recliner that used to be my husband's—and now, since his death, is mine.

I struggle with the long winters this far north, having never been able to embrace much about them. But I persevere, try to find comfort in the seemingly never-ending coldness, darkness, and stillness. The short days, endless gray skies, and absence of songbirds adds to my exasperation.

To make matters worse, I've never held a passion for any snowy sport to relieve the winter blues. I've tried skiing and sledding, but a combination of

a fear of speed and a fear of falling encouraged me to relinquish these activities. My ideal sport is to sit inside my warm home while drinking a cup of tea and crocheting, watching the snow fall silently outside.

On the occasional blue-skied winter day, I venture out of my nest to embrace the rare sunshine and marvel at the way the snow glitters like diamonds around me. The snow forms little puff balls on top of the dead yarrow and wood fenceposts, leaning precariously, waiting for just one snowflake to topple them over. I feed suet cakes and a mixture of seed and nuts to the poor unfortunate birds who, like me, must endure the winter. The black-capped chickadee, the flicker, the magpie and the Clark's nutcracker all have insatiable appetites. Perhaps, one day I too will fly south, following the migration of the meadowlarks, robins, and finches.

I am a Texas girl by birth, transplanted to this northern location by way of my husband in 1992. I originate from the hot and humid Texas Gulf Coast. I must admit that I prefer fresh clean mountain air over the stale polluted smog that hovered over the refinery-laden place of my youth. But I fear my blood is still attempting to adapt to the weather and the latitude; perhaps it always will.

It is my love for this place that grounds me and keeps me here. In spring, my spirit soars. Sunrise gleams over the mountains, days lengthen, and the sun sets in a magnificent symphony of color. Clouds fill the sky with the promise of rain as their shadows pass over mountains of green. A rainbow appears. Pine trees dance in the breeze and aspen trees unfurl their leaves. Meadowlark and robin song echo across the prairie; brightly colored bluebirds dart from fence post to nesting box, carrying food to feed their hatchlings. The chokecherry bushes bud profusely on the edge of my place where the old jack-legged fence is covered in moss. This is the season I have longed for, such joy to my senses and food for my soul.

The first wildflower to emerge on our land is always the buttercup. It stays close to the ground and blooms, spreading its beautiful waxy yellow petals despite the persistent cold. It will survive spring snows and re-emerge triumphantly after the melt. I admire its tenacity for life. Soon after, the yellow bells appear gracefully, nodding their heads like a ballerina taking a humble bow. I find a pasque flower patch blooming under a stand of pine trees. The wide purple petals open to reveal a bright yellow center. Slender stems emerge topped with a bluish-purple cluster of blooms; the wild hyacinth. The bulbs are edible. Once, I dug them up to taste them, but the mild onion flavor and small bulb made me reconsider the work it would take to dig enough to make a meal.

When shooting stars cover the meadow, it is a sight to behold. I search for the rare white amidst an ocean of purple. The variety of wildflowers that grow here is so numerous that I still struggle to learn all their names. Winter casts a spell and erases them temporarily from my memory, then spring rushes forward in green, my mind refreshed with their beauty.

Time passes swiftly, and soon the solstice sun is upon us, leaving winter's darkness a fading memory behind. Before the sun reaches 10 o'clock in its

long summer arc, I close the windows to retain some of the coolness for the warm day ahead. The bluebirds are raising their hatchlings, flying to and fro in a frenzy, hungry little mouths to feed.

It is the season of being outside; gardening, going for drives in the mountains, and picnics by an alpine lake or stream. Long walks, hiking and backpacking with my daughter, Sarah. Camping in Glacier Park and sitting on the front porch sipping iced tea fills the long days. I get ready for summer visits from family and friends by planting annual flowers in pots, weeding the perennial beds and cleaning everything in sight. I anticipate visits from my two sons and their families, grandchildren with ages ranging from two to sixteen; I know they will take me on some of my favorite walks. We will pack picnic lunches and find a turquoise lake to swim in. We will cook outside and toast marshmallows over a campfire.

I watch dark clouds drift by, distant thunder rolling across the mountains and plains. I pray for rain. Rainbows appear as I watch the sky. The prairie has devoured all the snowmelt and spring rains, leaving the ground thirsty for moisture. The driveway raises a choking plume of dust as the UPS truck delivers my eagerly anticipated hiking boots. The smell of rain, rich and earthy, fills my nostrils as it hits the dry earth, renewing and replenishing life.

My mother likes to go on drives in the mountains, so I pack a picnic and we load into my truck. We wind our way along Lake Koocanusa and turn to head up the Sutton Creek drainage. The roads are dirt and potholed, narrow, with sheer drop offs in places; built for access into the National Forest for logging, gathering firewood, hunting and recreating.

We wind our way up and up. I find a viewpoint near an old clear-cut where we can see the mountains to the east. We pull over and I get out to stretch my legs. It is still and quiet, just an occasional breeze moving through the pines and the sound of crickets. I peer through my binoculars finding reference points and searching for birds and wildlife. A raven glides overhead, a chipmunk skitters up a tree. A mountain chickadee flits from branch to branch. Since my move here, my mother visited on many occasions, until she finally decided to move from Texas to live with me. This was two years ago. Since then, we have gone on many drives in search of an elusive creature. We drive slowly, stealthily, searching the edges of the forest along boggy lakes and rushing streams. Not a moose in sight.

I have seen this large, gangly-legged creature only half a dozen times in the past twenty-seven years. It was fall when I saw the first one. I was raking leaves in the yard where we lived at the time, in an old ranch house near Swamp Mountain, north of Trego. I spotted a big bull moose lumbering through the pasture. When he got to the fence, he simply stepped over; no effort, just a step.

Another sighting occurred on my first backpacking trip with Sarah. We were approaching our campsite at Gunsight Lake in Glacier National Park. I was exhausted, having hiked over six miles with a 35-pound pack while gaining elevation gain of over 1500 feet, but the views were nothing short of amazing. We were approaching camp and suddenly there

he was; a giant bull moose standing in the creek at the foot of the lake.

He dipped his head, bearing huge paddle-like antlers into the lake. Water dripped from them when he came up, chewing the tasty plants he'd found. He didn't seem to mind us, but we remained hesitant. After patiently waiting, he finally decided to lay down to take a nap. We cautiously walked by.

As we drive along the gravel road, I find moose droppings and stop to show Mom. I get out and pick up a palmful of dried droppings, bringing them to her like a prize.

"Nope, not enough," Mom says. She doesn't have much left on her bucket list; seeing a moose is one of them. We give up on finding a moose and head down the mountain leisurely, windows rolled down to savor the pine-scented air. We have little to say, just quiet thoughts of our own. Enjoying our time together in Montana. I've come to realize, whether it be seasons or life, time is so very brief.

I make my camping plans in the dead of winter, six months in advance. My favorite spot is along the north side of Lake McDonald at Fish Creek Campground. My daughter and son-in-law hook up my little camping trailer after it's loaded with food, water, and supplies.

When we arrive, we make haste to set up camp. Trailer leveled, wheels chocked, awning out and rain fly fitted over the picnic table. Supper is grilled over the fire, the familiar smell of meat searing and the sound of juices hissing as they drip on the coals. The next morning, we wake to mountain birds singing in a cool and shady canopy of conifers. The lake is steps away down a short but steep path riddled with twisting roots of trees balancing along the edge.

Sarah, my son-in-law Vitaliy, and Juno take the canoe out for a morning paddle while I watch their old little dog, Mackey. I cook blueberry pancakes and eggs outside on our Coleman stove. When they return, we eat breakfast while sitting around a campfire, fighting off the morning chill. A deer walks through the campsite, and we hold the dogs still and quiet them from barking and scaring it away.

It will warm up by noon, and we will take a dip in the cold clean lake or cast a line in the creek. We can hear the constant din of cars and motorcycles driving the Going-to-the-Sun Road, reminding us we are still in a popular National Park. We wait until evening before driving up the Sun Road to avoid the crowds and full parking lot at Logan Pass. Days are spent cooking, swimming and canoeing in Lake McDonald, playing board or card games, going for hikes and listening to the outdoor amphitheater, talks led by Rangers which last until after dark. We make our way back with flashlights in hand to find our cozy beds.

One night, an unexpected and intense thunderstorm rumbled through the valley. It hailed pea-sized pellets and then poured buckets. I was thankful we had the trailer for some protection from the elements. We again drove over the Sun Road, heading to the trailhead for St. Mary and Virginia Falls, our destination hike for the day. We made a quick potty stop at the top of the Continental Divide where the temperature on the

dash registered 36 degrees. Only two days before, on the Fourth of July, it was a sweltering 94.

We drive twenty-eight miles north from our camp, down a dusty and potholed road to the rugged outpost of Polebridge. Remote and running on solar electricity, the mercantile is over a hundred years old, famous for its mouth-watering baked goods and the small-town version of a Fourth of July parade. The parade is simple and well attended, an antique fire truck leading the way, clanging its large brass bell. Model T's, horses with their cowboy riders and a Forest Service green truck carrying Smokey the Bear complete the parade. Afterwards, we make our way through the crowd and head toward the mercantile, painted barn red. Sweet smells of baking hit us before we walk through the door. That sugary sweet fruit deliciousness beckons us inside. The baked goods in trays on racks lining the walls and behind the immense glass case is a feast for the eyes as well as the nose. We inevitably claim our prizes: four huckleberry bear claws, a dozen coconut macaroons, and six giant snickerdoodles. The next morning, after the storm and sudden plunge of the thermometer, we savor our treasures with coffee and hot chocolate in the comfort of our camping trailer. Glorious Montana summer.

Heat, sudden dry thunderstorms, a lack of rain, dry tinder, and wind join forces. Unpredictable in timing and location, Montanans stay alert scanning the horizon for plumes of smoke from wildfires in the mountains. First, while at our usual camping spot in Glacier, we watched the fire that destroyed the Sperry Chalet. We were far enough away to be safe, yet it was chilling to watch. It started small, the winds picked up and its territory grew. At night, the flames shot high into the air as the tall pines ignited like torches. By day four, it had crested the ridge and headed toward the popular hiking area leading to the Chalet.

Valiant efforts were made by brave firefighters to protect the historic structure. It was wrapped in fire-proof material, but to no avail. A spark set off the fire, and that one spark led to its demise.

That summer also saw two large wildfires closer to home. To the east of our place, Gibraltar ridge burned and, across the lake, a fire came dangerously close to the community of the West Kootenai. We stood in awe, watching the thick gray smoke billowing up in slow motion to meet the Montana big sky, wanting to disbelieve what our eyes were telling us.

Soon, the blue sky is consumed with smoke and disappears completely, turning instead to a sickening yellow gray. The smell of smoke fills my nostrils and I shudder at the thought of the loss. The animals, plants, homes and possibly, the human lives.

"I hope everyone gets out safe," I tell my daughter and son-in-law. I rush inside to close the windows to keep the toxic unhealthy air away from my mother's fragile lungs. The sun turns into a bright orange red ball hanging in the sky. After dark, the winds die down and the air cools. We see the smoldering mountain in plain view. I hope for fall rains to quench the burning forest. To my surprise, I long for the grip of winter when snow will cover the charred remains of the mountain.

Sarah and I go for a late season hike as autumn arrives. We drive up Sutton ridge to the trailhead for McGuire Peak. An old restored fire look-out stands at the top, a reminder of a time before air patrols and computer lightning detection. Beginning in 1905, fire lookouts were built high atop mountains across our country. They were manned for the summer by both men and women who spent their days in solitude, searching for smoke.

Sarah, Juno and I are vigilant for bear in their hyperphagia state, eating as many calories as they can, in preparation for hibernation. We pack bear spray, but my daughter carries her Smith and Wesson pistol just in case. We see a tree marked with bear claw scratch. We see bear scat; full of berries, but not fresh.

The views at the top are so expansive that the peaks of Glacier Park and the Cabinet Mountains can be seen in the distance. The nearby mountains are clefted with deep valleys, rolling and changing colors from green to gold. In the distance, the mountains soften and turn various shades of blue into gray. Cotton clouds move across the bluebird sky, casting shadows across the mountains and the valleys far below. The wind whistles through the twisted trees, howling like wolves calling for their pack. Far away from the National Park, the hustle and bustle of town, the manmade din of constant sound, and the wildfires, exists this perfect peaceful place.

We take a break, sitting on a boulder on the edge of the cliff. A gentle breeze blows my daughter's curls around her beautiful face. Juno sits beside us, patiently waiting as we share our snacks. I embrace this moment and hold it dearly. An overwhelming feeling of serenity and peace catches me by surprise.

As the autumn breeze turns cold, I retreat to my place of warmth; my home on the Montana prairie where I wait for winter to cast its magic spell again. These joyful memories and the promise of spring will hopefully get me through yet another long Montana winter.

*Making It Work*
Aimee McQuilkin

Like the homesteaders before me, I fell in love with Montana and wanted to create a life for myself and my family in this rugged, beautiful place. I loved that it took 20 minutes to bike from downtown Missoula to the woods, where I could be with the bears and the Glacier Lilies.

Fourteen years ago, I opened a clothing store on Missoula's main street. At the time, my husband and I lived with our young daughter in a tiny, one-bedroom house. I was pregnant with our second child. With a degree in Psychology and Women's Studies, I knew that my employment options were somewhat limited, particularly in a highly-educated, college town like Missoula. I decided to focus on what I knew from years of working in clothing boutiques and watching my mom manage clothing stores in Portland, Oregon. So, while my family slept, I stayed up late at night working on a business plan.

My customers came from all walks of life—young moms like me, professional women, college students and travelers passing through town. I brought my daughters to work, nursing my newborn while working the cash register, outfitting my daughter Macy in a bike helmet as she learned to walk on the hard, concrete floors between the metal clothing racks. My little family was the reason I chose to work for myself. I craved work-life balance and a job that allowed me to be home by 5:00.

I stocked my shop with vintage-inspired dresses featuring wild prints and unusual necklines, high-heels that you could ride your bike in and funky jewelry. The merchandise reflected my style and taste, but selling $150 jeans made me uneasy. As a kid, my grandmother kept a closet in her spare bedroom stocked with dress-up clothes for my sister, my cousins and me. We spent hours pretending to be other people, carefully selecting clothes that magically transformed us. Thus began my love affair with second-hand clothing. As I got older, I discovered that not everyone's mom took them to thrift stores to buy jeans. I studied what affluent, cool girls wore and replicated their style with my thrift store finds.

After operating my business for several years, I found it harder and harder to reconcile my frugal, thrift store self with the person who now sold designer jeans. I started hitting garage sales most Saturday mornings in the summer, exploring basements and attics for one-of-a-kind treasures. I loved buying old man flannel shirts at rural, thrift stores and wearing them with new things from the shop. Although one of my favorite jackets was a crisp, blue, denim, cropped, jean jacket that I found at a yard sale, I refused to

stock the racks of my shop with jean jackets. It was my rule that some things had to be found second hand.

After years of playing with the idea, my partner Miranda and I opened a vintage clothing store in the back room of my shop. My multiple identities merged, and finally I could offer that cropped 90's jean jacket to the customer who wanted one. Now, my job as a buyer was not limited to trips to Las Vegas and LA in fancy showrooms run by perfectly coiffed women.

Buying trips meant traveling across Montana to Memorial Day flea markets, unlisted thrift stores operated out of kitchens, estate sales at beautiful homes, and the occasional sketchy trailer.

We drove along rivers, noting various species of birds and the changing of seasons, as we searched for the OG floral dress or white Reebok Princess sneakers, the ones that influence current fashion, because nothing is new.

We explored the bars and cafes of a Montana drastically different from Missoula and its vegan, trail running, "woke" population. We heard stories about the Unabomber from a bus driver in Lincoln who moonlighted as a bartender. In Stevensville, we were invited into the vast closets of an Argentine Flamenco dancer, who cooked elaborate meals in beautiful dresses from around the world. We gathered their stories in the same way we gathered old, worn out Levi's and 1970's polyester pantsuits.

Back home, we replaced missing buttons, patched holes and used science to remove stains. We cropped the sleeves of a men's Wrangler button-up shirt, size tall, and transformed it into a dress for a comedian in New York City. We sold thread-bare, rock and roll t-shirts from the 1980's to drummers in emo bands and hipster baristas working at cool coffee shops. Fashion has always borrowed from other cultures, honored ancient ways of manipulating textiles, and caused a ruckus. But we couldn't help questioning whether we were being respectful. Were we appropriating Montana?

I'd like to think we were taking unwanted burdens and sharing history. We took worn-out stuff destined to be thrown away or made into rags or stuffing for couches. We breathed new life into tired threads.

### King Kong Doesn't Live Here Anymore
### Robin O'Day

One o'clock in the morning, and I sit in a white dress. A wet head of hair at a trendy bar, ordering from the late night happy-hour menu on the eve of Easter Sunday.

I have just been reborn and I am alone. Thank God.

"What would you like?" asks the miniature bartender, who resembles a kindergarten teacher, not a bartender. She has no smile left to give.

"The falafel burrito, please," I say, and push the large rectangular menu towards her.

"And to drink?" She plucks the long menu and holds it in front of her chest, like a protest sign.

I clasp my hands in front of me. Not the familiar prayer gesture I've mastered over the last twelve months on my way to becoming a Catholic. This is a prayer of surrender. If I could rest my head on the bar, I would, but nobody likes a quitter.

"I'll have the Root Of All Evil," I decide, giving her a generous smile, enough for the two of us.

I've just dipped my brain in bleach and I'm watching the colors run. The only thing I want is to be alone. I haven't eaten all day, but I want a proper drink. A week of ash crosses drawn on foreheads, small meals nearing starvation for Lent, and a man nailed to a cross and then shoved in a cave to rot.

\*\*\*

It is 2018. My brother, John, has a twelve-inch staph infection in his spine.

"Two more days without surgery and you'd be paralyzed. Five more days and you would have died," says the Infectious Disease Doctor. This is serious. This is something bigger than all of us. This is the angst. This is King Kong.

Helpless, I follow the two nurses as they wheel my brother out of ICU, and into the elevator. He has no time. He needs surgery now.

I take the stairs to the main floor and cross the street to St. Francis Xavier church and the adjoining office.

I knock on the office door. I wait an entire minute, but finally the large oak door opens, a screen door between us.

"How may I help you?" I can hear her voice, but I can only make out the outline of the woman's body in the dim foyer entrance, the headquarters of the western Montana Jesuit Catholic division.

"Is Father Joseph available?" I ask.

"Umm…" she echoes.

I need to call God and let him know my brother is going under the knife. Earlier that year, I was told about Father Joseph by a friend, who thought he might help save my failing marriage. I never called. A year later, something bigger has failed. My faith. I'm glad I saved my golden ticket.

"I know it's last minute, but my brother is in the hospital," I say, a little too loudly. Without eye contact, the woman on the other side of the screen door makes my palms itch.

She does not respond. I can't fully exhale, like someone is strong arming my trunk, gigantic leathery fingers cross against my ribcage, tightening with every exhale. My quads begin to quake, as the winds out of the Hellgate Canyon pick up, another bitter March morning.

"Please…" I extend my hand, and open the screen door.

I see a woman with a Nancy Drew bob and eyes the color of Nutella. She's in her late 50's, dressed plainly, no make-up. She looks like the receiver of other people's bad news, sob stories, pleas for gas vouchers and spare change.

"He's really sick and I'd like to pray with someone," I whisper, despite her unwavering eyes.

"Father Joseph isn't available, but if you'd like to come in, I can see if Father Perry is free." She holds the wooden door open and I slip into the warm brick house.

The furnaces clank and hiss, a broken lullaby. I smell incense and sulfur from matches. I know I am in the right place. This is where you take the angst in the pit of your stomach. An already fatigued relationship with my brother, now exhausted by this sickness. Run this concoction up the flagpole. Take the angst to someone or something who knows what to do with it.

"Wait here." She gestures to a sturdy walnut tea table, surrounded by matching chairs.

She leaves to climb a tall staircase, and I examine an oil painting, hanging above the sitting area. It's not the typical Jesus, holding his hand out to a lamb on a mountain top. This oil painting requires more of me. It's a long staircase, and I'm grateful for the mental holiday. I stand, stare, and take it in.

It's an unlikely pairing of people, a cowboy and the Virgin Mary. Surely, the artist didn't mean to paint them together. The cowboy is dressed in an oilskin, three-quarter trench coat and a cowboy hat. He climbs a ladder with one hand and holds an oil lantern in the other, exposing the image of The Virgin Mary, held captive in a huge, oval stained-glass window. The more I look at Mary, the more it looks like she's rolling her eyes, irritated by the cowboy's lantern, thrust into her face.

The gold accent sconce above the painting lights and blinks with every step the receptionist takes up the staircase.

"Quite a painting, isn't it?" I turn when I hear the voice behind my shoulder.

"Yes, it is."

This is Father Perry. He is an inch taller than me, in his late 70's, with a generous upper lip, especially for a man his age. He is a soft landing for me.

"I can't figure out what's going on with Mary," I admit, gesturing to the painting.

"I think she's closing her eyes," he says thoughtfully, without judgment.

"Of course." I don't buy it, but I'm new here.

"Please, this way." As he walks, I follow him into a wood paneled den, couches that make me never want to return to the hospital.

A three-minute prayer.

A twelve-minute conversation.

I walk out of the den with conversion paperwork bundled in my arms.

I give Mary a nod on my way out the door.

"Sleeping," I whisper. "Whatever."

On the street, my angst is now just a faint thing, day-old perfume on the collar of a knitted sweater.

***

"Do you want to carry the top part of the cross, Robin?" Erin is the Easter Mass coordinator, and her freckles are a matching blueprint of my own.

"You bet," I say, enthusiastically. We should be sisters. Go with it, Robin, go all the way. Say yes to whatever is asked of you.

I have always been the type of person who leaves the concert before the last song to beat the crowd, the type who takes the service elevator at a New York theatre audition to beat the other 212 auditioning wannabe actors. I'm also the type who gets stuck for three hours in the same freight elevator, because it doesn't operate on the weekends.

But there's no cutting corners with Catholics. They even bring their pets to mass, to be blessed.

The dress rehearsal is a test of character, not just a preparation for the real performance. You can hit your marks, make your final costume alterations and change the gel on the lights, but you can never fully prepare for the performance.

I have been unraveling for months. This week I will be baptized, but I am a tethered and frayed thread. When I get pushed in a corner, I will ghost you, but I can't ghost the fact that I am married.

Divorce is a revelation. Eleven months and twelve thousand dollars in attorney fees, I have learned I am still in love with Jeff.

When I make mistakes, I make them big. I saw it in the faces of my mother's book club, when they heard I had moved back in with him.

"I wish you the best," they muttered in the quieted living rooms of their 1960's ranch homes.

"Bless your heart," followed by a sip of Chamomile tea.

"Father Perry will introduce you to the parish and then you and Opal will walk behind the altar with your Godmother. Then you will be baptized, and then it will be Opal's turn. Okay?" Erin looks up from her clipboard.

"Yes, of course." I have filled out the paperwork. It's official, and I can't run to the stage wings, and beg the heavy velvet curtain: "Help me. I think I am dying. Help me. If this is living, I'd rather die."

We stand at the altar, looking over the rows of empty church pews,

which will soon be occupied by the mumbling worshipers. Tonight is Holy Thursday, the Veneration of the Cross ceremony.

The church doors fly open.

"My lilies," declares Erin. "Finally." She hops down from the altar.

The cart in one hand, and the clipboard in her other, she plugs forward. Dozens of mature, white lilies bounce as the cart rolls towards the altar.

The long spear-like leaves tear, drops of water falling from the tips. The clouds shift and the sun knocks big chunks of prism-colored light through the stained glass windows. Erin consults her clipboard, as dust particles hang in the golden light.

"You're good to go," Erin pronounces.

My fool-proof introversion has nowhere to go. I am stuck on stage, the lead actress, Fay Wray, in the palm of King Kong.

If we are really, really quiet we won't wake the beast. Stay here with me, Erin.

But the show must go on.

I know my lines.

***

Opening night arrives, an ending to my year of devotion. I am converting from the church of King Kong, replacing it with new tricks: prayers, mass, spiritual lineage, ceremonials and saints. My Godmother is Diane, a girlfriend on loan. Nothing good ever lasts. Her heart is a prize, and I carry it in my purse.

Diane rubs my back, sensing that I am two shades shy of seeing crimson red. "Are they on their way?" She is referring to Jeff and Opal.

My parents and my brother and his wife are still not speaking to Jeff outside of pleasantries, a lingering hangover after the near divorce. Things were not left unsaid between them. They used all the words.

"They should be here any minute." I zip my royal blue polyester blend Baptismal gown over a white blouse and white pants.

My personified anxiety is starting to make the paper cups of water vibrate on the banquet tables with each approaching monstrous gorilla step.

I am getting that familiar feeling, large fingers around my rib cage, squeezing tighter with every exhale. When Ann Darrow was held in his grip in the original, black and white 1933 film, she simply kicked her ivory stems, while her paper thin, white negligee was torn off layer by layer by King Kong's curious long fingers. She put up a good fight. It is not lost on me that we both wore white.

Three Jesuit priests gather around the coffee and tea station, each holding three ring binders. This is their biggest performance, their starring role. Father Perry checks his watch.

Where is my lost tribe? My head hangs down, hiding my overly emotional state.

I hear a low pulsating hum above us in the church. King Kong is here. I will always be at odds with myself.

I look up. "What's that?" I ask Diane, my heart.

"It's just the organist warming up," she says, and gathers the hair from my shoulders.

Jeff throws open the basement door of the church, Opal on his hip.

"Thank God," I say, and Diane and I watch as Jeff shuffles around the banquet tables. He swerves around the huddled groups of people.

What is she wearing? Jeff passes Opal off to me, dressed in a soft black baby tiger sweater, charcoal grey corduroy pants studded with gold. She is not in her white baptismal dress.

"Hi, Opal!" Diane says enthusiastically, as Jeff hands me her scalloped lace dress, draped on a teeny hanger.

Opal clutches a battery-operated Christmas Minnie Mouse and a pale mint green dollar store plastic bag, filled with stickers.

She is nowhere near ready. Mass is about to begin.

"Opal, we need to get you dressed." I whisper in her ear, but she bucks in my arms like a horse, a sign she won't give up the toy.

Father Perry sweeps over, dressed in his white vestment, a gold embroidered stole draped over his shoulders, and hanging down his chest.

"Great, everyone is here." He smiles at us. "It's time to go upstairs." He quickly moves on to another group of parishioners, also waiting to be saved.

"Jingle Bell, Jingle Bell, Jingle Bell rock..." screeches Minnie Mouse, a high pitched voice, plastic feet moving back and forth in Opal's arm.

Opal smiles proudly. Frantic, I open up Minnie's velcro dress and find the battery door, smooth along my finger tips. I flick the button, and Minnie Mouse is silenced.

All the candidates, their mentors, the priests, and the coordinators walk up the stairs of the basement to the front of the church. Diane, Opal, and I sit down in the second pew, behind the priests.

Mass unfolds before my eyes, and I am not present. I'm only a spectator, not a participant. My vision has fuzzy frames, there are no sharp corners. Unlike Ann, I don't fight in King Kong's hand. I am just a rag doll, tossed from side to side in his palm.

When I am called, I walk with Opal to the converted horse trough, covered in blue cloth, surrounded by white lilies.

Father Perry holds his hand out to me. Diane takes Opal and Minnie Mouse and the dollar store bag. I step into the warm water. Father Perry is stronger than I had imagined, and I give him the entire weight of my body. He stands wide-legged in the trough, facing the congregation as he dips me. I immerse, full body, water sealing my hairline. One, two, three times.

"The Father, The Son, The Holy Spirit," Father Perry repeats each time, as he releases my body into the water.

I hear the congregation applaud loudly. I stand on the stage, soaking wet.

"Congratulations." Father Perry embraces me.

Diane attempts to pass Opal to me, but my daughter has just watched this strange, public bath and wants nothing to do with it.

"No, no, no," she says.

I hear laughter behind me.

"She won't get in," I tell Diane.

"It's okay," responds Diane.

Father Perry addresses the waiting congregation, and there is more laughter. In this moment, I thought I'd be as high as the Swiss Alps, bathed in the golden sun. Instead, I feel like I'm strung out in the bowels of a water canal in San Bernardino.

I step out of the trough, water rushing down my legs from the soaking blue polyester gown.

Diane, Opal and I leave the stage, and descend downstairs, where Erin is waiting.

"I'll head upstairs with Opal," offers Diane. She's had six children, and there is no room for King Kong in her life.

I pull my white dress over my head and tie my hair back.

I'm sure I have mascara running down my cheeks. Pretty soon they'll add sacred oil to my forehead and then I'll really look reborn, like the Lower East side punk I really am. Patti Smith, my Godmother, the full circle of life.

When I return upstairs, Opal is sitting on Diane's lap, several sheets of stickers in one hand. The other little hand carefully decorates Father Perry's stole. Unknowingly, he sits as Peppa The Pig, rainbows and stars are carefully applied to his vestment.

Opal turns to me. She places a star on my forehead, between my eyes. My daughter knows where my third eye should be.

"You're the star, Mama," she says.

I could cry, but I don't have tears left.

I turn in the pew, and look behind me, past all the parishioners. I look for my best mate, King Kong.

He is nowhere to be found.

*Brimstone*
Kirsten Holland

The scribbled note told us to cross the railroad tracks, take the left fork in the road, and another 100 yards to the cattle guard. We rumbled across it in the big diesel pickup and slowly rolled to a stop. Lolly whined between us, panting and anxious to run. Neither of us said a word.

360 degrees of heaven. Meadows of rich, green grass. Rolling hills thick with stands of larch and lodgepole pine. A seasonal creek hidden by cottonwoods, aspens running down from the sheltering mountains in the east, feeding into a half-acre pond where families of Mallards, Common Goldeneyes, and Canada Geese stopped on their way to warmer country. 320 acres, surrounded by Forest Service land on three sides.

Home. At least for a little while.

We'd only lived in Montana two months when a friend told my husband, Randall, who everyone called Red, that Brimstone Ranch needed a caretaker. We could keep our jobs, since there were no cattle to tend, just five retired performance horses, gophers who needed hunting in the overgrown pastures, and fence and grounds to maintain. My own horses lived with friends in Kalispell, since the landlord's wife didn't want them grazing down the grass.

This ranch was five miles up Trego. We entered the caretaker's cabin to find filthy carpet, filthier appliances, and one tiny bathroom/laundry room/mudroom. As soon as I saw the six outdoor paddocks with run-in sheds, five cross-fenced pastures, six-stall barn, and a heated indoor arena, I forgot about the cabin. The back gates led to miles of trails and old logging roads. We could ride for hours without hearing a human voice. We would be caretaking the main house, located just past the front gate. Our cabin was tucked away in the back, closer to the barn. The ranch's owner had made his fortune in the portable toilet business, but he was unlike most wealthy out-of-staters, who treat Montana like their personal playground and the locals like personal assistants. Although he raised cutting horses, he was mostly involved in local politics in Illinois, and only visited twice a year, for a week at most. When he and his wife arrived, they kept to themselves and expected the caretakers to carry on as if they weren't there.

It was not a tough decision.

Six months earlier, I'd been on a plane in Kalispell, headed back home to Oakland after visiting my sick father. As the flight attendant gave the safety speech, I buckled in, pleased the seat next to me was vacant. Just as she reached to close the bulkhead door, another crew member stopped her. We

heard the announcement: a passenger had been delayed at security. A tallish man in a black cowboy hat and oilskin duster appeared at the front of the plane, stomping down the aisle. I could see nothing of his face, only sharp red sideburns and a neat goatee. When I realized he was heading for the only vacant seat, I quickly repositioned myself to stare out the window. He collapsed with a hard thud. I immediately sensed his energy, radiating like dryer static. Crackling, annoying, and uncomfortable. He turned to me, drawling in a thick southern accent. "Do I look like a goddamn terrorist to you?"

I cocked my chin and quickly examined him. A redneck.

My response was flat. I did not want to engage. "I don't know, do you think you're supposed to have a dot on your head. Or a turban or something?"

"You must be from California." His face softened, and a slight smile crossed his lips.

"I am," I replied.

"Then you must be a movie star."

***

I guess I was easily charmed. We moved to Montana and six months later, I gazed out the kitchen window at my horses grazing in belly-deep grass, now part of a herd of seven. I'd found the real reason to come to Montana. That red-headed man made it an easy decision.

We moved to the ranch in April. Those first weeks we discovered that in addition to the high-bred quarter horses put out to pasture after suffering competition injuries, the ranch was home to coyotes, raptors, elk, and plentiful deer. Red went out at night, throwing cracked corn to his "nannies," his name for the does who knew the ranch was a safe place to raise their fawns. They emerged from the thick woods by the dozens, conjured like a dream. Once a month, our sleep was interrupted by the wolves, plaintive howls shattering the stillness, mystical and haunting.

Red was from Georgia, a slightly crazy country boy who fixed everything with duct tape. He didn't believe in throwing anything away. "Better to have it and not need it, than to need it and not have it," he said, quite often.

He was a natural fit for the job and tended the ranch like it was his own. An exiled city girl, I learned more from him in those months than years of riding lessons and weekend hikes in the East Bay. Fence work, sawing up deadfall for firewood, putting up hay; we were newly married and every chore felt like play. We went to bed exhausted every night. He trained my young gelding while I groomed and tended to the others. His daddy taught him to trim and shoe horses when he was a boy. Thirty years later, he trusted me enough to teach me.

The ranch was divided on the southwest side by a Forest Service road, creating 120 acres isolated from the main property. We rode there from time to time, flopped down in the grass as the horses grazed. We dreamed in that spot, made plans for when the owner died, convinced he would leave Brimstone to us.

In the fall of 2004, Red found a massive buck decapitated on the 120.

The poacher left the meat to waste, just to take the antlers. Red staked out in the underbrush several nights in a row, sitting, fuming, praying greed would cause the wastrel thief to return to take another. Red considered every critter, every leaf, and every blade of grass on Brimstone to be precious, needing protection. I thought I'd married a redneck cowboy, but as I watched him wait in the darkness, realized I had married a sensitive conservationist.

The year went by, slow and peaceful. When the owners returned, they went to great lengths to let us know they were just there for a visit. We continued our life as usual. Some rich people are funny that way; as long as they know their property is there, they don't necessarily need to be. They always thanked us, grateful their Montana home was well-cared for, even if they only saw it twice a year.

In July, a late model white pickup came across the cattle guard, passed the main house, and stopped at the barn. The driver looked like Hollywood's version of a cowboy—a tall hat, dinner plate belt buckle, and shiny pointy-toed boots. A petite woman with long, dark hair emerged from the passenger side. The man clearly knew his way around as he pulled open the heavy barn door. Red dropped his tools. He crossed the driveway, tucking a pinch of snuff into the corner of his mouth.

"Can I help you, sir?" Red unleashed his southern charm.

"Yeah, I'm showing the ranch to my client." The man barely looked at Red, instead turning his focus back to the prospective buyer as they headed into the barn.

Red crossed his arms. "Pardon me, sir, I'm the caretaker, Randall Holland." He stood straight. "Now I don't know you or your client, but no one told me you were comin', so I'm gonna have to ask you to leave."

The woman appeared in the doorway, the man pushing past her.

"The ranch is for sale, I'm the realtor. For years, it's been listed. I'm not surprised Nelson never told you."

Red's jaw clenched. "No, I did not know the ranch was for sale and like I said, I don't know you. It's my job to take care of Brimstone, so until I speak to the Nelsons, I'd appreciate it if you don't just show up here."

The real estate agent laughed. "I'll show up whenever I please. You can go back to whatever you were doing. I'll let you know if I need anything."

The woman took a step toward Red. "You didn't know the ranch is for sale?"

"No, ma'am," he replied.

"How long have you lived here?"

"Just about two years."

She turned to the agent. "You didn't tell him we were coming?"

"I don't need to tell the caretaker when I want to come up here. I'm friends with the owner." He leaned back against the hitching rail, crossing one shiny boot over the other.

She looked at Red. "I'm sorry for barging in on you like this. We're leaving."

The agent started to protest, but she just walked back to the truck and slammed the door.

He glared at Red, fuming. "You'll be seeing me again soon."

"Yep," Red spit tobacco juice at the giant belt buckle, hitting the easy target dead center, then turned back toward the shop.

The agent stuttered, yelling at Red's back. "Nelson's going to hear about this! You'll be out on your ass in a week!"

That night, we spoke to the owner. He admitted it had been on the market for the last six years, long before we arrived, but not advertised. Just listed in case the right offer came along, so he never thought to mention it. Now he needed to sell, so we should expect more visits, but not from that particular agent. He apologized before he hung up.

Something had shifted. Now there was an expiration date. Every ride felt like it could be the last. Red's plans to remodel the cabin were scrapped. He stopped feeding the nannies.

In September, another agent showed up, but she was alone. The seller's agent. The ranch had sold. The buyer, a business owner and city councilman from Texas, had shown up while we were both at work, and we never even knew. A week later, the new agent let us know the buyer wanted us to stay on.

We had another golden fall, thankful for the reprieve. The ranch had sold for less than half of it's appraised value.

In late November, trucks showed up with heavy trailers to take the equipment away, all sold at auction. The new owner didn't want anything left on the ranch, including the tractors.

He mostly avoided us, even as he spent one weekend a month at the property. I wouldn't know he had come unless my old dog, Pea, tore off over the hill bellowing at the unknown intruder.

The owner had a habit of calling the night before he was to arrive, with no concern for our time. In late winter, he called from the Kalispell airport, asking me to turn the heat up. I spent a frantic two hours vacuuming up the flies that accumulate in every log house, making sure things were ready for his arrival.

Without the tractors, we had to hire someone to plow the road. It had been our job. In the spring, despite having no equipment, Red remained determined to keep the ranch well kept.

One time, worried the owner would show up, he ran the weed eater around the main house, then used it to mow five acres of lawn. It took him nine hours.

In April, we began cleanup work, burning the fence line. A clear, cool day with no wind, perfect for the task. Red tended to the work and I left to the cabin to make lunch. Moments later, he raced up the driveway on our four-wheeler.

"The fire's out! The fire's out!"

I misunderstood, thinking the fire had died, but he meant out, as in out of control. A rogue wind kicked up, and the fire burned a few acres of

pasture before we finally got it contained. We collapsed on the ground, filthy with soot and sweat. We gasped for breath, palms covered in blisters from beating back the flames with shovels.

In May, we sat on a big fallen Cottonwood, looking out across the lush meadow for what would be the last time.

The owner had decided he wanted someone less "colorful" than Red to run his Montana ranch. When he saw the grass, Red explained what happened.

"You never should have burned without the requisite fire equipment on site!" The owner barked.

"You took away all the goddamn equipment!" Red responded, seething.

It was only the second time I'd heard Red say "goddamn" since the day he sat next to me on the plane.

They argued a bit longer, but I walked away. I was tired of watching my husband struggle to show his worth, and angry that the city councilman from Texas never saw my loyal, capable man. He didn't know what he wanted, but he didn't want us.

He gave us 60 days to move out. I asked for 90. He didn't budge.

\*\*\*

The day we left, I sat in my truck at the bottom of Brimstone Road and clutched a receipt, handwritten in pencil, for two nearly 20-year old horses. I took what mattered the most, and left the rest behind. The horses moved in the trailer as I turned onto the main road.

We found a place just outside Eureka, a simple dull grey house with an enclosed yard for the dogs and perimeter fencing for the horses, a run-in shed, irrigation: Everything we needed. We only planned to stay on the five acres for a year or two, and then flip it.

13 years later, we're still here. I painted it barn red six years ago and we have a new roof, a better fence, and a bigger run-in shed. Nature's stunning beauty is a little farther from home, usually in the alpenglow on Poorman Mountain or looking north to the Canadian Rockies. The ranch horses are buried in the back pasture. I lost the last one in March, just a month shy of 31. The only wildlife who visit other than birds and geese are the deer who come to pick through the neighboring apple orchard. Red doesn't feed them. He doesn't want to lure them across the highway. I have to trailer the horses when I want to ride into the woods. But when the wind rustles the big birch tree in the backyard, or I catch the sunset reflected in my mare's deep brown eyes, I realize there is splendor everywhere.

It's just five acres, but it's ours. Home, for as long as we want it.

*How Ancestry.com Ruined My Life*
Ame Boyce

Let's start at the beginning. I was born in Billings, MT on February 20, 1975. I spent several months in a foster home and my adoptive family came to get me on April 21. I was described as a mellow baby, a good first timer. My birth name was Maggie. There's a lot a name says about you, and I imagine the name Maggie would have led me to be one hell of a quilter and an office manager in a vinyl siding business. My life as Maggie from Billings was short-lived, however, and I am eternally grateful to my parents for that.

My parents feverishly began working on the nursery when they started the adoption process. They were informed that it could take up to five years to actually adopt a baby. The idea of staring across the hall into an empty nursery for five years sounded horribly depressing to my Mother. She decided to take a woodworking course instead of focusing on the nursery, carving out her desire for a child into some very functional shelving. Six months later, my parents received a call that they would be parents to a baby girl. They might have had handcrafted shelving, but they were completely unprepared for a baby that was coming four and a half years early. My Mother put up the wallpaper in the nursery while I slept on the couch. It is interesting what we all do with expectation and hope. We try not to have high expectations, so we don't hang the wallpaper. We don't get disappointed, but are completely unprepared when we get what we want. Investing ourselves into something we so desperately want is frightening and vulnerable, and there is a price to preparation and anticipation.

This young couple got onto an airplane, something neither one of them had done very much, and went to pick up their baby girl. I can't even imagine how that would feel. My Dad told me that he was not really concerned with the mechanics of taking care of a baby. He had two younger sisters. In fact, he could even put a diaper on himself, which landed him at the principal's office, but that is a story for another time. The important thing is that they had shelves.

My Mother, however, was very contemplative of the responsibility involved with adopting this baby. She prepared herself to be the Mother that my birth mother wanted her to be. My Father said that he saw my mother transform on that plane. She looked softer, deliberate, she looked like a mother. And from the moment she held me, she was.

Three photocopied pages: "Information For Adoptive Parents, Re: Maggie," were the only link my parents or myself had regarding my birth mother. According to these documents, my birth mother had been allowed to see,

hold and feed me before she relinquished her parental rights. This was 1975, not 2019, and things were very different. In 1975, there was nothing "open" about adoption. My birth mother must have been a strong, capable and grounded woman, if the hospital and adoption agency allowed her to hold me. In her own words, my birth mother reported: "She is not my possession to keep because of my own emotional needs."

This has always resonated with me, because it sounds exactly like something I would feel and say. She placed me for adoption because she loved me, and wanted me to have a stable family. She also wanted to finish college, something I've always hoped she accomplished. My heart aches for that young woman. She was never detached from the truth, and stable enough to make a decision to give away a child she loved. I will always be grateful for the sacrifice she made in order for me to live the life I do.

I am incredibly lucky. My adoption was ideal. My friend Shannon reminds me of this after a lot of glasses of wine. Shannon was also adopted, but never had a connection with her adoptive family. I think her family felt like having kids was just something that everyone did, regardless if they wanted to. My family was the opposite. They were supportive, showed me that I was valued and wanted. "Exactly like you," points out Shannon.

I have always felt like I had an advantage over kids who weren't adopted. I have never known what having blood relatives is like. Anyone close to me feels like family, and this has afforded me deep relationships with people, without the normal familial constraints.

When I gave birth, this idea of family forever changed.

My son was the first person in this world who looked like me. I wasn't able to hold him immediately after giving birth; he was born early, and had some complications breathing. I could not wait to see my son's face. The magnitude of holding a child that was my blood was overwhelming. The nurses offered help getting dressed and a wheelchair to take me to the NICU, but I was already halfway out the door. This child, this part of me. Did he have my eyes? My nose? Did he have my dark skin? Yes, he has my eyes. Yes, he has my nose, poor kid. At that point, he was actually a lovely shade of jaundice, so we were unsure about his skin tone.

I have always been curious about my own ethnicity. I was envious of those people who knew they were Irish, Italian or Lebanese. They knew where they came from, and could claim a heritage I would never know. In college, I got tired of having a vague idea of who I was and where I came from, so I created my own. I lied about my ethnicity because I didn't know what I was. I didn't want to be left out of the conversation. I held this secret for a very long time, and finally came clean when I was ready to marry my husband. I couldn't marry a person who didn't really know me. It was embarrassing to admit I lied, but the real truth was going to remove the sting.

I always wanted to try DNA testing. I received my 23andme test, but was ambivalent about taking it. The truth could not be better than the story that I had made up. I waited six months before I took the test, the same amount of time my parents waited for me. When I received the results,

they were pretty vague. I didn't know much more about myself than when I started.

I decided to try Ancestry, a last attempt for a clearer picture of my ethnic identity. I sent my saliva off to their lab, and waited for an eternity to get my results. Although my husband and I took our tests at the same time, he received his results within a month. Finally, I received an email informing me that my results were inconclusive. I would have to take the test again. This happened a second time. And then a third time. A year after I took the initial test, I finally got the results. I didn't find out much more about my ethnicity, but my DNA had matched with someone, a relationship reported as "Parent/Child." When I read this, my heart zipped right through my chest. I got light headed. This person was my father.

I had expected to maybe find a second cousin, but never my biological father. I had to keep repeating the test, because Ancestry wanted to be certain. Finally, they confirmed the fact: This man was my father. Thank you, Ancestry.com. I never had any intention of looking for my biological family, never a yearning desire to find my biological parents. I know who my parents are, and never felt like I was missing anything, missing anyone else.

After the initial shock of finding my biological father, I had to figure out what to do with this information. If I had found my biological mother, it would have been different, because she obviously knew that I existed. But this man might not even have known my birth mother was pregnant. I really didn't want to approach him, and could only imagine the conversation: "Hey! Looks like you had a daughter, and it's me. Surprise!"

He must have felt something similar, because he waited a long time to contact me. Thankfully, he did. When he reached out, he hesitantly offered his name and phone number. "If you don't want to call, I understand."

I hate talking on the phone in general, so the idea of talking to my birth father on the phone was terrifying. I told him I wanted to leave the line of communication open, but phone calls were too much for me. At first, we started with texting, but finally it led to a phone call, and I was so scared that I was shaking. The conversation itself was nonchalant, but he said something that struck me deeply. He confessed that when my birth mother became pregnant, they were too young, and he wasn't ready to be a father. He convinced my birth mother that adoption was the best choice. "I think she had a really hard life," he said. That statement broke my heart. It was not what I wanted to hear.

I had imagined my birth mother graduated from college and became a writer, a teacher or Gloria Estefan. It never occurred to me that she would just walk out of the hospital, determined to live her life to the fullest. She might have been broken by the choice she made.

I wanted a choice, too. I wanted the choice to free her, to give her the same gift I had been given.

Several months after I had contact with my biological Dad, I received a message from another searching relative, who believed I was a cousin he hadn't known about. I had been relentlessly pouring over my Ancestry

report for months, and suspected he was my uncle on my birth mother's side. I had no idea how to address this. I didn't know if she had kept it a secret from her family. I still don't. When I returned his phone call, I could only report that I had been adopted in Billings in 1975. There was a chance we were related.

More waiting. A few weeks later, I finally got a message from my birth mom.

She wanted me to know that she was my mother. She offered contact in whatever form I was comfortable with. I sent a brief email to her, and explained that none of this was planned, but I would love any kind of conversation. I never received another email.

On Mother's Day, I reached out again. I wanted her to know how grateful I was, that I supported the decision she had made. I wanted to wish her a happy Mother's Day. I never received a reply.

I have always thought that I was comfortable being adopted. I have always known that my Mother and I will celebrate April 21st, the day I was adopted, for the rest of my life. Truthfully, I felt like it was my super power. I love being adopted. My parents CHOSE me. When my own biological mother did not respond, I recognized that the feelings of inadequacy throughout my life, my fervent desire to be liked and accepted, was a subconscious reaction.

On good days, I am excited to meet a whole new family, on my birth father's side. My uncle has been open and inviting, and I have learned about my mother's roots. My maternal grandfather was a famous scientist. He was friends with Darwin, and the irony of evolution is not lost on me.

On the bad days, the silence from my birth mother still hurts. Is it possible to be rejected twice? In my head, and in my heart, I acknowledge that this must be equally difficult for her to navigate. But the little girl inside of me feels a familiar pain. Once again, I'm not good enough for her.

Ancestry.com did not ruin my life. It opened it up, and left me with unanswered questions. My journey has just started, and I look forward to finding my birth family. I look forward to finding myself.

*Zoetrope: A Drinking Memoir*
Sharma Shields

## One: Traveling Companions

One evening not too long ago, a kind man arrived at my house to drop off my son after a playdate. As we stood chatting in our living room, it came up that he was sober for more than twenty years; I told him that in March I'll be sober for three.

Meeting another sober person is like traveling in a remote part of the world and running into someone from your hometown. It's a pleasant surprise, an unexpected relief. There is a language shared, a history that's tacitly understood. You find yourself opening up, so much shared experience to illustrate, so many mournful arias to chorus.

It comforts me, these moments of companionship, because it's easy for me to grow tired of my identity as a sober woman. Now and again I become as ambivalent about not drinking as I do about romanticizing booze. Frequently, enduring a conversation about sobriety with puzzled parties, I turn to my husband, who dealt with the brunt of my addiction, and I enlist his help.

"Sam will tell you," I say. "He saw all of it."

But even he didn't see all of it.

Not even I did.

The blackouts made it so that sometimes no one saw anything, and it would just be a miracle the next day that I made it home alive, or that I only bloodied but didn't break my nose when I fell into the dresser, or that I didn't die choking on my vomit despite bursting a constellation of blood vessels in my eyelids.

Sam, for his part, stands by me but doesn't elaborate. He won't speak ill of me, not in front of me and not behind my back.

No one is perfect, of course, but he's the best sort of husband.

I haven't always been the best sort of wife.

## Two: Big Bad Loves

My husband and I met at The University of Montana, an MFA program as renowned for its long nights of drinking as for the quality of its writers. Sam was the quietest and kindest in our classroom, capable of giving helpful criticism without withering a writer's confidence. I was a loud-mouth, full of opinions and ideas without the writing chops to back them up. He

thought I had a great vocabulary and nice legs. I thought he was an anomaly, a brilliant hunk. We made one another laugh. We spent a lot of hours drinking together, shooting pool, playing ping pong, talking about our lives before graduate school, his in New York City and Michigan, my own in Seattle and Spokane.

We frequented a bar called The Union Club. Over whiskeys one night, I gave him a copy of Larry Brown's Big Bad Love. It reminded me of the spare, punchy lyricism of Sam's own writing. He loaned me First Love and Other Sorrows and So Long, See You Tomorrow. He was dating another woman; I had a boyfriend back in Seattle. We kept our distance but the attraction grew.

When we finally hooked up, drunk at our friend Alex's house, all of our previous ties were cut. We wanted one another. A friend later told me, half-annoyed, "You two will get married, I just know it." Marriage was not something I'd ever had in mind. I didn't grow up dreaming about it the way some girls did. But I liked it when my friend mentioned it. I was in love. Startlingly, even skeptically, I'm in love, still.

These are my best drinking memories, the most romantic of the bunch. But even they are flawed. There are black moments in them, times where I wept or attacked him, times when we drunkenly fought. My wretched hangovers became more and more frequent, entire days spent in bed, and they worsened in my late twenties. The fantasy land of the MFA program ended; we went to work. I stopped writing. Sam worried for me. I began to suspect that drinking would kill me in one way or another. Even so, I courted the blackouts. I craved how they shuttered my anxiety, how they silenced the endless river of narration that flooded my skull. Despite the rules I enforced on myself (no drinking during the workweek, no hard alcohol, a month-long break here and there), I hurtled further into the darkness.

My last night of drinking involved my two children. I drove them home from a playdate when I was blacked-out drunk. I woke the next morning, head pounding, to crawl to the toilet and begin an-all-too-familiar day of wretched vomiting. My husband couldn't even look at me. I was filled with poison and self-loathing, trembling and sick, and I wanted to die.

From my miserable perch, forehead touching the toilet basin, I heard my son ask my husband, "Why is she always sick?"

The unknowable scope of my love for my daughter and son has always shocked me. How limitless it is, how irrational. Mothers will talk of this, the hearts walking around outside of their bodies, how we wince at any threat, any particle of pain that strikes them. We are meant to cherish and protect them while they cultivate endurance, fortitude. It has always been difficult for me to step back and allow them to learn from the uncomfortable: My instinct is to absorb it all, the darkness, the threats and cruelty and unfairness, to grow heavy with it, to sink so that they can rise.

And now, in nearly every regard, I was failing them. I'd put their very lives in danger, and if I kept drinking, it would happen again.

## Three: Everything Changes and Everything Stays the Same

The first ninety days of sobriety were, for me, a lesson in panic and desperation and patience. But I made it through them, with the help of a women's group and of my mom-in-law, also in recovery, and especially with help and love from Sam. After a time, sobriety became easier; it was now the norm. A sense of relief ballooned: For the first time since I was a teenager, I wasn't letting myself down all of the time.

Life sober very much mirrors life as a drunk: up and down, confusing and alienating, stressful and sometimes empty. Every now and again, an ache for alcohol rises up—not merely to enjoy a sip or a drink, but to ruin myself with it, to get fucking tanked. But the feeling, so far, has been quick to subside. The key is patience: If you wait long enough, the grip inevitably loosens.

I've found, too, that life sober mirrors life as a drunk in exhilarating ways. The things I worried I would never feel again, excitement and wildness, freedom and connection, are all there, only this time I'm sober and can embrace them without shame. Enjoying a dinner with friends and coming home clear-minded, certain I won't be sick the entire next day, is a novelty that I continue to marvel over.

Once, I asked my husband if he missed the Drinking Me, if he ever wished we could relive our first months together back in Missoula.

His answer, as firm as it was loving: "No."

My sober years have been our best years.

## Four: Another Year, Another Lifetime

I stood with my sober friend in the living room and discussed many of these revelations and aches. He continues to endure all of these tribulations, even twenty years later. And while I'm still relatively new to them, I've grown accustomed to them in my own right.

"It's wonderful," I said, "that you didn't involve your kids in this stuff."

He shook his head, resolute. "Don't look at it that way. Look at all you've given them now, now that you're sober."

My daughter and son played with his son, each taking a turn holding our new kitten. They passed the kitten from one to the other like a precious gift. The kitten blinked sleepily at them, pleased or merely tolerant, it was hard to say.

My friend and I talked quietly about gratitude. Our Christmas tree was already dying, many of its needles drying out, but it shone cheerfully there in the corner, multi-colored lights gleaming.

I didn't tell my friend that I have this persistent voice in my head that wonders, cruelly, if I should start drinking again, as if this short handful of years have been long enough, as if I'd be in control of it at all once it reignites the dormant fuse in my bloodstream.

He has no doubt heard that voice, too.

We focused on our gratitude instead. There was plenty of it to go around: our homes, our marriages, this stable life in our hometown. Our children twirled like the figures of a zoetrope all around us, faces shining even in the shadows we cast.

We're lucky, yes, but it's more than that: we've made, for once, a good choice. How intricate a choice is, how fragile and how powerful. It's much bigger than a simple New Year's resolution. We're talking about an entire life here.

## Down the Dearborn
### Joyce Hocker

"This is high water. Anybody check the CFS?" Trish inquires.

"The river already crested," Elise reassures, "but its still running high."

By June 22, the water should have receded. It still looks daunting to me; no one checked the flow. As the group leader, I feel guilty for not even knowing to check anything out.

"What does CFS mean?" I ask, clueless.

"Cubic Feet per Second," Elise informs me. "How much water is flowing and how fast."

It's a Saturday in June, 2002. Our group of six women began our trip today by driving up the Blackfoot River, over Rogers Pass, and then down into the plains Charlie Russell painted in hues of blue and rose. Our plan is to float our raft down the Dearborn for an overnight at Elise's ranch.

Our journey together began in 1986, in my psychology practice in downtown Missoula. I organized a group of women to meet together to explore life issues. In the 1980's, following the second wave of feminism in the 1960's and 70's, women continued to claim our own journey through life, different from the masculine hero's journey. We needed each other to become clear, strong, and courageous.

After meeting for a while, someone declared the group needed a name; brainstorming resulted in a proclamation: "We are the Heroines." Together, we have grieved losses, analyzed bad boyfriends, weathered the trauma of divorces, and changed careers. We have laughed and cried over poetry, especially Mary Oliver's supportive challenges, which guided us to claim our lives for our own. We delved into dreams and encouraged each other to speak with authority.

While I led the group for years, the participants eventually took it over. Now they met on their own, for reunions, retreats, feasts, and trips like today. We take heart from Mary Oliver's reference to "the fires; and the black river of loss." These women, all warriors of the heart, declare themselves ready for the next phase of life. We are women of a certain age, and proud of it.

All of these women live as heroines to me. Elise is a singer, landscape artist, and ranch owner. Katie helped start a Community Health Center and now works in end of life care policy. Trish pioneers midlife women's health in her medical practice. Nancy raises llamas; her duties take her out in the freezing winter to help llama mamas give birth. Jane once won trophies for her archery, but now she nurtures women as an esthetician. All the

.omen devote themselves to the emerging feminine in their own lives and in culture. I grew up a preacher's kid in Texas, proud of my parents and their stands on social justice. Finding my way north to teach college, I never returned to the land where five generations of my family lived.

I'm a psychologist, not a river guide. Years of looking to me for a different kind of leadership might have blinded them (and myself) to the limits of my expertise. Once I capsized in our canoe on the north fork of the Blackfoot; nearly losing my life, but saving my husband's Sage fly rod. My only river rafting experience included a wild ride down the Pacuare River in Costa Rica, guided by whitewater cowboys. I paddled for my life back then; the Dearborn looks tame compared to that majestic jungle river. On this waterfront, I will hang on, try not to drown, and hope for the best.

As we planned the trip, Trish offered her raft and rowing skills. Elise transported our gear to her ranch a few days earlier. We dragged our raft down to the Dearborn, just off Highway 287, near the Rocky Mountain Front. When Elise and Trish return from dropping a van upstream, we are ready to set off on our expedition.

The float begins right at an historic site. In 1983, Mike Curran ran over a raft and a woman's leg with his truck. The disgruntled owner of the 70,000-acre Dearborn Ranch, he was furious at the perceived incursion of boats and hikers on the river that flowed through his private property. Before this incident, boaters, anglers and hikers enjoyed informal access at bridge crossings and within the high-water mark. After the guide was injured and public outrage coalesced, the Montana legislature codified public access into law in 1984.

Not only does the river look fast and dark, we notice an ominous grey sky with rain clouds looming. Regardless, we're up for the adventure. Knowing Trish is the rower, we all look anxiously at her cast. Trish broke a bone in her left hand a while back, but she assures us that the cast holds it steady and she can row.

"OK, Heroines, let's earn our name!" yells Nancy. We push into the current, toppling aboard our raft.

We float through the massive Dearborn Ranch, spread wide with sparsely populated rolling prairie. It's dotted with abandoned ranch buildings, herds of black angus, antelope, deer, and a few elk. While we are technically in grizzly country, we don't spot any.

Despite our calculations, we arrive at the ranch surprisingly early, drenched with rain during the final part of the float. The water carried us as rapidly as a Styrofoam cup tossed out of a car window.

While Katie and Jane build a fire in the raised fireplace, I happily prepare to cook in the outdoor log pavilion. Gazing at the wild Montana skies, my gratitude swells. I remember church camps in Texas. I also recall summer vacations in Colorado, where our family of five erected three tents for our month-long escape from the Texas heat. My body registers the delicious tingle of possibility at the beginning of each new camping adventure.

As we set up, we carry the Girl Scouts and Camp Fire Girls we used to be inside our midlife bodies. We cook our burgers in the fireplace, glad for the shelter of the log pavilion. We laugh and grin at each other around the picnic table.

The wind comes up, blowing hard as dark gray clouds carry a scent of more rain. A storm is brewing; we feel the chilled damp air. Knowing that we plan important group work tomorrow morning around the fire, an early bedtime beckons. No one wants to sleep under the pavilion; we've all seen Montana rain blow sideways. Cold and tired from an early day and several hours on the river, everyone decides to bed down in the large wall tent—except me. I ask Elise if I can sleep in the partly finished log house. She takes me up the trail to look at it, and I immediately take a liking to the structure. Log walls help me feel secure; the sub-floor and roof are intact. Holes for the doors and windows yawn open, but I think I can position my sleeping bag and mat under the center beam to escape the rain.

Retrieving my gear, I set up my home in the woods. Laying out my mat and bag, I set out a water bottle, the candle lantern, and some lip balm. My red silk pajamas are present, too. You can take the gal out of Texas, but not Texas out of the gal. I'm a fifty-seven year old happy camper.

I watch the storm come in over the Front Range to the West. As I situate a folding chair out under the eaves, the sky darkens. Rain pelts down amid thunder crashes. Soon, lightning illuminates the sky. I begin to wonder whether the logs will protect me from a strike.

As the lanterns go out in the wall tent down the trail, my solitude descends with the rain.

For quite a while, I am content to watch the downpour pound the metal roof and ground in front of the open doorway. Then I remember our talks about unseen creatures in the raft. Grizzly bears, even mountain lions. I find some comfort in the fact that Jane has her .357 Magnum, until I realize that she could not possibly hear me yell if I need help. I don't have bear bells or bear spray, but I recall that we make lots of noise on hiking trails in Glacier, so I start to sing.

Dozens of hymns and camp songs live in my brain. When I can't sleep at night, I sing them to myself in my mind. Now I sing out loud. Really loud, a quaver in my used-to-be soprano voice. "Oh God, our help in ages past, our hope in years to come." Or rather, "my help in hours to come." I launch into 'Abide with me, fast falls the eventide,' but this is entirely too mournful. 'Brightly Beams our Father's Mercy,' a hymn from the 1920's, rises up. I sing the one true Texas song, of course, clapping along at each beat. "The stars at night, are big and bright, deep in the heart of Texas! The sage in bloom, is like perfume, deep in the heart of Texas!"

I hope any local bears follow a different religion or might be repelled by my voice. While the rain drums the roof, I finally feel exhausted. Reassured by reminiscence and songs, I sleep deeply and well.

In the morning, Nancy peers over the windowsill, blonde bangs making her look like a teenager. She reports back in her Georgia drawl: "Hey girls,

she's alive." The rain has stopped just in time for breakfast, and one of our favorite rituals.

Everyone has brought papers that no longer serve us: journal pages, letters, notes, answers to discernment questions in the group, and anything else that the women have brought for release into a cleansing fire. We find enough dry wood to make the bonfire by scattering out to collect the lower branches of huge pine trees. We want a big, glorious fire to burn up those quandaries, piercing heartaches, brave questions, and poignant disappointments.

Despite the dearth of rowing skills present in the group, us Montana women all know how to make a fire. We pull up logs, rocks and chairs to gather around the blaze. Each woman describes what she is releasing as the rest of the circle of women witness the days, months and sometimes years of life that the burning items represent. We are back in our life stories. Joking as we try to keep the soggy wood burning, we speculate whether the pages contain too many tears to burn.

"Get back there," Jane declares, using a sharp stick to poke pages flying from the fire pit. The past shrivels with each page and photo. We honor and bless the life they represent, and then let it go. I look at each face, knowing their struggles, and blessing their lives that will unfold from here.

As we pack up and prepare for the short float to the Missouri River, we notice that the Dearborn is definitely higher than when we arrived. The rapid increase lights a different kind of fire under us. Packing our belongings into duffel bags for Elise to retrieve later, we pile into the raft. Despite the tense situation, we feel lighter now. We left heavy burdens of the past—and unneeded gear—behind.

The river flies us along much more rapidly than yesterday. Patches of blue sky start to show through the clouds as we head into Dearborn Canyon. Trish expertly manages the oars. The river roils, tumultuous and dangerous; we exchange worried looks. The raft floats perilously close to the limestone walls on the left. Not thinking about broken legs, we push off the cliffs with our Teva-clad feet to keep from crashing into the rock. As we careen toward a sharp turn, the raft tips ominously.

"Everyone out!" Trish bellows. Dropping the oars, Trish executes a flat dive off the river side of the raft. The rest of us just look at each other, but then rush to the high side of the raft. Agonizingly, the raft settles back into the river, sparing us from flipping over. We realize in terror that no one is on the oars. We're out of control. Instinctively, Jane scrambles back onto the rowing frame and takes hold. I ask if she knows how, recognizing a silly question as I pose it.

"No, but I'll do my best," she replies.

"We have to reach Trish," Elise yells. Trish paddles frantically towards the raft. Nancy and Katie pull Trish up to the raft's edge; she uses her strong arms to crawl back in. Jane maneuvers us to a grassy landing where we can reconnoiter.

"Let's rest here for a while before we go to the takeout," Trish counsels. We climb out of the raft, glad to be on land, relieved no one was hurt. We

spread our sopping wet outer clothes on the bushes along the bank, lying in the grass to catch our breath and dry off.

"The takeout is just below," Elise explains gently. We climb back into the raft and somberly finish our float, Jane rowing us the rest of the way. We're still wet and subdued when we climb into the van, beginning our drive back to the put-in place under the bridge on the Dearborn.

Riding back on Highway 200, the raft is stowed on Trish's truck. Our worries more at ease, we begin to fantasize about hot food. Highway 200, which meanders around the Blackfoot, must be one of the most beautiful drives in Montana. Giddy, adrenaline and joy take over.

Pulling into Trixi's Antler Saloon, named for a trick horse rider and roper who bought the saloon in the 1950's, we climb out. Trixi must have been a Heroine just like us. Trish voices her first worried complaint about her sore hand and sopping cast; we will find out later that she re-broke the bone.

Feasting on burgers and chicken fried steak, the five of us recount the trip. We laugh and shiver, remembering our close call. We raise a toast to the Heroines. Our float trip gave us wisdom to plan, courage to forge ahead, and to trust in our life saving connections. We are full of life, ready for the next emotional rapids in our renewed lives.

## The Rooms
### Alena Gostnell

❉

The glass shimmers like bubbles in the sun. Through the ancient windows, the warped view of Hellgate Canyon proves that glass is fluid. It can age into a rainbow. The steep climb to the upstairs classrooms reveals the creak of old wood that has been sanded and refinished. How many feet have climbed these stairs? So full of history, the smell of thousands of sweating students permeates the rooms of Jeanette Rankin Hall at the University of Montana.

I have a room in my memory, full of my history. Warped like the windows in the classroom, it is a room I avoid.

\*\*\*

My Aunt Geneva painted the room yellow—like a canary in sunshine. It smelled of lemon-scented Pledge and moth balls. Shades of green shag carpeting covered the floor. In one corner, a plant hung in a macramé hanger. An amber colored bubble-glass chandelier dangled in another. It never worked. Framed, embroidered yarn flowers decorated the walls. My grandparents' wedding photo perched atop a lace doily on the standard four drawer dresser. Their eyes watched, young faces frozen in bliss.

A rose-colored chenille bedspread dressed the king-sized bed—so high I couldn't climb in by myself. Tall posts flanked each corner, anchored by a massive, carved headboard. Crocheted in colorful, patchwork patterns, an afghan draped across the foot of the bed. It was scratchy, not soft. Transparent curtains skimmed the high, postage-stamp windows. A small closet, just big enough for a child to crouch, completed the yellow room.

The room became a living being. It breathed a dark invitation. I memorized the cracks in the paint, and the holes where pictures had hung. I watched as the bed became smaller, the room became smaller, and I became smaller. The yellow room was my normal.

\*\*\*

Uncle Virgil sat on the crushed velvet sofa, a pattern of brown and burnt orange flowers. Carved wood armrests curved beneath his fingertips. Wearing my homemade pajamas, I snuggled on his lap. Edged in ricrac, my lightweight cotton top hung like a long-sleeved summer dress. My bloomers resembled oversized underwear. Uncle Virgil's hairy arm pulled me close. He smelled like Old Spice. His deep, hollow voice whispered in my ear. "Merry Christmas, Alena."

I felt his scratchy sideburns and his warm breath on my cheek. His hand moved down my back and lifted my nightgown. He rubbed my back in small

circles. I giggled because it tickled. He looked at me with his numbing smile, a smile that never reached his eyes. His hand slid inside my bloomers and he rubbed my naked butt.

He lifted me up in his arms, and made an announcement. "I think she is tired. I'm putting her to bed." Scooping me up, he carried me to the yellow room and laid me in the middle of the king-size bed. He lifted my nightgown and blew on my belly. I laughed like any other three-year-old.

***

Uncle Virgil sat in his olive-green swivel chair. He watched television—a shiny wooden console. Crisscrossed slats concealed the speakers. I sat on his lap. A scratchy crocheted blanket covered me. We swiveled until my eyes grew heavy. I felt his hand on my belly. It rubbed back and forth, back and forth. My eyes closed. His hand traveled lower. The blanket dropped to the floor. I was glad. It was itchy. His hand touched my tiny, innocent childhood. He stroked and caressed it like a cheek, or a soft head of hair.

***

I looked forward to spending these summer vacations with my cousins, Genie and Deanna. The lush, cool mountain air in Libby, Montana, was a welcome relief from the hot, arid summers of Shelby. In addition, my cousins' house always had a supply of sherbet popsicles from the Schwan's truck.

My Aunt Geneva kept a spare bike for me. It was a yellow girl's bike with a glorious long banana seat. The handlebars extended higher than my shoulders, so I usually pumped standing up. My cousins and I raced along the forest trails. I could barely see the sky through the thick, dense jungle. Our favorite trail, a three-mile ride through a mysterious thicket of trees, emerged at the junior high school. We flew our kites.

One summer, we packed a lunch every day and walked 7 blocks to the public swimming pool. We ate our sack lunches at the baseball field next to the pool. Two years older than me, quiet, dark-haired Genie led the way. Neat and tidy like her mother, she fussed with her clothes while Dee and I splashed through mud puddles. Dee dared us to bust the teenagers who were kissing in the dugouts.

My brother resented my summer vacations with our cousins in Libby. Stuck at home in Shelby with our parents, he was never allowed to stay at Aunt Geneva and Uncle Virgil's house. I promised him that when I got home at the end of the summer, we'd collect rattlesnake rattles with our wrist rocket sling shots. Maybe we'd set a new record.

***

"Do you want to play Monopoly?" Uncle Virgil asked. This was his code. My cousin Dee and I accompanied him into the yellow room. He smelled of sweat and Old Spice. I knelt in the closet as instructed. The winter coats hung over me, waiting for snow. A pair of boots stood guard like ghosts. The green shag carpet crept between my toes. I wore shorts and a tank top. They smelled nice, like Aunt Geneva's laundry soap.

"Pay attention, Alena." Uncle Virgil commanded. He took off his pants and stood naked in front of me. He looked stunted—his legs bowed; his arms

79

have privacy. Virgil always waited for my aunt to go to work, or go shopping, before we played our game. She didn't like Monopoly, he said.

He laid Genie in the middle of the bed. Her dark hair fanned out around her head. Virgil spread open her legs. He asked me to lick Genie the same way I licked him. "Make sure you do it right," he cautioned. "It will help her enjoy this." He whispered to me in his secret voice. "She will do this to you when it's your turn."

He asked Dee to lick him while I licked Genie. He stood at the foot of the bed with his hairy hands wrapped around the bed posts. Dee knelt before him. It seemed like we licked forever. He finally climbed onto the bed. Dee stood on the right side and I stood on the left. We watched carefully, curious. We knew one day it would be our turn.

"This may sting, but it won't last long," he said to Genie. She nodded. He entered her. "Are you okay?" he asked. She bit her lip and mumbled but nodded yes.

When he finished, he pulled out and rolled over. He asked his daughters to give him a kiss. They each kissed him on the cheek.

I noticed the red stain on the blanket. It looked like cherry Kool-Aid. I worried my aunt would be mad. She was so concerned with cleanliness. The house always smelled like Pine-Sol and bleach. The floors were spotless. Virgil didn't seem worried about the red stain, neither did my cousins. I assumed I shouldn't worry about it, either.

***

I wasn't there for Dee's special day. I guess I wasn't important enough to be included.

My special day happened the summer I was 7. I felt smart because I completed 2nd grade and could read. My teacher said I was advanced for my age. My parents dropped me off at my cousins' house for the summer. I was so excited! My grandmother bought me a new swimsuit from J.C. Penney. It was a dark green paisley print bikini with a halter top. I felt so grown up.

Virgil arrived home later that afternoon. "Alena, it's your turn this summer!" he announced. "I can't wait to play Monopoly with you!" I was so excited. I would finally have my turn in the special way, just like my cousins.

That night, we snuggled together in Genie's bed, talking. "It will be better for you," Genie said. "We have been working all year on how to make it easier for you."

The next time Aunt Geneva left the house, Virgil shouted. "Genie! Deanna! Alena! It's time for Monopoly!" We entered the yellow room and removed our clothes. It was a familiar ritual. I began to crawl up on the bed, but Virgil stopped me. "We're going to do this differently. You'll like it. Don't worry."

Uncle Virgil lifted me up on the bed—my head toward the wall. My bottom rested at the edge, as my legs hung over. The soft cotton bedspread had been removed, replaced by an old wool army blanket. The blanket was itchy.

"You are so beautiful and special. I am glad we get to play Monopoly today," he said. He asked Genie and Dee to stroke my vagina. Their tiny hands

81

obeyed his command. He stood with his back against the dresser. I couldn't see the picture of my grandparents. I stared at the ceiling. I noticed a small crack in the corner by the chandelier. I hadn't noticed that one before.

"Close your eyes and feel what they are doing to you," he said.

I closed my eyes. I tried to focus on each hand, each finger. He told Genie to spread open my vagina. He told Dee to insert her fingers. "Dee is making it bigger, so it won't sting as much," he explained.

"It really does help, Alena. We practiced all year." Genie reassured me.

He instructed Genie to lick me, just as I had licked her. He asked Dee to arouse him. He always preferred Dee for this; I guess she was better. When he was big, my cousins climbed onto the bed with me. They held my hands, and kissed my mouth. I tried to figure out why, then I felt the sting.

Moving inside me, Virgil lifted my legs. He pressed a hand on each knee, pushing them apart. I wanted to yell that it hurt, but one of my cousins had her tongue in my mouth. I kicked my legs in protest.

"The worst part is over," he crooned. "I promise. Just relax. If you fight, it will hurt worse." I believed him. I shouldn't have.

Genie and Dee stopped kissing me and just held my hands. I squeezed them tight. It burned so bad. I wanted to be brave like Genie, so I didn't cry or fight. My cousins looked proud of me. I felt something warm and wet down there, but it still burned. He pushed into me, faster and faster. When he stopped, his head dropped backward. The end of the game.

He pulled out. I felt a rush of warm fluid go with him. He released my legs, and my cousins released my hands. For an instant, I felt abandoned and alone. When I opened my eyes, they were all there—smiling and proud. I did it! I finally had my turn!

"You did great!" Virgil said.

"You won this round!" Genie cheered. "This is going to be a great summer!"

We didn't tell anyone about our games in the yellow bedroom. Those walls kept a dark secret. My grandparents' photo sat stoically on the doily. They watched, smiling, the only witnesses to the crimes. It was our secret for six years.

*Logging Camp*
Teresa Lundy

❋

We camped alongside the Spotted Bear River in Montana's Bob Marshall Wilderness, four hours from our home near Troy, a tiny logging and mining town near the Canadian border. In 1984 the logging industry was booming, but as a 14-year-old girl, spending a summer in the woods with my parents and a bunch of loggers was the last thing my sisters and I wanted.

At first, we slept in late, then spent the day slumped in our camp chairs, pouting and complaining to Mom about all the fun we were missing out on at home. Mom, always working on an afghan or reading, even while camping, grew sick of our whining. "Here. Make yourselves useful and go catch us some dinner," she said, thrusting Dad's fishing pole into Bekki's fist. "I'd like a little peace and quiet." We headed off to the river to fish and smoke cigarettes and swim and skip rocks. Soon, lost in our activities, we thought less and less of what we were missing at home.

The temperatures soared into the 90's during the day and dipped down near freezing at night. Dad, along with the other hard-working men who were camped nearby, woke up hours before daylight to fall and buck, choke and yard logs, then load them on trucks to haul to the mills. While they were gone, and with Mom busy with her own activities in the bus, we were free for twelve hours. The men returned, bone-tired, caked in sawdust and dirty sweat, in the late afternoon.

"You girls going fishing today? Better get your worms." Dad would wake Bekki, Noni and me before he left for work at 3:00 each morning, so we could catch nightcrawlers in the dark, while the ground was still wet and soft. We bundled layers of clothes over our pajamas and carefully tiptoed around so we wouldn't wake Mom, lifting stray pieces of wood strewn around camp. We shone the flashlight beam on the fat worms underneath, grabbing them before they could slide back in to the ground. We filled our coffee can quickly, then hurried back to burrow into our sleeping bags, still warm.

Every morning, as soon as the sun hit our camp site, the frost disappeared and steam rose in slow, thick wisps from the wet grass. Mom cooked our Malt-o-Meal over the camp fire, as there was no stove on the bus. We washed our bowls and spoons with river water. The bus had no sink or running water, just a dinette set and a couple of fold-out beds.

By midmorning, the temperature was perfect to head to the river; just warm enough for shorts and tank tops; barefooted as usual. True to our ages,

83

Bekki always lead the way. At sixteen, she was already engaged to be married and considered herself grown up. She stomped her way down to the river, scaring away any snakes that might be sunning themselves across the trail. She walked the same way no matter where she was. She always made her presence known.

I followed behind Bekki as I always did, no matter what the situation. She was my protector and example, good or bad. Noni, eleven, came last. She was always a good sport, game for any adventure. We pushed our way through the dew-drenched branches of the Douglas Fir trees, inhaling the poignant smell and shivering from the wet, we were thankful for the sun's heat as soon as we broke through the trees and onto the rocky beach.

We only had one pole to share between us. Bekki, always first, waded twenty feet into the river to cast her line. In less than a minute, that first whitefish bit. After pulling it to shore, she handed the pole to me. How I hated smooshing that wiggly worm on to the hook. I'd cast my line, and reel in the fish, and smack it over the head with a rock. I pulled out the hook, and hand the pole to Noni. The ice-cold river was barely a foot deep where we fished. It rippled over the rocks, drowning out the distant whine of chain saws.

By the time the sun was directly overhead, we were starving. We cleaned our catch, slitting the fish's bellies with a pocket knife and ripping out the slimy insides. We threw the guts back in to the river to float downstream, and gave the fish a final rinse. We stuck close together as we headed back singing as loud as we could to warn away any bears. At camp, we put our fish in a cooler. With no ice available, we used jugs of cold river water and stashed the cooler in the shade of the bus. We downed the peanut butter and jelly sandwiches Mom always had waiting for us.

An hour later, we returned to the river to swim and bathe. We stripped down and jumped in the river with a bar of soap, a short way downstream from where we fished, where the river was deeper. We made sure to be dressed and back at our own camp before the loggers returned. They headed to our spot for their own baths, washing away their work. We rarely saw the men as their camps were separate from ours. From a distance, we watched as they slowly made their way towards the river, exhausted from a long day of back-breaking work.

After Dad had his bath and donned clean clothes, he stoked the dinner fire and added wet wood for smoke. He arranged the whitefish on sticks and covered the pit with wet canvas bags. As darkness fell, Dad played his banjo and Mom read by the fire. Bekki, Noni and I toasted marshmallows over the coals on green sticks and ate as many as we wanted. Tired from hours of fishing and swimming in the hot sun, sleep caught us easily, soon after dark. By morning, dozens of flaky smoked whitefish waited. Dad brought most of them to share with the loggers, but he left plenty for us to snack on.

One of the loggers, Jim, drove home to Troy on the weekends, and some-times let Bekki and I squeeze into the front of his little red pickup. Our parents didn't trust us to stay home alone all weekend, but they thought we'd be fine hanging out at Jim's with his wife and daughters. Little did

they know that Jim and his wife drank hard all weekend, and never paid any attention to what we were doing.

We went to keggers in the woods, as Tom Petty songs blasted through the open doors of a pickup, and beer flowed freely. Bottles of MD 20/20 and joints were passed around. If we were lucky the party wouldn't get busted. When it did, the cops just confiscated our alcohol and left. Within an hour, a new party started at a different location, lasting until dawn.

We dragged ourselves back to Jim's on Sunday. The three of us, tired and hungover, made the four-hour trip back to logging camp. On Monday, we ate our Malt-o-meal and spent another day at the river.

## The Fire
### Gladys Considine

❋

The faint odor of smoke in otherwise clear skies. Hot afternoon winds and parched vegetation. No rain since May, rendering our spring-fed ponds to dried, cracked mud. Tree leaves curled inward. Grey sage turned crisp, giving aroma to the hot air. In Southeastern Montana along Powder River, farmers and ranchers are jumpy and on edge, constantly on the alert for an increase in a burning smell or a plume of ashy smoke on the horizon.

August was unusually dry in 1971, when my two older sisters and I co-ordinated a visit to Mom on the Third Creek sheep ranch where we grew up. After Papa died, my oldest sister Alice and her husband, Albert, shared ranch work with Mom from their home forty miles away. Irene and her daughters came from Wisconsin; I flew in from Seattle with my sons, the baby just 20 months old.

Mom lived alone in the house she had set up when she married my father nearly forty years before. Comfortable and happy, at age sixty-one she was where she wanted to be—taking care of her sheep and a growing menagerie of peacocks, turkeys, guinea hens, and mixed-breed chickens.

The sky had been clear through the first day of our visit, but darkened just as we finished supper. The wind blew strong from the south and west and gave the air a slight chill. Thunder growled in the distance. Closer to us were sharp snaps and pops as lightning flashed and crackled, leaving a sulfur and brimstone smell in the air. Unfortunately, there was no rain.

"We'll be lucky if it don't start a fire someplace," Mom murmured, watching the heavy clouds roll on east over the hill.

The party-line telephone clanged, all of us jumping at the sound. On the line was the neighbor to the north. She told Mom to go look outside, warily announcing that she could see smoke.

We all hurried outside, gazing from the yard towards the horizon. Black, grey, and white seethed and boiled over the first small hill from the house. I cast a glance at Mom worriedly.

"Well, I guess we just ran out of luck," she muttered tonelessly. "Let's go see."

Like most of the area ranchers, Mom kept her little red pickup stocked with fire-fighting equipment—cream cans filled with water, an assortment of gunny sacks, and a couple of shovels. She jumped into the pickup, Irene joining her. I loaded the kids into the Maverick my older sister loaned me. When we ascended the hill, we could already see fire and smoke flashing near the other side of Third Creek.

86

"Gladys. Go call Alice," Mom called to me. "See if you can get the fire department in Broadus." Without even awaiting my response, my mother went speeding down the ranch road toward the creek crossing, leaving a trailing cloud of dry dust.

I drove back to the house, jumped out of the car and burst into the house. Running past our cooling supper, I dove for the phone. I broke into a party line conversation as I lifted the receiver.

"I'm sorry to interrupt," I babbled. "I'm Nora LaRiviere's daughter, Gladys. A fire started out here, but the house is safe. Mom told me to call Alice in Ashland and to call for help."

Most of the neighbors had known us as children. They knew a long-distance call to Ashland wouldn't work if another party-line was open. One by one, they hung up their phones. My call to Alice went through.

\*\*\*

The Deputy Sheriff for Ashland, my brother-in-law Albert, had already fielded a call on his police radio from the Broadus fire dispatcher. The hard wind was racing the grass fire straight toward Broadus; fire fighters there had called for help from surrounding communities. The Montana State Patrolman my sister ran into confirmed a big fire south of Broadus, on "that ranch owned by the woman with the funny French name."

"The LaRiviere place?" Alice asked him.

"Yeah," he replied. "That's the one."

"That's my mom," Alice clarified, voice tight. With widening eyes, he responded. "Oh, my God. How can I help? Are you going over there?"

With the patrolman as an escort, Ashland Volunteer Fire Fighters sped to Broadus in their small tank truck. Alice and her family flew past their flashing lights in their big heavy Mercury. The car was outfitted for almost any emergency, adapted as a cop car.

They cleared the forty miles to Broadus in less than a half hour. As they nearly flew over the Home Creek Divide, the glow of the fire lit up the eastern skyline, twenty miles away.

When I finally got off the phone, Irene's girls, baby Wayne and I piled into the Maverick. I drove out to the county road where we could see what was happening. Ahead of us, ravenous fire ate hungrily through next winter's sheep feed. My heart was racing as fast as the flames; I stopped the car well behind the fire. We rolled the windows up to shield ourselves from the acrid smell of flaming vegetation.

Through the smoke, the town fire truck lights flashed and swirled. Water sprayed and beat out the fire a half-mile from where Mom and Irene were working. Neighbors and firefighters with their pickups and water trucks did their best to smother the flames.

Like flint to tinder, the lightning had struck rocks on the hill just to the east of Third Creek. Dried grass sparked into flames that mushroomed and bolted, driven by afternoon winds. Across the pasture, we saw that Mom had maneuvered her pickup into an area that was already burned. Mom and Irene flailed at the flames with gunny sacks, wet down from the cream

cans of water. They beat back the fire spreading downhill toward the trees of Third Creek. The little girls with me gazed at their mother and grandmother with growing fear. A neighbor steered his pickup along the east side of the burning patch, his teenage son balanced in the back to spray the fire with water from a portable tank.

***

The graveled county road served as a fire barrier. Everything on the east side was burning, but no fire had jumped to the west side. Fortunately, most of the sheep were on the west side of the road, down in the river bottom, under the trees.

Not all the sheep were safely tucked to the west side. Our neighbor had been moving cattle when he saw the fire and left to help. Keeping tight control of his wild-eyed and snorting horse, he tried to force twenty or so of Mom's sheep to the safe side of the road. The sheep wouldn't go; they barreled around the horse instead, so terrorized by fire that they ran crazy. They crashed into the fence that separated our ranch from the neighbor's property. Bleating and coughing, they bunched up together against the fence, only a short distance from safety. Heat, smoke, and the frantic actions of his fire-panicked horse rendered the rider's heroic actions futile.

The fire burned right through and over the little band of sheep and blazed on. He pulled back and calmed his horse as he rode to Mom, reluctant to tell her that some of the sheep were caught in the fire.

We returned to the house to find three of Mom's neighbors waiting with food and coffee. They stocked wash tubs full of ice, soft drinks, and beer. The tired neighbors and kinfolk who had stayed to clean up spot fires arrived at the house after dark. In came the men with red and tearing eyes, faces and clothes blackened with soot. They gobbled down a sandwich, and guzzled Coke and coffee.

Some went home to tend their own nighttime chores. Some stayed, planning to go back out, to clean up burning fence posts, dig up smoldering sage brush, or to join others putting out spot fires in the miles of burned pastures. The women returned to their own homes, thankful that the fire had not consumed the grass in their pastures—this time.

***

I tended to the children while our family tackled the fire. I put the kids to bed in the little camping trailer Mom used as a guest bedroom and waited. Way after dark, Mom and Irene finally came back to the house, Alice and Albert right behind them.

Mom was black all over, her new white tennis shoes charred and torn. Exhausted, she spread a big bath towel on her bed and fell on it, fully clothed. She was asleep before her singed hair hit the pillow. Whether we had been fighting fire or not, we were all traumatized and exhausted.

A little after five the next morning, I heard Mom ease her aching body from the creaking bed. In her sooty, fire-blackened clothes, she tiptoed outside into the cool dawn to survey the fire damage in daylight.

We were just finishing our pancakes when she returned. Her jaw was

clenched so tight that her lips disappeared; not a word budged past them. She reached around behind the kitchen door and pulled out a rifle. Stretching way up to a high porch shelf for a box of rifle shells, she jammed them into her jeans pocket, turned around and poured herself a half cup of coffee.

"It's bad," she finally spoke, quickly swigging down the bitter brew. "But, it's a thing you kids need to know about, and something I've gotta do. Get into the back. We've got to go take care of my sheep."

With her kids and grandkids safely settled in the bed of the pickup, Mom drove out to the county road. Once across Third Creek, she left the road and down into the pasture. Ash littered the ground in lieu of grass, leaving a gray rooster tail in the air behind us. We liked fire in our pleasant campfire circles or our fireplaces, but this was vastly different. The smell was ugly and threatening; our noses filled with soot, dirt, and filthy acrid leftovers. The pickup bounced over blackened humps that had once been sagebrush, and melted patches of prickly pear cactus. Occasionally, Mom stopped so Irene could grab a shovel, tearing out a still smoldering root.

Mom slowed the pickup to crawl past the burned sheep. They were still huddled against the pasture fence where the fire had swept over them. We got a close-up look at what fire can do to animals. Melted wool clumped together, the smell of it mingling with the horrible scent of burned meat.

Mom wouldn't let us get out of the pickup. She drove over a little hill that blocked us from the sight. She told us to stay there.

***

She only took her gun. We sat in tentative silence, shattered by sporadic shots. Irene and I climbed out, leaned against the fender, both fighting tears. Without success, we tried to be calm, as fatalistic as our mother.

"My God, Mom," Catherine said. She climbed from the back to the comfort of Irene's arms. "Is Grandma shooting her sheep?"

"Yes," was Irene's tight-lipped reply.

"But why? They made it through the fire."

"Some of them will die anyway. Sometimes their lungs are burned so bad they can't even breathe. She is taking care of the ones that are suffering."

Mom, a good shepherd, had learned through hard experience what had to be done. This agonizing task was one that my mother, Nora Gladys Wetherelt LaRiviere, would not foist upon anyone else.

89

*Montana Music*
Audrey Koehler Peterson

❋

For several reasons, it was an unusual rehearsal. On a sunny afternoon in 2000, I sat among 130 musicians—about twice the number I was used to as a violinist in the Missoula Symphony Orchestra. We were crowded on a soundstage that had been trucked in from somewhere east of the Mississippi, assembled and set up that morning in a natural lawn amphitheater on the Carroll College campus in Helena, Montana.

The stage faced south into an intense August sun, and I remember fussing with my violin as the strings stretched randomly in the heat. Perspiration caused the instrument to slide out from under my chin at unpredictable moments. It was our first rehearsal away from the Helena Civic Center, where we had met the past two afternoons. The change in venue was disconcerting, because the sound dissipated in the great outdoors, making it difficult to hear cues I had come to rely on in earlier rehearsals. The pressure was on; the next night's concert would be broadcast live on Montana Public Television. It would also be recorded for the subsequent marketing of CDs of the performance.

Consequently, each music stand had a microphone attached. That mic was intimidating, a huge ear eavesdropping on every note. We were instructed NOT to say anything to our stand partners, and to be careful when turning pages, in case of dropping pencils or accidental bumps into the stand. As if all that weren't enough distraction, technicians roamed through the orchestra while we rehearsed, often blocking my line of sight to the conductor as they adjusted mics, strung wires, and tested lighting and camera angles for the set-up of two full-size movie screens on either side of the massive stage.

Strangest of all was our preparation for our guest soloist, appearing at the third annual Montana Power Summer Symphony concert scheduled for the next evening. We rehearsed the *Armed Forces Salute*, a collection of military theme songs, among the programmed concert selections. The medley included the 'The Army Goes Rolling Along,' the Coast Guard's 'Semper Paratus,' 'The Halls of Montezuma' honoring the Marines, 'The U.S. Air Force' ( 'Off We Go Into the Wild Blue Yonder ') and the Navy's 'Anchors Aweigh .' Our guest artist would appear during the concert performance of the medley, but was unavailable for the rehearsal. This was largely due to the fact that the soloist was an Air Force pilot.

The instrument? A fighter jet.

While directing us with one hand, conductor Uri Barnea of the Billings Symphony was holding a telephone with the other, working with personnel

at Malmstrom Air Force Base in Great Falls to coordinate the timing of the jet's flyover with the orchestra's playing of the *Armed Forces Salute*. Ideally, the jet would arrive at the same time that we played the Air Force song.

We rehearsed and timed the whole series of military tunes several times at various tempos, all the while consulting with stopwatches and the contacts at Malmstrom. It was eventually decided that if the jet was sitting on the runway in Great Falls with engines running, ready to take off when the conductor in Helena gave the downbeat for the *Salute*, it should arrive over the concert venue in Helena at the right time. That meant that we had to time the whole concert in order to get the pilot to the end of the runway at the right moment. Aside from miscalculation, miscommunication, system failure, human error, or inclement weather, what could go wrong?

I was a part of that rehearsal in Helena because of my membership in the Missoula Symphony Orchestra, a community orchestra then in its 45th season, comprised of area musicians along with University of Montana music faculty and students. The Missoula Symphony is one of seven symphony orchestras in Montana, the others being the Billings, Bozeman, Butte, Great Falls, and Helena Symphonies, and the Glacier Orchestra in Kalispell, all of which work together through the Montana Association of Symphony Orchestras (MASO).

In 1998, the Montana Power Company joined with MASO to sponsor a Montana Summer Symphony, comprised of players and conductors from all seven symphonies. This composite Montana symphony would present a free concert to be held outdoors on a summer night at Carroll College in Helena, and also broadcast live throughout the state on Montana public television.

The program would feature all of the conductors and include popular favorites: show tunes, patriotic songs and marches, Montana college school songs, ballads, traditional American frontier and folk tunes, light classical. Many of the selections would be scored specifically for the event—especially the grand finale, the *Montana State Song*. That first concert, held on August 8, 1998, was deemed so successful that the Summer Symphony became an annual event through 2002, each concert advertised using posters created by Montana artist Monte Dolack.

To assure that the Summer Symphony would include a balance of musicians from all seven Montana symphonies, players were asked each year to apply for a seat on the stage. If you were chosen, your music arrived about a month before the concert. Your expenses were paid, including transportation to Helena and food and lodging in the dorms at Carroll College for the week of the concert. I was fortunate to participate in three of the five annual events, reliving the music camp experiences of my youth, enjoying the camaraderie of musicians from all corners of Montana.

Montanans have a long tradition of making their own music. Like many aspects of life with wide-open spaces and long distances, if you want something, you probably need to figure out how to do it yourself and then 'grow your own' for future insurance. That tradition was good fortune for me.

My journey to that stage in Helena began 45 years earlier when, as a

nine-year-old, I was finally big enough to wrap myself around a violin and old enough to enter Missoula's public school music program. My size (and my mother) dictated the selection of the violin as my instrument.

My first teacher was Helen Wunderlich, an orchestra director who traveled to all of Missoula's elementary schools to give fourth-graders the opportunity to play orchestral instruments. Missoula public schools were also fortunate enough to draw on the commitment of music faculty from the University of Montana. Through the all-city grade school program and later, the Missoula County High School orchestra, I had the opportunity to be directed by and study with dedicated music educators who were passionate about bringing up new generations of orchestral musicians. They made sure we kids had the opportunities to participate in local, state, and regional music festivals and camps and competitions, which allowed for traveling and meeting fellow music students from across Montana.

I joined the Missoula Symphony during high school and continued playing through college. During those years, I often traveled to Butte and Helena to help augment their symphonies when a few extra players were needed (and to earn a little extra cash). It's just what you do as a musician in Montana, lending credence to the old adage that Montana is indeed a small town with very long streets.

The morning of August 5 dawned clear and bright, promising another hot day and hopefully a pleasant evening with a cloudless sky for the 2000 Summer Symphony event. Headed to the cafeteria for breakfast, I glanced outside the Carroll College dorm window onto the stage and sloping lawn amphitheater below. I was surprised to see a colorful patchwork of unattended quilts already laid out on the lawn. Before 7 a.m., early risers had stopped by to stake their claims for seating at the evening concert. They were obviously confident that those claims would be respected by others who came later.

Throughout the day people gathered, some with tables and umbrellas, portable grills, champagne ice buckets, and decks of cards; others with blankets, lawn chairs, coolers, boom boxes, toys and baby carriages. It was something of a carnival atmosphere, people happy to fritter away the hours on a summer Saturday as the sun made its way to the west. Ushers appeared later in the afternoon, asking folks to move this way and that in order to create aisles for safety and access as the amphitheater filled up. The audience seemed to arrive from all over Montana. (The next year, at the 2001 Summer Symphony, it was reported that a crowd of over 20,000 were gathered on that lawn—equivalent to the crowds typical of the annual Grizzly-Bobcat football rivalry. It was even touted as the largest gathering ever for a Montana event unrelated to sports.)

The concert began with The *National Emblem March*. We worked our way through the early program selections. The *Armed Forces Salute* was the tenth selection on the concert program for 2000, situated about halfway through the two-hour program.

When it was finally time, the announcer invited those in the audience

who were members or veterans of the various branches of the military to stand when the song for their particular branch was played. At the downbeat, I thought about the jet taking off in Great Falls and had to admonish myself to pay attention to what I was doing. It was probably fortuitous that the jet would come from the northeast, its approach not visible to us sitting under the shell of the stage.

As we finished the modulation into the Air Force song and launched into 'Off we go, into the wild blue yonder,' it was all I could do to keep my eyes on the music and the conductor. We played it all the way through—but no jet arrived above us. 'Anchors Aweigh' was the only military song that remained on our setlist.

When we approached the last chord for the Air Force Song, I wondered what we would do at the end of the Salute. Would we stall and wait for the jet, or just move on to the rest of the program? In the middle of my doubts, I sensed the agitation and shift of attention in the audience as they spotted the jet coming in low over the top of the stage.

The crowd jumped to its feet, cheering as the jet flew over, a perfectly timed exclamation point at the completion of the Air Force Song. The backwash from the jet engine thundered into us with that primal, throbbing percussion of sound that makes one gasp, and drowns out all but breathing and heartbeat.

In the wonder of it all, I think some of us in the orchestra may have briefly stopped playing, sitting agape, but no matter—we were just part of the whole. Nobody was listening as our guest soloist stole the show. The orchestra pulled it together to play 'Anchors Aweigh' as the jet banked east. After one brilliant silvery flash of reflected light from the setting sun, it disappeared into the purple summer twilight of Montana's big sky.

I felt a little sorry for the Navy personnel present, as their song got lost in the aftermath, but no one seemed to mind. Our soloist remained anonymous and didn't get to take a bow, but I hope there was at least a fist pump in the cockpit to celebrate the successful mission and perfect timing.

It was an unforgettable moment of music and magic, quintessentially Montanan: a stage of local musicians and an audience of friends and neighbors scattered on a grassy hillside, watching mountain majesty under an evening star. All of us—players and listeners—found ourselves bound together in soaring sound that evokes the common history and traditions of our life together in this place.

What does it take to make music and magic? In the technical sense, it takes focus, simultaneous attention to many details, mathematical precision, and the management of sound waves to create emotion. Dissonance eventually resolves into some level of closure, harmony, peace. One can create sound and melody by oneself, but I wonder whether one can truly make music alone. Music requires givers and receivers—a generosity of spirit in the willingness to stop everything else and be in the moment of shared experience, whether producing the sound or listening to it. If you're the musician, the notes are simply the medium. The essence lies in the ability and

willingness to blend one's voice, both human and instrumental, into the voices of other musicians. The music and magic come from shared experience: listening and watching together, shaping sound and contributing exactly the right blend of self, skill and emotion to the larger whole. If you're the listener, music demands your immersion in the moment; your willingness to be present and open to receive whatever the experience turns out to be. Montana audiences know this. Their responsiveness has been a big part of the magic for me.

Now I am 74. The years and arthritis have taken their toll on my ability to play my violin, and I'm dealing with the inevitable frustration of not being able to play as I once could. It often discourages me from playing at all. I left the Missoula Symphony a few years ago, not willing to risk an embarrassing error, not realizing until later that I had left a part of my soul behind.

We musicians are taught to be self-critical and to strive for excellence, patiently practicing the same passages over and over to set the neural pathways that assure accuracy and consistency in tempo, quality of sound, intonation. We want to play well, fulfilling our responsibilities to our fellow players, and to the composer of the music. But I'm coming to understand that there is an essential balance: if we are unable to be forgiving and encouraging of ourselves and others, we will be lost in the mechanics and miss the music. I may not be able to perform as I once did, but perhaps I still have something to give and to gain if I'm willing to risk something new.

Fortunately, I'm in Montana, where I now have a group of similarly-aged friends who gather weekly to play chamber music. One of them even travels to Missoula from Hamilton in order to join in. Some are learning their instruments as adults; some are picking them up again after a long hiatus. Maybe we'll play for an audience and maybe we won't, but we are still giving and receiving, still making music under Montana's big sky.

*Digging My Grave*
Ashley Rhian

❋

I laid in the snow, the rattle of a fence shaking close to me. I didn't know where I was, but I knew I was cold. I glanced around through the dark. I saw a headstone, then realized there were many more. Gray stone of various lengths and shapes stuck out from under a pile of snow. Some were worn down, chipped, and old, while others looked newer, the text hadn't faded away yet. I turned my head toward the rattling. A man shook the fence, his voice becoming more clear.

"Get up! Get up!" he yelled. He looked tall, with a black coat and a beanie on his head. I was frozen. The fence where he stood seemed far away. When I looked down at my feet, I realized my shoes and socks were gone. Snow blanketed my body. My skirt was soaked and knifed through, torn a few times. I still wore my jacket, but no gloves. What was I doing out here? And where were my shoes?

"Get up! You need to get up!" he shouted to me. His voice was high and frantic. "Come here to me. I'll help you out!"

He shook the fence once more, pacing as I tried to connect the dots. My feet were numb, but I managed to crawl towards him.

"You need to climb the fence!" he exclaimed. Small strands of blonde hair popped out from underneath his beanie. I felt like a zombie, unable to respond. I tore more pieces of my long, cotton skirt as I straddled the barbed wire on top of the fence. When I lifted my leg over, I found myself falling, landing on the snow on the other side. My rescuer slung me like Prince Charming, picking up another damsel in distress. He carried me to his apartment, the streets as listless as I felt inside.

He gave me one of his large shirts to change into and some fleece pajama bottoms. A blanket and a pillow were set on his couch in his living room. He kept a small, sparse apartment. A single poster of some band stared back from the wall. A big TV with a video game system sat across from me. With the company of someone else's possessions, I laid down and passed out for a few more hours.

In the morning, it all hit me with new vigor. I was in a home that wasn't mine. The stranger from last night sat across from me with two steaming cups.

"Would you like some tea?" he asked, holding a cup toward me.

"Yeah, sure," I murmured, letting out a chilled sniffle. My voice was hoarse and deeper than normal. I grasped the teacup he offered to me.

I glanced across silently at my rescuer. He wore jeans and a t-shirt and

his long, blonde hair fell just above his shoulders. His hair was damp from a shower. Behind him, food wrappers and a pizza box sat on the counter in the kitchen, clothes scattered about the rooms. It smelled like vanilla air freshener. For a moment, the details of last night abandoned me. Why am I here? Did we sleep together? I didn't think so; I always knew when something bad happened. Guilt and shame, familiar feelings.

"What happened?" I asked him. I was barely able to look him in the eye.

"I found you laying in the cemetery," he replied. "I was high on mushrooms and decided to take a walk in the snow."

He was high on mushrooms? Who was this guy? I had passed out in a lot of random places in my life, but the cemetery was a first. I stared down at my cup of tea, playing with the end of the tea bag.

"I ran up to the fence and yelled for you. I thought you were dead," he said. My stomach dropped. I sunk even lower into the couch cushion. "I saw you move, so I shook the fence hard and kept yelling. I hoped you'd wake up," he continued. "I noticed your shoes were gone so I looked for them, too. I only found one."

He got up to fetch something from the mess, retrieving a burgundy clog from his room. I felt cold and faint all over again, taking the shoe from him.

"Thanks."

"What were you doing out there?" he questioned, eagerly. I looked around the room as if it might hold an answer.

"I don't know," I said. "I wish I could tell you. I really appreciate what you did for me."

"Yeah, it's really no problem. I'm just glad you're okay," he said. He got up, and inched down beside me on the couch. He leaned in closer, but I scooted away from him.

I put the cup of tea on the coffee table and put my head between my knees, rocking back and forth. The mystery of the cemetery occupied my blurry mind. Instead, I tried to recount the night leading up to it.

A few of my friends and I had been drinking beers at their place to pre-game for a party that night. We had come together over our love of music. We were young artist types, trying to find a place to fit in. A couple of my friends were musicians who played in a local band, which gave us free passes to parties with an older, crazier crowd.

I loved going to these parties. I loved the weird music, wild dancing, and the drugs. I adored the piercings, crazy hair, and the tattoos.

The ancient Victorian house where the party was held was located across the street from a dairy factory in a rundown residential area, a few blocks away from downtown. It was a cold night, so I wore some knit tights and one of my favorite long, brown skirts.

There was a theme at this party- heaven and hell. People talked and smoked cigarettes on the massive porch as we approached. Partygoers wore black and white masks. Some had wings, others wore white or black spandex, and some people only wore underwear.

Despite the party, the inside of the house felt scholarly. There were

wooden details and tons of books and expensive rugs. The upstairs and downstairs of the house were split into two dimensions. The upstairs was lit with bright fluorescent lab lights and cotton balls were spread everywhere. People wore wings and dressed in tight white clothes. I saw a couple kissing and fondling each other in a corner and others swaying from side to side. Dustings of cocaine rested on a table and red cups were abandoned everywhere. I doubted that real heaven would feel so down and out.

I grabbed a couple of the abandoned cups to drink from as I headed downstairs. The descent was lit with candles and nightlights. Some people wore horns and others dressed in only black. Someone breezed by in a cape, as techno blared from the speakers. As I walked through a hallway, observing the party goers and searching for the main beer source, a streaker ran by me laughing like he was possessed. I continued through to a room where multiple people stood nude in a circle, talking and drinking. Someone lifted a goldfish to their lips and dropped it into their mouth.

I finally located the kegs, pouring myself a cup of heavy, stout beer. I knew the darker the beer, the stronger the alcohol content. I brought it to my lips with a wary feeling brewing in my stomach. Drinking was like a game for me; I blacked out most nights, but I kept gambling.

Alcohol and I had a love-hate relationship. On some nights, I felt so alive after drinking a couple beers. I danced to music, I kissed boys, I wasn't afraid to start a conversation with a stranger. I left my reserved self behind when things were good with alcohol.

When things were bad with alcohol, it was rotten. I woke up in alleyways in the back of bars, or naked on the bed of a stranger. I was eighty-sixed from several places for being too disruptive. I'd spent a couple days in jail once for drunkenly wrecking my car and then mouthing off to the cops at the scene. I hated myself when I was like that, but alcohol was the only thing that could take away the guilt and shame. I continued to gamble.

The night of the party was another game of roulette. I sat outside on the porch, smoking a cigarette and drinking out of the stolen red cup. After I saw those naked, tattooed strangers, I wished I had enough courage to do the same. I finished my beer with one long swig. After that, the details remained fuzzy, until I woke up in the graveyard.

My midnight Prince Charming kept up the conversation as I sipped my tea, listening to him but lost in my own thoughts. I couldn't believe I passed out in a cemetery. My friends had probably been relieved to be free of my incoherence and stumbling.

Another night I won't be able to get back. Another morning swamped with dirty clothes and bruises from God knows where. I've spent too many mornings like this.

"Would you mind giving me a ride home?" I questioned. I still didn't know his name.

"Yeah, of course, no problem," he replied. He got up from the couch to grab his coat and keys. I let out a long held breath.

"Thank you so much," I murmured.

I didn't live too far away, just south over the bridge. We pulled up to the front of my house and he got out of his small white sedan to open my door. "Can I get your number?" he asked.

My mind raced. Why would he want the phone number of the biggest piece of shit on Earth? I gave it to him anyway.

"Thanks!" he said. His excitement made me uncomfortable. "Cool if I call you sometime?"

"Yeah, that's fine," I muttered, as I walked to my front door. I waved goodbye as he drove away, knowing it would be final.

My granola roommates listened to college radio bluegrass as I entered. The room smelled of bacon, toast, and eggs. They were happy as ever, oblivious that I might have just experienced the worst night of my life.

"Hey," I greeted quietly. "This might sound weird, but will one of you give me a ride to the urgent care in the mall? I can't feel my toes."

"Yeah, no problem," Doug volunteered. "Let me get my stuff."

I lived with Doug for several years, just as platonic friends. I trusted him, and we continued to sign leases. Doug was a smart guy. He was tall and lanky, freckles sprinkled about his nose, brown hair and a red beard. He was definitely handsome, and an awesome cook, too. I left Spaghetti-Os and Hamburger Helper behind after I met him.

"So, what's up?" he asked me. I assumed he was referring to our trip to the urgent care.

"I passed out in the snow last night. In the cemetery," I said. "My toes are pretty numb."

He was silent. He was not an easy person to shock, but I knew I had done it. I sunk into my seat.

"How'd that happen?" he asked. "I mean, how did you pass out in a cemetery?"

"I don't know," I said. "I can't remember."

More silence. He interrupted it with an awkward grimace and a sigh. "Dude, you can't be doing stuff like that." He looked at me with a forgiving face.

"I know," I replied, softly.

We pulled into the parking lot of a small urgent care office. I knew they took patients who didn't have insurance. We left the cold behind and entered the clinic, scouting out a few chairs in the lobby near an activity gym for kids. Doug and I sat next to each other as we waited for the doctor to call me back. We flipped through random magazines until a female nurse in pink scrubs called my name. "Ashley?"

The wait for the doctor didn't take too long. I stared down at my toes, wiggling them gently. My weird long toe next to my big toe was a light grayish color. The others looked pink. The door swung open, the boisterous energy making my head throb. "So, I hear you may have frostbite on your toe?" he asked. "How the heck did that happen?"

I paused a moment, scraping up an answer hesitantly. What was I going

to say to him? "I was just out hiking for a while and... snow got in my boots."

I don't know if he believed me, but he didn't ask more questions. He took a look at my toe and poked it with a metal instrument.

"Well, you do have frostbite," he told me. "Luckily it's just on that one toe. It's pretty minor. You will need to keep it warm consistently and try to run it under warm water for a while. Not hot, just warm."

"I don't need medication or anything?" I asked. He shook his head, leaning back with another bright smile and a shrug.

"No. Sometimes we give a tetanus vaccine for frostbite, but I think yours will heal up just fine," he said. "Swing by if it doesn't get its color back by tomorrow."

I explained things briefly to Doug as we set out for home, his hands drumming the top of the steering wheel, waiting for a light to turn green. "Well, I'm glad you didn't have to amputate any of your toes," he joked.

"Yeah, me, too." It was the first time I had laughed all day.

As the light changed, I looked out the window and thought about the first time I got drunk. I was in high school and a few of us decided to drink at a friend's house. We didn't hang out with the popular crowd. We got good grades and did all the extracurricular activities.

After a couple beers, I had gotten chaotic. I broke a lamp on purpose and ripped down a few posters, finally passing out at sunrise. My heart felt empty with the memories, so I asked Doug to turn the music up a little louder.

When we got home, I sped past my roommates and walked straight to my room. I shut the door and sat on my bed, questions creeping into my mind. Was I trying to kill myself? Or did I just pass out in the snow on accident? I couldn't ignore this or drink it away like I normally did; the questions kept returning.

I got up from my bed and paced the room. I shut my curtain, unable to bear the light. My head hurt and sweat started to drizzle on my forehead. Eager to busy my shaking hands, I took out a box of old pictures and started to look through them. They were mostly from high school; I never took the time to take pictures of my life anymore.

I stopped at one in particular. All of my friends, eating lunch together, a ritual. I liked that girl I used to be. She had dreams of being more than what she knew. She wanted a husband, kids, a dog, a family of her own. I shook my head and started to cry. I was only twenty-two years old and I was throwing my life away one night at a time. What happened to that girl?

I took the mirror off my desk and looked at myself. My blue eyes looked dead, my skin too pale. Dark circles sat below my eyes. My hair laid in a ratty mess and my face was swollen. I hardly recognized the person I was staring at. I thought about the lightness and the darkness and which life I really wanted to live.

I needed help. I needed to change. I wanted that girl I recognized in that old photo back in my life.

I decided to take a bath to warm up my toe and drown out the sound. I drew some warm water, not hot, as my body started to tremble a little

more. I stripped the borrowed clothes off my body and put them next to the tub, slipping into the water. It felt good to be warm again.

I sat there, staring at the tile in front of me, in awe of myself and my situation. I wanted more than anything to be like everybody else. I wanted to drink and have no problems. I couldn't imagine my life without alcohol, but I knew I couldn't have it in my life anymore. I dipped my head under the water and opened my eyes. I blew a few bubbles and held my breath as long as I could bear it. When I lifted my body and gasped for breath, I knew what needed to be done.

I would stop drinking today.

## First Night in Our New Home
### Jane Peterson

❈

An early September chill crept through the hills surrounding Evaro, Montana, an offbeat collection of houses and mobile homes, a couple businesses and a few farms. The community's allure was not the Buck Snort Restaurant, although the food was more than passable. It was rather the forested hills and 20-minute proximity to Missoula. It matched our criteria for a retirement location; in the mountains, but not far from civilization.

Wafting through the evening air was the faint but unmistakable odor of wood-burning stoves, a smell that evoked comforting memories of campfires and s'mores but also carried the promise of not-too-distant snow. It was a momentous occasion; we were spending the first night in our new home. The guest yurt, to be exact—one of three interconnected yurts. It had been more of a design idea than a reality until, that day, when the builders installed frames for the windows and doors. Once secured, they provided the structural support to position the lattice between the frames and hold it all in place with airplane cable. The lace-like webbing now served as walls.

Eager to escape our claustrophobic truck camper, Eileen and I were determined to sleep on the concrete foundation of our new home. Having sweet-talked two wooden shipping pallets from a Missoula manufacturer, we laid them side-by-side to improvise a box spring in the center of the room. On top of the pallets, we placed a mattress we'd lugged down from the cabin at Flathead Lake. I was ready to crawl under my grandfather's faded Hudson's Bay blanket, but first we piled on the plaid sleeping bag we'd snagged for $4 at the thrift store. Swathed in hoodies, sweat pants, and wool hats, Eileen and I finally snuggled into the long-awaited softness.

The thick mattress was a luxury compared to the 2" camper pad we'd slept on for the past two months. Kali, our 8-month old puppy, who had whined and cried every night as soon as the camper door was closed, wasn't even whimpering now that she was no longer confined inside. The camper had served its purpose as a temporary home, but we were much happier in the not-quite-yet-finished yurt with all its fresh air. Our roof was the stars; they would have to suffice until the beams were installed.

An assortment of train sounds moved through the little valley below. They let out a dull roar as they approached, the rhythmic clickety-clack, screeching with steel-on-steel as they braked to round a bend. Then finally, the whistles. Like bird songs, each train whistle had a distinct variation rending the nighttime silence; from short, assertive blasts to extended, plaintive

101

moans. A lover searching for a mate, trailing down the valley. They were reassuring, a touchstone in a world that shifted around us daily.

The surrounding forest, draped in blankets of green pine and golden larch, was a vivid contrast to daytime's cloudless azure dome. Silhouetted against the last light in the western sky, the dense woods quickly gave way to a kind of darkness I was not used to. A darkness in which objects and space melded into an indistinguishable inky blackness that refused to reveal its secrets. The darkness was coming earlier with each successive evening. Our compensation was an unobstructed, front-row seat of the Milky Way, a jeweled bracelet strung across the sky, sparkling in the cool mountain air.

The labored sound of another train cracked the pervasive silence, revealing its enormity. There had always been ambient sounds where we'd lived in New Jersey, suburban white noise we'd learned to ignore. This silence was deafening in its utter absence of sounds. It would take some getting used to.

The temperature was in the mid-30s, but sure to dip further during the night. Hoping it didn't go below freezing, we each pleaded with the all-powerful camping goddess that we not have to pee before daylight. Getting up in the middle of the night had been a production in the truck camper—especially for someone in their mid-60s. I thought back to those nighttime expeditions with a grimace.

First, I flailed my arm around in the dark until I bumped against my LED headlamp. I tugged it on to get out of bed—which in the case of the camper was climbing down from the 'loft' bedroom—found my shoes and jacket, and steeled my resolve to go outside to find an appropriate location in the woods to relieve myself. Of course, the entire process had to be reversed to get back in bed. The distinction between my physical needs and wants, especially on cold nights, was morphing into an obsession: an indoor bathroom.

There was no time to lose sleep over worry. I gazed at Kali in jealousy, the pup sound asleep tethered next to the mattress. I dwelled in worry that the yurts wouldn't be finished before colder weather set in for good. Worry that we would be snowed in for most of the winter and go stir crazy. Worry that we didn't know a single soul in Missoula.

Eileen turned off the lantern, letting the darkness envelope us. Just as we were drifting off to our first uninterrupted night's sleep, Kali roused sharply. She began barking and growling, straining at her tether. It wasn't the kind of barking that announced someone she knew; these sounds came from some deep recess within her puppy body, a primal growl. I prayed that the tether would hold, since she wasn't well behaved enough not to run off after whatever was out there. My puny headlamp couldn't penetrate the darkness surrounding us, and I wasn't sure I wanted to know what riled her. Eventually, Kali settled down and we all went to sleep.

The next morning—after my first cup of coffee—Eileen confessed she saw what had left Kali so undone. The unmistakable yellow eyes and distinct body of a mature mountain lion, fifteen feet from the yurt's lattice.

*Wisdom*
Beth Cogswell

I didn't expect to break their living room window when I egged my neighbor's house. I also hadn't anticipated that Steve West, the junior high school quarterback, would spring to his feet and bolt after me.

He was always lounging around the sprawling colonial-style Wisdom residence, lying on the living room couch and silently watching TV in a house that wasn't his own. I never knew why except for a vague explanation of his 'family problems.' Steve seemed comatose, lulling me into thinking he was complacent in all scenarios—except for this one.

I ran toward home, but Steve easily caught me with his choppy, rapid strides. He grabbed my purple down coat and dragged me back towards the house despite my writhing, unceremoniously depositing me in the living room where a lurking figure stood. Dr. Wisdom's gaze met me silently, arms folded across his chest.

Dr. Wisdom was an Air Force physician who moved to our neighborhood the year before. He was stationed at Malmstrom Air Force Base in my hometown of Great Falls, Montana. Accompanied by his wife and five kids, plus two Basset Hounds, they made their way here from Little Rock, Arkansas. Evangelical Christians with pronounced Southern drawls, they were the most exotic people I had ever met in my twelve years.

"Miss Beth, what's going on kid? Why did you do this?" Dr. Wisdom questioned.

I tried to answer coherently, but instead blurted out, "I don't know. I'm so sorry." All I wanted to do was run and hide. I was ashamed and confused. I had been inside their house every week for the past year for Bible study, or to be with their daughter Jennifer. Although Jennifer could be mean as spit, the family had always welcomed me into their home.

Jennifer Wisdom befriended me on the bus during my seventh-grade year. I was vilified as a nerd and bullied due to my boyish face, short hair, and developed breasts—a freckle-faced boy with tits. I couldn't fathom why Jennifer felt drawn to hang out with me.

It was in early September 1977, the first week of school. The bus picked us up at the edge of an expansive park lined with Cottonwood trees. The crisp air hinted at the colder days ahead. Jennifer had approached me on the bus without hesitation. She plopped down into the seat next to me and dove straight to conversation. "I love your hair. How do you get it to do that?"

She was referring to my perfectly feathered hair. I remember exactly what I was wearing, too. A brown and green striped knit cowl-neck

underneath brown denim overalls. Jennifer had thick, wavy dark hair that she wound around her index finger when she spoke. Her green eyes were lined in black eyeliner that stood out against her pale, freckled face. A pair of jeans hugged her hips and accentuated her round ass.

Fashion was lost to me, partially due to my mother. She had no interest in clothing or makeup. I remember being embarrassed that she would often be wearing the same outfit on Tuesday and Wednesday as she wore on Monday. She kept her hair in a pixie cut that required no styling at all.

I spent a lot of time at the Wisdom household. Mrs. Wisdom hosted weekly Bible study gatherings for teens. Not only were the cutest boys there, but the junk food was plentiful. I was enamored with Mrs. Wisdom, the spiritual center of these evenings. She spoke softly with a Southern drawl. She had an oval face, small and perfect. Her porcelain skin was accentuated by long, jet black hair that she wore in a tight bun. She was tiny and often wore clothes that belonged to her daughters.

She captivated everyone circled around her, speaking in hushed tones about the Lord as if she were telling us precious secrets. I rarely spotted her except for during Bible study. She was always in her bedroom at the top of the stairs. She only descended to ask for things. "Rand, can you bring me a Tylenaal and a Docta Peppa?" she'd call down the stairwell. This was her cure for frequent headaches.

***

I remember driving somewhere in their family's paneled station wagon, Dr. Wisdom at the wheel. I was squished in the dark of the very back with a boy named Todd. After some nervous glances and a growing boldness, Todd and I inched closer and closer to one another. Eventually, we began making out.

Dr. Wisdom kept looking at us in the rearview mirror. We made eye contact, but he never said a word about it. A sexual current ran through the Wisdom house. The way the boys looked at Mrs. Wisdom with rapt attention. The tight jeans and long, flowing hair and swaying hips of the Wisdom girls, so practiced and perfectly executed. The Bible study nights were often pretenses for teenage hook-ups. Dr. and Mrs. Wisdom had gotten married and started their large family when they were just teenagers themselves.

The Wisdoms ate at a dining room table piled high with papers, magazines and newspapers, and it seemed impossible to find room for people to eat. The first time I ate dinner there, Jennifer opened the freezer and showed me a variety of Tony's pizzas and asked me to choose one. It was just the two of us sitting on bar stools at the white, Formica countertop in the kitchen eating our pepperoni pizza.

This scenario repeated itself whenever I was there. When someone was hungry, they ate. No dinner time, no family meal, just a constant supply of junk food. They had all kinds of chips—potato chips, Doritos, Fritos, you name it.

At my house, we sat down to dinner in our formal dining room, my father seated at the head of the table. For breakfast, we ate a fried egg and wheat

toast, or a bowl of Raisin Bran or Grape Nuts. If my sisters or I wanted a snack, it was a peanut butter sandwich or a piece of fruit. My mother had a sprawling vegetable garden and found all kinds of ways to annoy us with zucchini.

The Wisdoms bred Basset Hound puppies, and every few months there would be a new litter. One afternoon as I lay on their living room rug watching a rerun of the Brady Bunch, a puppy pooped on the carpet inches away from me. I crinkled my nose and jumped to my feet. Soon after, the mother Basset Hound waddled up to the pile of poop and ate it. "That's so gross!" I exclaimed.

"It's not bad. The mama dog always eats the poop," Jennifer replied. She went on to tell me that her parents let the dogs poop and pee on the carpet, but they would have the carpets cleaned as soon as all the puppies were sold. Regardless of her explanation, I avoided lying on the carpet to watch TV.

Jennifer and her older sister Tammy had countless outfits between the two of them: Gloria Vanderbilt jeans with the iconic swan on the pocket, Hash bell bottoms with big stars sewn on the rear. I coveted the Crazy Horse Shetland sweaters and Izod polo shirts with the iconic alligator logo.

I had grown up wearing Levi 501 jeans paired with flannel shirts and sweaters. The Wisdom girls, with their expansive wardrobe, never wore the same outfit twice. They piled their clothes on the double bed they shared and pushed them off the bed to sleep. They doused themselves in sickly sweet perfume—White Shoulders, Anais Anais and Love's Baby Soft. I think their parents had to sell Basset Hound puppies to afford their daughters.

Jennifer taught me the essentials of life for a junior high school girl. How to wear makeup, fashion dos and don'ts, how to wiggle my butt when I walked. Despite our friendship, I was slowly drifting away toward new friends and Jennifer didn't like it; she often shamed people, critiqued their hair and clothes, or spread rumors that someone was a slut.

Over time, she began making fun of me on the bus and encouraged others to do the same. I developed a sick feeling in my stomach before climbing the bus stairs. Once, on the way home, a boy spit a goober on a bus seat and pushed me into it. Jennifer laughed with her head thrown back.

The boys would occasionally push me down on the walk home and hold my face in the snow. Jennifer always laughed. This behavior let up on days when Jenny Ickes rode the bus home with me. Jenny was a cheerleader and the most popular girl in 7th grade. She and I were becoming close, but Jennifer seemed to try to inch between us like a good friend. She layered on the sweetness and compliments when Jenny was with me. Eventually, she invited us to stay the night at her house—an offer we naively accepted.

The night of the sleepover, we ate junk food on the Wisdom's pee-stained carpet while watching *Charlie's Angels*. Despite how pleasant the evening began, things took a turn for the worse. Jennifer began slapping my face repeatedly and pulled my hair. I yelled, "stop it!" as Jenny Ickes giggled nervously with a confused look on her face. Even amidst Jennifer's cackling laughter, no adult showed up to stop her.

I jumped up and ran out the front door. In my pajamas and bare feet, I shivered and walked two blocks towards my house beside the Missouri River. It stood silent and dark in the night. I didn't want to ring the bell and wake everyone, so I shivered in the back seat of my mom's red Saab until the sun came up.

***

I kept my distance from Jennifer after that, but I felt the pull of Bible study and the allure of her beautiful mother and continued attending. An Evangelical preacher had spoken at our school assembly about a loving God. He was a small man with thin, greasy hair and square glasses that overwhelmed his face. He promised free pizza at the evening show, so Jan Wisdom offered to drive a group of us to hear him speak to a packed auditorium at the local community college.

His sermon was wildly different that night, his loving God turning vindictive. He screamed into the microphone, telling us we were sinners and warned us to repent, or the flesh would be burned off our bodies in the Rapture. "You will be left on earth to burn in hell," he screamed, and shook with rage. I was terrified when I realized we were locked in. Mrs. Wisdom looked stricken.

There was no pizza. As soon as the doors opened, we rushed out. For nights after that, I had nightmares that God would choose to leave me behind when the Rapture came.

I never returned to the Wisdom's house after that. I was tortured by questions that plagued my growing mind. *Am I wearing the right clothes? Is light blue eyeshadow a good idea? What is my relationship with God?* The entire Wisdom family had the answers to my various teenage inquiries, and I hated them for it.

It was a cold November evening when I attempted to egg the Wisdom house. On nights like these, I often roamed the neighborhood, interested in catching glimpses of people through lit-up windows. That hobby was out of the question for tonight. I stuffed a couple eggs in my mother's down jacket without considering what I might do with them.

Steve West looked at me with disgust as he dragged me inside to face my consequences. Dr. Wisdom was gentle with me, arms still crossed over his chest. I said I was sorry, and I would pay for the damage. I needed to separate myself from the family that both intrigued and confused me. One egg launched through the air drew a line between us; I knew I could never go back.

*Naked Bears*
Jessica Spears

❉

"Alden and Isabel," Shane called as he unloaded the last of the gift bags out of the trunk, "You can carry some presents in too."

Exhaled breath rose around our mouths. The stars cast a blue glow onto the stiff sheets of sparkling snow that enveloped my grandma's lawn. Cale, then three years old, held my hand. I gripped as many gift bags as I could with my other arm.

Cradled close was a large paper plate of shortbread cookies I made earlier that day. I used the same recipe my mom used to make these cookies every Christmas when I was growing up; it was the first time in my entire life that I had ever used lard. Plastic wrap sucked the edges of the plate. A red, tin bow wiggled on top.

Alden, then six and a half years old, dragged a black garbage bag bursting with wrapped packages up the sidewalk. His thick, blond hair flopped around his face. Isabel, then five years old, walked beside her dad with her thumb in her mouth, still sporting the haircut Alden gave her. Isabel's hair landed at all different lengths now, little blond spikes sticking straight out.

Isabel had been diagnosed with autism about five months earlier. She had a tendency to bang her head on things—ceramic tile, the bars on the fronts of grocery carts—which was dangerous enough, but which occasionally posed other safety concerns as well. On more than one occasion, she got away from me in a grocery store parking lot and threw herself down onto the ground behind a moving vehicle, banging her head repeatedly onto the asphalt.

After her diagnosis, Isabel began to receive various therapies. We put her on a gluten/casein free diet. Since then, the head banging had nearly stopped. She started talking more coherently, and could even tell people her birthdate.

Cale had been diagnosed with autism and an intellectual developmental disorder, just ten days prior to this visit. We started him on Isabel's gluten/casein free diet immediately. We didn't yet know that the things that worked for Isabel wouldn't do squat for Cale. We didn't yet know that no matter what we would ever do, no matter how hard we would ever fight or how many different diets and therapies and medications and fads we would try, Cale would never learn how to talk. He would remain non-verbal, functioning at the level of an eighteen month old.

All the houses on my grandma's block were identical. My grandma and grandpa had this house built after my grandpa's stroke left him bound to

a wheelchair, focusing on wide interior doorways and a ground level floor plan. My grandparents lived here together until my grandpa passed away. A few years after that, my grandma married a man named Cliff that she attended church with.

Alden rang the bell. Shadows shifted behind the blinds on the living room window. My mom's black and white shitzu, Panda Bear, let out her high pitched howl. Shane glanced over at me and took a deep breath. He and I had been married about twelve years, and still his dark green eyes made me want to be alone with him.

I had this recurring nightmare, probably once a week or so, in which Shane and I wanted to find a place to be alone together, but we were being chased. Eventually, I always found some broom closet for us to climb into. Every time I got my hands into those soft brown curls on his head, to pull him in for a kiss, someone always opened the door. In our waking lives, we were never alone for more than a minute before we were found.

"Well, hello there!" My grandma beamed, pulling the front door open. A rush of warm air engulfed us. We hugged our way through the little greeting line that met us inside. My mom and dad had been divorced for years, but my dad still occasionally celebrated holidays with us at my grandma's house. My mom gave me a long squeeze, her lanky, silver locks brushing the side of my face. My dad, who loved to talk about different foods he sampled on all the trips he took now that he was retired from truck driving, kissed me on the cheek, his coarse beard tickling my jawbone.

Cliff was in his nineties, yet still over six feet tall. He struggled to stand up from his recliner, and walked like his legs were stiff and sore. He had chiseled features, bright white hair and sapphire blue eyes. He seemed to forget about his legs while he chuckled and hugged each of us. Cliff's daughter, Gwen, and his granddaughter, Tyna, greeted each of us as well. Gwen wore a small pair of silver glasses on her nose and often carried a look of tension on her face. Tyna, our sole high schooler, held a little gray schnauzer dog. My brother wasn't there yet.

***

One of the best things about my grandma's house: Things didn't change quickly. The same stockings that belonged to my mom and aunt in the sixties hung from a gas fireplace mantel. The forty-five year old Christmas tree ornaments dangled dutifully from the branches of the Christmas tree. The wooden manger, with only a few strands of straw left sticking to its miniature rooftop, sat beneath the tree on a skirt made of cotton.

Baby Jesus and his parents had the misfortune of having their butts superglued to the floor of the manger by my grandma thirty-five years ago. It took Alden about twenty seconds to discover the manger and attempt to lift the figures from their cemented perches. Cliff sat up a little straighter in his recliner. My grandma glanced over, but then looked away, pretending not to notice. I didn't worry; no one has ever been able to free baby Jesus.

We waited for my brother for over an hour. Gwen vented to Cliff about the HOA. Tyna discussed grooming techniques for the pudgy, gray schnauzer

while it sat on her lap, staring at everyone with a bearded gaze. Shane followed Cale around endlessly, trying to keep him from breaking knick knacks.

My parents tried to keep Alden and Isabel entertained by playing tug of war with Panda Bear. My children squealed when the dog lunged, her black and white bangs flopping above over her eyes as she seized the sock ball with her pointy little teeth. My grandma watched from the edge of a sofa, delighting at their laughter.

I watched it all from what felt like a great distance. I kept slipping into a strange heaviness. My thoughts had been trapped in a loop anytime I wasn't distracted by something else, ever since Cale's diagnosis ten days earlier.

Two of my children have autism. How can everyone just carry on like nothing's happening? Why, God, would you give me children with autism? I've never even known anyone with autism.

"I hope your brother's coming," my grandma said, as she shuffled over to the kitchen peninsula, and set down my plate of shortbread cookies. My mom stood next to her, arranging crackers onto a plate. "He said he'd be here," my grandma glanced from my dad to my mom, "but you know how that goes sometimes."

"Don't worry," I put my hand on her shoulder, "He'll be here. He's probably still doing his Christmas shopping."

A short burst of laughter escaped Gwen, shaking the curls around her face. Tyna smiled and glanced from her mom to me. They seemed to think I was joking.

My brother was diagnosed as learning disabled in the 1970's, which explained his continuous academic difficulties and the fact that he never learned to read beyond a third grade level. There were so many other things that it never really explained—his extreme aversion to certain foods, for example. Or why, one day when he was younger, he fell out of a treehouse and broke his arm, yet didn't mention it to anyone. He drank glass after glass of water all afternoon instead, which I didn't think much of. He was always doing bizarre things. My mom noticed him holding his arm later that evening and asked him what was wrong with it. It's broken, he said. She took up to the emergency room. The learning disability diagnosis never explained why my brother's social communication skills were always so extremely limited.

Layers of social understanding come into play with gift giving. There are rules that no one seems to think much about. Do your Christmas shopping before Christmas actually arrives, for example, so your family doesn't have to wait around for you while you do it on Christmas Eve.

Gwen and Tyna had no way of knowing my brother didn't always know the rules; of course, they thought I was joking. My mom pushed the glasses up on her nose, and glanced at my dad. He leaned back on his bar stool, crossing his arms. My grandma glanced away from my parents, turned on her heel, and opened the refrigerator door. "Do we want sweet mustard on the table?" she asked.

Gwen realized I was being serious and stopped laughing immediately. Tyna's face straightened out as well. They sunk back into their protective

cocoon of chatting with each other. Alden stood in front of me all of a sudden, a pained expression in his gray eyes. "When are we going to open presents, mom?" he asked.

"We're still waiting for Uncle Mike, sweetie," I replied, wiping his thick hair off of his forehead. My grandma put her hand on Alden's shoulder. "Why don't you and Isabel start sorting each family member's presents into separate piles?" she encouraged.

A smile grew on my face. Years ago, my grandma had my brother and I do the exact same thing when we grew impatient to open gifts on Christmas eve.

Isabel didn't seem to realize that there were names on the presents. She picked up a package, examined the wrapping paper, and seemed to decide from there which package should go to which person. My grandma sat down on the sofa nearby with her hands in her lap, seemingly torn between her desire to correct Isabel and her delight in how cute the mistake was.

Alden didn't correct Isabel either. He waited until she turned her back to him and then switched the presents into the right piles. I felt myself smiling again; I used to do the exact same thing with my brother.

My mom walked in through the back door. She had been outside smoking a cigarette, but wanted us to believe she was outside cooling down. She met me at the peninsula. "God, it's hot in here," she said.

Platters of crackers and dips, candies, and cookies sat on the counter. My mom examined the shortbread I made earlier, her long hair hiding the expression on her face. She pushed her glasses up on her nose and then picked up a cookie. I leaned toward her and whispered, "You do you realize your cookies have lard in them."

"Shhh!" she exclaimed. The doorbell rang.

"Oh!" My grandma stood up from the couch, and shuffled across the room as fast as her hips allowed, pulling open the door. "Hello there!" she said.

Mike was six feet tall, with dark hair and big, brown eyes. Gifts bags hung from both hands, and he balanced three unwrapped boxes on one arm. He walked carefully, holding his body more erect than most people, as if one leg was slightly shorter than the other. Mike deposited his gifts under the tree and then moved around the room, delivering stiff hugs to everyone. "Sorry I'm late, the mall was crazy."

Gwen and Tyna glanced at each other curiously. The rest of us, so glad he showed up at all, hugged him and kissed him and asked how work was going.

I don't think my brother had eaten all day. I sat with him at the dining table while he stuffed crackers and cheese into his mouth as fast as he could chew. My mind looped again.

Two of my children have autism. How can everyone just carry on like nothing's happening? Why, God, would you give me children with autism? I've never even known anyone with autism.

I lowered my arm onto the table and decided to tell him the news. "Isabel and Cale have both been diagnosed with autism."

My brother found my eyes. "Oh yeah?" he swallowed whole chunks of cheese ball, yet maintained direct eye contact. I assumed this was his way of saying he cared about this topic, but he didn't know what the word autism meant.

I realized immediately that I couldn't explain it to him anyway; I didn't know much about autism myself. I was studying it now, of course, but the criteria for being placed on the autism spectrum seemed both complicated and somewhat vague to me. The books I had read on the subject talked about developmental delays or repetitive patterns of behaviors. It mentioned hypersensitivity, or a lack of processing of sensory information like textures or foods, and clinically significant deficits in social communication and interaction.

Mike swallowed again. "That's too bad," he murmured.

"Yeah," I sighed, my elbow on the table and my chin in my hand. "Too bad."

"Are we ready to open presents, Mom?" Alden burst in, hope in his tone. In his hands, he held one of the unwrapped boxes my brother had brought for my kids. The name on the box read, Build-A-Bear Workshop.

The smile drained out of my eyes. I knew, even before my kids opened these boxes, that my brother had missed the point. I knew there was a naked bear inside each box.

The biggest problem with loving someone with communication deficits is the lack of communication. My brother experienced increasingly intense bullying throughout his junior high and high school years, for example. I knew this from the school reports and the notes my parents wrote down, the police reports, and the documentation provided by psychologists. Because of the nightmares. The night terrors, actually, when, in his sleep, he screamed like he was dying and punched holes in his bedroom walls. They lasted for years.

Yet, after each thing that happened to him, Mike could not tell me what happened. My mom and dad and I coped by creating a concept we called "Mike language." We asked ourselves what his limited strings of words and facial expressions meant in "Mike language," trying to piece together details of what might have taken place. I grew up traumatized, not by the things that actually happened to my brother, but by the stories I created about the things that happened to him.

I imagined my brother trying to purchase three naked bears from some well-meaning salesperson at Build-A-Bear Workshop. I pictured the salesperson explaining to him, in front of all the other customers in the store, that the whole point of going to Build a Bear Workshop was to build a stuffed teddy bear, and to dress that bear in little clothes and accessories that would give the bear a distinct personality to please the child it would belong to.

The salesperson might let him know the cost per item of clothing, and perhaps they'd want him to make snap decisions about which items he wanted. Considering Mike hadn't eaten yet that day, my guess was that he

111

had a limited amount of money. The cost per item of clothing was hopeless to multiply in his head, especially since he was supposed to choose multiple items for three different bears. I pictured everyone standing there waiting for him, wrestling with their own guilt about buying presents at the last minute, and wondering why the hell this guy hadn't just gone to Target for three naked bears. He'd finally say, "I'd just like to buy them like this." People might gawk, scratch their heads, or roll their eyes. Then Mike would leave the store, relieved to have something to bring each of my kids for Christmas.

I clenched my eyes shut for a long moment, attempting to dispel the image from my head.

When we finished opening presents that night, my brother sat at the dining table again, scooping cheese with crackers and popping them into his mouth. My brother found my eyes, but only for a moment this time before directing his gaze back to his plate.

"Build-A-Bear Workshop, huh?" I asked.

"Yeah," he said, a furrow sinking in between his eyebrows.

The overlapping voices of my family chatting and laughing filled the room. Half empty platters of cookies and crackers littered the tables and counters. Another pot of coffee brewed in the coffee maker, the thick, nutty smell rising into the air.

My brother shook his head, and said, "they wanted me to put clothes on the bears."

In "Mike language," this meant that what I thought happened at Build-A-Bear Workshop was close to the truth.

"Clothes?" I replied, "Well, that's just silly."

Isabel walked up to the table, and stopped in front of my brother. I tried to brush her hair down with my hand, but the shortest spots bounced right back up again. Her little facial expression was so flat that I couldn't tell what she was thinking. She lifted her arm straight out in front of her and started waving her little hand. Her arm didn't move at all; only her hand waved.

"Hi! Hi! Hi!" she cried out. In response, Mike lifted his arm straight out in front of him and started waving his big hand. His arm didn't move at all; only his hand waved.

"Hi Isabel," he replied.

My vision blurred, the entire room going white.

Somehow I didn't faint as our entire childhood flashed before my eyes. My gaze froze solely on my brother and daughter's outstretched hands as color trickled into the world again.

## Cinquefoil
Sav Shopay

✳

Rain patters down, bubbling off of the brim of my baseball cap. I drag a muddied hand over the front of my saddle, leather slick under my fingers. As I shift my seat, I manage to steal a glance to the sky. Our latest summer storm broils over the top of The Sleeping Giant. Clouds crawl across the mountainous belly, pine trees wheedling their ascent up towards the rocky nose. Lightning splinters near the toes, threatening to jolt the myth awake for real.

The mountain refuses to budge, but the horse beneath me riles. Milo springs to the side as thunder crackles above us. His muscles tense, a cord pulled too tight. His nervous prance leaves behind soggy hoofprints stamped into the earth.

Across the field, a horse lurches into action, carrying my new riding partner.

Sophia and I are the only summer pupils of Romi. The sole Japanese cowgirl of Helena, Hiromi—called Romi by anybody who knows her well enough—has owned this acreage for years. A family friend, she offered for me to live for the summer as a farmhand. Sophia arrives in the mornings to labor alongside me for the day. She stays for the occasional overnight, both of us clustered onto an air mattress on the porch to save space. Our reward is riding lessons—rain or shine.

The day after high school graduation, I climbed into my little red pickup and scrambled to Montana with a duffel bag in tow and my Thoroughbred in a horse transporter's trailer. Sophia, a Helena High School sophomore, was already there when I arrived. So was her prized friend, Hidalgo; a spoiled quarter horse, but agile, and a chronically stunned expression.

Sophia gives a sharp kick to Hidalgo. The paint's hindquarters buckle down as his body tears from a standstill to a bolt. I spur Milo, urging him to cross a cattle feeder brimming with wildflowers, erupting with a splintered stump.

Romi scrutinizes us from across the pasture, leathered face doused with rain and a scowl, as she wheels her little black mare around.

"Sav, get a leg around him! Sophia, deeper into your corners." Our instructor orders, frustration building in her tone. I sullenly wonder if she'll give us each a bucket and make us dig up rocks in the back pasture again. My teeth grit together, and I bend my calves to secure a closer hold onto Milo's sides.

Sophia tears past me with a sunshine grin, the only light in the gloom.

Errant pieces of hair escape her damp brunette braid as she sinks into another tight turn. Romi lets out a whoop, a grin sneaking over her face. "Excellent!" she calls out.

My brow folds into one troubled line. Sophia gleefully rounds another corner, calling out something unintelligible to Romi that makes them both share a short peal of laughter. A jolt beneath me rips my attention back to my steed; Milo swerves last second to avoid the first barrel, his head tucked with a disobedient snort.

"Sav!" Romi barks my name once, sharp and chastising. Sophia thunders down the field again, embarking on a victory loop that lassoes our instructor's attention again. At the very least, it seems to make Romi forget my distracted blunder. Sophia flies past me gleefully, the threat of a challenge rising in her light eyes.

I catch a sharp turn around a barrel and spin after Sophia; Milo fumbles for traction in the dirt. We trail behind them—thanks to Sophia's head start—but at the sight of our impromptu competition, Romi flings up a hand to halt us.

Sophia slows to a more leisurely pace beside me, chuckles barely heard over Hidalgo's heaved breaths. Scowl aimed straight ahead, I disregard her approach.

Romi spits as soon as we are close enough to be suitably chastised. "Heads up your asses," she hisses. I wrinkle my nose, rivets of cool rain dolloping across my feverish ears. Romi snatches a hand around my reins, keeping my horse anchored. The closeness forces my attention to her dark eyes. "Work together. Stop ripping after her and making it a race."

A sharp laugh from Sophia as she tries to smother it with a work glove. Romi doesn't break our staredown to chastise her. Sophia's eyes glint, mocking me like a rabbit evading a trap, her shoulders squared back confidently.

I dismount rougher than usual, saddle creaking with the movement. Together in exhaustion and frayed nerves, Milo and I march across the muddied pasture.

Romi and I enter the pea-green farmhouse, our boots caked in brownie batter muck. I shuck off my shoes by the door and leave them in a heap beside Romi's, stalking behind her in my socks. Sophia lingers outside, methodical in her attempt to rid her shoes of every piece of mud.

Romi's house is small, a mixture of ancient decor and improving renovations. A bookshelf looms across from me, littered with horse training books and worn out novels. On the top is a tattered photo, the child in it beaming back at us from beside several stalks of bamboo. Romi in Japan, prior to her adoption, and her move to Montana.

Romi showed this picture to me on my first day here, nonchalant in her explanation. Her father, a military man stationed in Japan, took such a liking to her and her brother that he wanted to bring them home. He assured Romi a horse of her own if she'd come with him—and that's exactly what she badgered him about mercilessly the second she landed on American soil.

An old television sits on a small stand in the forefront of the living room, reflecting the rest of the room back like a dusty mirror. A ragged maroon couch occupies the space across from it, an afghan thrown over the back. I resist the urge to flop into it, sulking into the kitchen. Now that Sophia is out of earshot, the words spring from me.

"I don't like her."

Romi considers me testily, swiping moisture from her leathered face. She brings down a mug from the crowded, white cupboard, filling it from a coffee pot plugged in beside a toaster older than me. She takes a sip before speaking. "It's not a matter of liking her or not liking her. You need to work together. A three ring circus out there today, both of you."

I twist away to smother my scoff. I fan my waterlogged tank top out from my back, feeling it cling like a needy lover. On the porch, Sophia hums a blissfully unaware tune while she wicks mud off of her boots. I sputter a low retort.

"She was showing off."

"Pot calling the kettle black. You're practically twins out there, down to the horses." My instructor gives a low chuckle, but I fail to find the humor she's found in our situation.

I can find similarity in our steeds, maybe. Two young geldings splattered in white and coppery red, both set in the basics but learning how to operate to a higher standard. Sophia and I know how to throw hay bales or scrape up manure, but we are just teenage girls etching our place into the riding world.

Thoughts of our lesson bring a swell of angry heat over my cheeks, simmering down to my chest. The way Sophia pops her head to the side coyly when Romi praises any turn she pulls off, or any lead she picks up—or any word that comes out of her mouth.

The front door opens, Sophia humming her way into the room, but I refuse to greet her or even recognize her approach. I amble towards the fridge, gazing into the cold box to numb my broiling temper.

Stacks of butter wrapped in film; a carton of eggs marked in sharpie with 'ANA'S FARM $2.50.' Grapes cluster in a bowl, a violet clique. Several bottles of Corona. I scoot the beers to the side, eyebrows furrowing. "Where's the leftover mac and cheese?"

"Oh, I finished it," offers Sophia.

Rigidly, I straighten my posture and hone in on her, lips tensing into a taut line. She flicks a sliver of dirt out from under her thumbnail; I dig my fingers into the handle of the refrigerator hard enough to ache.

Sophia looks up at me, her grin immediately faltering. The fridge door slams shut, beers clinking against each other. Sophia scrambles around and launches back outside.

"Sav!" Romi snaps after me. I tear through the entryway and onto the soaking front porch. My shoulder barrels into Sophia's back, sending us both careening off the steps and into the mud.

Romi issues a list of chores as punishment. We spend the day an acre apart from each other, clunking rocks into buckets and carrying them out

to dump in the ditch. We refuse to even occupy the same side of the trailer while we heave hay bales onto it, scowling darkly across the growing stack.

Unfortunately, we end up only a foot from one another on an air mattress on the back porch. The ravenous summer rainstorm strips across east Helena, but tonight is quiet. Chores leave us stagnant, muscles aching. Shreds of hay burrow into our hair; I pluck one out of my dark waves, untangling it and flitting the leafy portion onto the drying porch boards.

The air mattress gives a miserable groan as Sophia rolls over, thumping down hard enough to lurch me upwards. For a full minute, she lays still. Then she's tossing aside again, shimmying down the blankets. Seasick, I let out a grunt, flinging an arm across her stomach and pinning her in place.

"Stop," I growl, sleep thick in my voice. She scowls up at the cosmos, but doesn't wriggle another inch. I chisel a glare toward the North star, willing it to transport my brain somewhere else. When it fails, I close my eyes and hope for sleep instead.

In the darkness, horses snort out in the pasture. Bats fly above us, flapping and settling inside the ramshackle livestock trailer parked beside the house. Sophia slowly sighs, words trailing behind. "Are you gonna miss this place?"

My eyes remain shut, and I inhale the scent of alfalfa and rainwater. Cool air swathes over me like a second blanket. In two months, I'm due back to my mother's cookie cutter suburban condo, bought in the wake of my father's suspiciously lengthy trip to the grocery store that he never returned from. The wreckage of our family, a crumbling closet of skeletons, makes me ache for space. Everything is bigger in Montana, and I long for it to be true. The sky, the mountains, the moon impeding and bright. My heart spread, and thrived, since the day I arrived. I respond to Sophia reluctantly, my gaze halfheartedly sinking out of their typical gray-eyed scowl.

"I'm gonna write a book about a girl who runs away to Montana."

Sophia's whisper curls its way through the dark. "I'll read it."

The mattress lurches as Sophia adjusts her pillow, but this time I don't chastise her.

Small green stalks climb skyward from the crumbling dirt. They spread voraciously, blooming into petals of several different hues. The rain last week has brought out the wildflower population in full force. Purples, reds, and yellows blossom over the slim path that crosses from Romi's ranch all the way to York Road.

Sophia and I meander along the trail, eager to take a stroll out instead of practicing in the rock-riddled pasture. I rein to the left to angle Milo down into a ditch, reaching out to tug a fistful of yellow sulfur cinquefoil out of the side. Leaning forward, I urge Milo upward again, joining Sophia on the trail. Hidalgo swivels to the side and peers at us incredulously, snorting when Sophia gives him a nudge forward.

"What a dork," I chuckle, watching Sophia pat a reassuring hand onto her horse's neck. Her lips tighten and flicker, but she bends it back into a smile. She slows him down a few strides, bundling her reins into one hand.

"Give me one," she demands, giggling and swatting a hand out to capture my flowers. I pull them back, backing up Milo and holding them away from her.

"No! Get your own," I reply, a taunt wiggling into my words.

We glance around for another sprig of yellow flowers. Farther down the trail, where the ditch dips down into the creekbed, sits a thick bunch waiting to be plucked. The water has ceased it's rampant flow, down to a slow dribble. Sophia swivels towards the bed of the creek without question, turning around in her saddle to direct a mocking glance in my direction.

The mud beneath Hidalgo's feet plummets up to his knees. Sophia reels back around, hands doubling down to grab for mane to hold onto. She lets out a shout, muck sloppily gasping out a sucking noise with each thrash Hidalgo makes.

"Go right!" I call out, angling Milo towards higher ground. Sophia finds a divot of earth leading out of the creekbed, tamed and dry. She cranes Hidalgo's head around and gives him a kick, rocking forward as he rears up and lunges out of the slick earth. With feet planted on dry ground, her horse stumbles out with wide eyes and a huff of air, bobbing Sophia on his back.

A moment of hesitation; birds chirp obliviously in the distance. We both lock eyes, mouths agape in astonishment. Mud drips off of Hidalgo's chest, plopping down into the grass. "Don't tell Romi," Sophia sputters out.

"Don't tell Romi," I agree, tugging a flower out from my makeshift bouquet. I hand it to Sophia; she sticks it into her hair, hand still trembling.

\*\*\*

Lingering clouds of a Utah snowstorm swirl over the tops of the Bountiful mountainside, loitering long after the storm drowns the valley in white. It's my birthday; November snow is my gift. My work uniform reeks like burnt popcorn from my shift at the bustling new movie theater. I pry it off immediately when I get into my pickup, revealing a ratty black tank top underneath.

I peer through the cracked windshield, turning gently on the roadway still slick with snow. My back tires spin a few times in a scramble for traction, thankfully catching on eventually; I squeeze my legs by habit, as if I'm astride a horse digging its hooves into the mud. In the rearview, I watch my swiveled tire lines recede further and further behind.

The chiding tone of my cell phone rings from somewhere beneath my seat, fallen there during the slushy roadway scuffle. Inching towards the side of the street, I reach for it, refusing to wreck my truck—not with twenty-seven minutes left on my eighteenth year.

"Sav," Romi greets hoarsely. Hesitation in her tone, peppering my heart. "Happy birthday," she tacks on halfheartedly. I swallow back a knot in my throat, fingers kneading my steering wheel. My worry becomes a ghostly whisper.

"What happened?"

Romi hums, balking, but continues with careful consideration. "Hidalgo got caught up in a corral panel. Broke his hips. He didn't make it."

117

My tongue feels bloated and lethargic in my mouth, lips parted for words that won't come. I shift the phone to my shoulder. A small Honda speeds by, pumping their horn once with an annoyed bleat.

"How's Sophia?" I blurt out. I scramble for what to offer, what to do. Romi's dark hair rustles into the receiver with a crackling noise. "She's not well. Nobody would be after that."

A flash, and I feel a sunny day on my skin again. Wildflowers in our hair. Fingers wrapped around the same bucket handle, heaving rocks towards the creekbed. Laying on top of a stacked mountain of hay, blisters ripe on our hands. Sophia's unwavering whisper at my side, months ago under another night sky.

I crank the key in the ignition. The truck thunders to life. "I'll leave now. I'll be there by the morning."

## The Lookout
### Sarah Aaronson

Matt builds a fire in the woodstove.

In the few minutes it takes me to unfasten the hammered steel latches and remove half of the heavy wood panels covering the windows, the fire lookout is warm. Panes of late afternoon sun wash the interior, revealing the white curve of a snowdrift on the vinyl twin mattress. I sweep it off with a broom. Twenty feet below, snowdrifts form continents over the scoured outcroppings of granite.

Wind works with intention up on the Divide.

Five summers ago, I'd come up here as a trail work volunteer, levering boulders with a rock bar and pulling a crosscut through deadfall. I had climbed the tower then, just after the Forest Service completed renovations. I hoped to return someday as a guest.

The hike in was easy. Until it wasn't. Matt wanted to veer off the sunlit logging road to the Continental Divide Trail, which he assured me would take us right to the tower. The last mile became a frustrating meander through the forest, post-holing in virgin snow and ferreting out trail markers on the pines. I stopped to catch my breath and let a football field of silence separate us.

Having met only a month ago, our trust is still fledgling.

Darkness arrives early the week before winter solstice. From the lookout, the city lights of west Helena create disorienting constellations on the ground. I unfurl our sleeping bags side by side on the bed while Matt unlaces his Army issued combat boots. He steeps pho broth on the propane stove in his socks, and invites me over.

I tear cilantro and squeeze a half moon of lime into my bowl. The food repairs the quiet between us.

"Sometimes, I'll need to push myself too hard," he says.

"I'll learn to let you."

We take turns draining the small box of red wine and spend the evening moving in clumsy orbits around the Osborne Fire Finder—a plexiglass covered topographic map which crowds the center of the single-room cab. I light votives and place them like sentinels on the tabletop and ledges. Suspended above the winter earth in glass, Matt and I talk the way new lovers talk. Still, I question my instincts to bring Matt here, if being artificially confined together is premature. Outside, clouds shuttle across and gray the night sky. The breeze accompanies our voices. After all the candles have burned down, we sidle into bed, perching on our hips and shoulders to fit.

119

We wake to howling.

The remaining window shutters slam against their frames. It's midnight, but the blizzard lightens the sky, making the hour imperceptible. A gust strikes our faces. Matt rises to find a window has been blown ajar, the rapid accumulation of snow and ice preventing its closure. He resets the window sash, sealing it back into place as only a carpenter can. The tower shakes and rattles on its struts. Matt traces the windowed walls, checking for other leakages and dangers. He stokes the fire.

"I hate the wind," I whimper.

"I don't think we're in any real trouble."

I'm not comforted because I'm with a man. My life in Montana is largely defined, as one friend said, "by being a woman doing man things"—most frequently and happily, alone. Often, when I'm joined by men in the wild, I've been the more observant, prepared, and even fearless one. What bothers me now, is that I think I'm comforted because the man I'm with disposed bombs in Afghanistan, and this is not how I was raised. War is not a means for security.

I tuck into Matt's side.

He reads the tension in my torso, the torque in my jaw.

"How about the lullaby I sing to my daughter?"

His ribs receive my nod. I reposition my head and attend to the soft melody passing from his lips, centimeters from the coil of my ear.

Our sleep is fragmented, no more than 20 minutes at a time. We wake wide-eyed each time the gale ratchets to a higher pitch. It shrieks on all sides of the lookout. The hammering of wood on wood becomes deafening. The quaking relentless. If the sole purpose of a lookout is to spot danger from a distance—hundreds of miles away, even—what happens in a direct assault? I remind myself the lookout has withstood decades of high elevation exposure. Hints of woodsmoke hang inside the air, eerily still, confusing the senses. I roll makeshift earplugs from a scrap of toilet paper. The buffer is minimal. Any dreams steer into nightmares: all the windows shattering, the rooftop ripping off, being carried away to some obscure fate.

By 4 am, we are delirious. With the night mostly over, we resort to mimicry. When one of us gets up to check the fire or slug water, we wail and shout to each other across the floor, as if by making noise we might be certain that noise alone will not harm us. I contemplate torture. The lookout, our stress test.

We nestle back together and wait it out.

By the whiteout of dawn, I am desperate to get off the tower. Out of the violence of the storm. The woodbox needs restocking. Trying to reclaim my sense of grit, I open the door and step gingerly through the metal grate in the catwalk, onto the main staircase. A force strikes my back and I sail into the railing of the first landing. My hands catch me before my head collides. Breathing becomes a chore, and I hold it down two more flights until I stagger onto the concrete base. The rounds of the woodpile are within reach, but an opposing force halts me. I wrestle and lean, wait for a lapse in the wind,

120

then lunge for three small logs. Turning, I'm lifted back to the base. I climb the stairs, low and burdened.

I batter the door with the logs in my arms. Matt tugs it open to find me standing breathless, my hair in knots. The tight wool beanie I'd been wearing is stuffed into my pocket, after the wind robbed me of it.

"I want out of here."

Matt boils water for coffee then initiates movement foreign to him this early in the morning. We take turns hauling armloads of firewood, each trip taking an embarrassing number of minutes. Buttoning up the lookout, I follow Matt outside and take to the lee side of the tower; Matt moves toward exposure. I'm shocked to find all the shutters I'd taken down are still lying flat on the catwalk. When I finish my wall, I shuffle to the corner and check on Matt. His movements are calculated as he replaces each shutter, careful not to let the panels be caught broadside.

We are both out of breath as we pack our gear.

I watch Matt dress for the descent, wrapping his desert scarf around his face and neck. Bearing the weight of my pack, I move down the tower after him, anchoring each step. An injury now would be ruinous. Ankles and skulls intact, we stand at the base and laugh, watching each other make failed plays for the woodpile. With the promise of escape, our relief takes the shape of momentary horseplay.

The bleached sky peels back, making the timberline visible. I yell at Matt to pick the route. We hike apart, each searching for solid footholds. Within yards, my hands sting from cold. I could finally cry. Matt hears me holler, then pauses long enough to gift me his glove liners, and slips a neck gaiter up over my cheeks to shield from burn. With tears in our eyes and the tempest at our backs, we're swept down the mountainside, uncertain how the wind will deliver us.

*The Number*
Emily Johnson

❋

On the scale.
Off the scale.
94.
The scale must be lying. That's too much, the earth is going to collapse underneath me. What did I eat today? Dried Cranberries. Rice cakes. Salad. High fiber cereal. Steamed eggplant, balsamic vinegar. Fish oil supplement, 10 calories.

If my hip bones don't protrude like a bird's beak, I have eaten too much. How many bowel movements have I had today? Only 2. Maybe I'll drink some Epsom salt, despite the sting. I can't keep my eyes open but I need to go on a hike. I can squeeze in two miles but I have to be in bed by 11. I need sleep, without waking from the voices in a constant nightmare: Wake up, Emily. Why don't you have some toast to settle the stomach?

I will fight it. Get the toast away from me. The carbohydrates are going to seep through my skin and into my thighs. I don't need food. Human, glutton. I need to be less dependent. I cannot drink caffeine. I cannot drink things that dehydrate me. More water. Water is better than food.

Everyday. Scrape the avocado off the rice cake, too much fat. In restaurants, I ask the same questions: Is that regular or nonfat? I need nonfat.

Carbohydrates slow me down, block my plumbing. Can't. Won't. Not worth it. Even in the day, the nightmare: What are you doing, Emily?

Nightly crunches and leg lifts. Can't sit still, have to keep moving, I haven't had enough exercise today. I can't stop looking at pictures of perfect skinny women, fantasize about having their legs. Am I a lesbian? I would trade my arms for those legs. Give them.

Please don't ask me to eat the pasta. Please, please, please. 90. That's all I want to see. Okay, maybe six less. Maybe 84.

Why don't you eat something, Emily?

No thank you, I'm fine.

***

There is a feeling when you are suddenly aware of your breathing. You listen closely to the inhale, followed by the exhale. Soon, you have forgotten what it is like to breathe without thought. You are aware of your lungs. You would like to watch them expand and contract.

Once, you were able to inhale air without consciousness.

I grew tired of hugs from family members with ulterior motives.

They counted my vertebrae, empty shelves, stabbing when touched.

I moved to another state, but so did all the problems. I took my eating disorder with me, packed it carefully. Knowing it was safe, I could breathe.

I finally unpacked it, left it at the door of the nutritionist's office. When she weighed me, the number terrified me. I wish I hadn't asked to see it.

107.

The nutritionist comforted me, assured me that bread, meat, and avocados meant survival. The doorbell rang, the alarm went off, and I woke from my hunger strike.

That day, I realized what I was really starving for. Comfort. Assurance. Longing for those things manifested through my body. Control. Life would be too easy, if everything was just the way it was supposed to be.

I crawled back to my family and friends, another kind of addict, another kind of eighth step, recovery. I crawled through my selfishness, and found a new definition of power, a new meaning of control.

I always wanted cheese the most.

*Float On*
Shelly Carney

I was incarcerated three hundred and fifty miles from home and had just been through as much heroin addiction treatment as the Montana Department of Corrections could provide. I finished my last group session when an inmate walked up to me and told me my son had called—and it was urgent. My heart sunk, my stomach turned inside out, and I knew.

I stood ten deep in the long line of payphones, listening to inmate conversations only three feet from each side of me. The narrow area was loud with the clamor of inmates' arguments with their boyfriends while I needed to make the most important phone call of my life.

Every inch of me trembled with fear. I wanted to puke. I was shaking so badly that I could barely dial. I could feel the paleness in my face and in my body. My eldest son answered. "Mom, you better sit down."

"Please, don't say it!" I pleaded with him.

"It's true, Mom. I'm looking at her right now."

He told me my daughter was dead.

I fell to the floor and I shrieked. I was screaming and crying so loudly; I could not hear what else he said to me. The inmates gathered around and stared at me like I was a new interesting piece of gossip to pass around. When the prison staff overheard, they realized it was serious and locked the other inmates in the cafeteria. They told me to hang up and that we could call from one of the back offices.

I was limp. I was hysterical. I was broken. I wanted to escape to come home to see her and say goodbye. I wanted to use and be numb. But most of all, I wanted it to not be true.

Immediately I called back; there was so much confusion. Everyone was there but me, her mother. The one she was closest to her entire life. I thought she overdosed, but there were not any answers yet. They thought she bled to death. She had miscarried a baby less than an hour before she died.

After the autopsy, the coroner said she had died from a massive heart infection. Endocarditis; a bacteria that spreads through your bloodstream and damages your heart. My sweet Emma passed away on December 19th, 2013. The holidays have not been—and will never be—the same.

My furlough application to go home to grieve my daughter's death took ten days to be reviewed and approved. I was allowed a thirty hour furlough to come home for her funeral. I traveled three hundred and fifty miles each way. The stipulations were that I could spend a few short hours with my family, but I had a curfew and had to sleep at the jail.

My children's father would not allow me to attend the funeral, so my mom and dad hosted a separate memorial at their home. At least we could be together a few short hours in Emma's memory. The cops came to make sure I was there. I was already angry at the thirty hours, but being interrupted by the police was an unnecessary pain. I was finding it very hard to be grateful for being allowed to be there. But I was an inmate after all, and I was treated like one.

***

While I did not introduce Emma to heroin, I enabled her and showed it was okay through my own addiction. She discovered the drug after I had relapsed after a nine year period of sobriety. I had walked in on her in the bathroom as she was sticking a needle in her hand. "If you can't beat 'em, mom, join 'em," she stated. I had never felt so guilty or ashamed of myself in all my life. I hated myself.

Sometime after that, I started using with my own daughter.

In addition to being a fellow addict, Emma was a severe epileptic. I was with her day and night. For a few years, she slept next to me. She would have up to seven seizures in a twenty-four hour period, so I would not let her out of my sight. I even sat with her while she showered. I could keep Emma safe from the seizures, but I could not keep her safe from the dope. What a damn contradiction. I told her every day: "This is not okay. Using together is not okay."

I had picked up another drug charge just a year and a half after completing a ten year prison sentence. I could not wait to go back to jail. I needed to be safe from myself so I could get clean again and be the mother my children deserved. The worst thing that has ever happened to me was losing my daughter; the worst thing I have ever done was to enable her and to use with her.

I never grew up thinking addiction was okay. I never thought my addiction would be a part of my children's lives. Every time I had been clean previously, I had relapsed. Even after nine years of clean time. I was always such a disappointment to my children. How does one teach her children to be a good parent if one cannot be one herself? On many levels, I was a very good mom. In regards to addiction, I was not. My addiction has cost me everything: my children, two husbands, friends and family, my health, and my freedom.

My first husband is the father of my three children. After seventeen years, he had enough. Towards the end of our marriage, my using was out of control. The very last straw was waking up from a coma in the hospital. I was told I had HIV and hepatitis C. That same day, he asked for a divorce. I was still so loaded, I didn't quite feel it.

I had a friend I had used with who had AIDS. Once I was so sick in withdrawals that I used one of his needles. I wasn't thinking or caring, only desperately needing the fix. I didn't care about the consequences. It was 1998, and I knew nothing at all about HIV.

After my first husband told me he wanted a divorce, he followed it with a restraining order for unsupervised contact with my children. I had to leave

our home because I was injecting drugs in the house. My children were all I cared about. I thanked God for this terminal illness, because life was not worth living without them.

I used as hard as I could, hoping I would overdose. I couldn't get it done no matter the amount I used. A few months later, I was sent to prison. I wrote letters to my kids every single day for three years; each child got their own letter so they would feel special. I had weekly phone calls, but I never talked to my husband.

My kids told me he had started seeing some of my longtime friends. I was shattered. Prison is the loneliest place. After getting off the dope, all these feelings I had kept far away began to surface. I was a mess, I was alone, and I was nothing; an empty shell of a woman, completely hollow. I could not have been in a worse place; prison is a three ring circus sideshow of freaks. All I wanted was for the HIV to kill me.

After three years, I got an AIDS diagnosis. I refused to take the medications. At some point, I decided to take advantage of what was being offered me; so many groups, so many ways to heal. I could see it in the lives of other women.

I did the work. All the childhood sexual abuse, physical abuse, a bad mother-daughter relationship, my kids. I worked through it inch by inch and started being accountable for my behavior and stopped blaming my parents and everyone else on the planet.

Slowly, a different person emerged. I actually liked myself. I finally went to pre-release in Missoula and had visits with my kids, family and the few friends I had left. I saved every nickel and got a four bedroom house. The restraining order had not been lifted, but I was confident it would be. I knew people would see a very different Shelly, an honest Shelly with a good job. I was finally released into my own home. After prison it was a big space and I had never been without a partner, but I did not want one. I wanted to continue to love myself and focus on my children.

I met with my children's father, after four years of no contact. We talked; I told him I had AIDS. The next day, he stood in my living room and examined what I had worked so hard for and what I now could offer my kids. The restraining order was dropped. It really works; you do good things, and good things come to you.

My oldest son moved in right away. He was about to graduate from high school. Emma followed soon after, because she wanted to be with her mother. My youngest was there on weekends, as their father did not want to lose all of his children.

About that time, the most beautiful man walked into my life. It really was love at first sight. Shane only had sixty days clean, so I was still leery. The love and friendship was so powerful, more than I had ever had with any human. We were both on parole and he moved in. I was in awe everyday, and three years later, we were married.

My kids adored him. Shane, thirteen years younger, was a better father to my kids than their own. We were a real family; so happy, so in love, so

complete. My journey through the correctional system had paid off. Shane had a great job, and plenty of money to provide for our large family. All the kids lived with us. Shane went to father/daughter dances and paid for everything they needed and wanted.

But things were getting complicated.

I was a stay at home mom, suffering on and off with symptoms of my disease. He worked twenty hour days, and then slept for four hours, until he did it all over again. I was alone. I missed him and our family time. I relapsed right before my nine year sobriety date.

I used in secret for many months. The guilt ate me from the inside out, so I finally confessed to Shane I had been using. He was beyond devastated; our entire relationship had been based on sobriety. He said he would stay and support me, only if I got clean. The lies flowed out of me very naturally, telling him I was clean when I was not. Over and over again, I had to admit that I couldn't get it together.

I was lonely, he was gone. My health deteriorated. My kids were growing up and spending time with friends. I was all alone on a nine hundred acre ranch with too much time on my hands to feel sorry for myself.

Months later, Shane relapsed. We used together for about a year. Everything had changed. When I broke the news to my kids that Shane and I were using, they left. Angry and hurt once again, feeling like they would never be a good enough reason for mom to keep her head out of her selfish ass.

Two weeks before Christmas, Shane told us he was leaving. We were killing each other. That event, until Emma's death, was by far the most devastating thing that had happened in my life. I turned into a psychotic, bawling, crazy bitch. A woman came into his life and I made threats. I was homicidal. At that time in my life, I believe I would have killed her, if given the chance.

Once again, I screwed it up and lost it all. He left and I had to move. Of all the kids, Emma was the most broken after Shane left. Feeling rejected her entire life by her dad and her brothers, she began using. I started using and selling dope like never before.

In spite of our drug use, I had truly beautiful times with Emma, while I waited to be sentenced. We watched movies, we gardened, we went for late night walks, my English lab, Alabama, always at my side. Emma was a self-taught musician. She played her guitar for me every day and the beauty and passion in her voice brought tears to my eyes. It was warming and comforting to listen to her sing; Modest Mouse was her favorite.

Her using was unlike anything I had ever witnessed. She was reckless, far hungrier for it than I ever was. I performed CPR on her countless times after overdosing. I finally realized she was doing it on purpose. She was terrified to be without me. I warned the family repeatedly that she was going to die.

"Please take care of her while I am gone. She cannot be by herself," I told them this over and over. I was conflicted. I wanted to go to jail to get clean so I could help her do the same, but I did not want to leave her.

On sentencing day, my mom and my children were there. When they took me to the cage, my family stood to leave. Emma sat there, staring at

the floor in disbelief. She refused to leave. I hated myself, I hated Shane, and I hated the world for what we had become. But I was determined to get in and do the work. I could do this.

While in treatment, I chose to use Emma as my "victim," which is a concept I learned during a mandatory Victimology class. The focus of the class was to write letters to your victim, and letters from the perspective of your victim to you. The letters never got sent, but were a way to apologize and hold yourself accountable. I worked hard; I was a few months away from coming home, almost done with pre-release.

As it was, they let me out two months early. I was given a little more time to figure out how to live life again without Emma and without Shane. I swore to not lose focus on what was important to me: My recovery, my children, my family, and myself. I loved myself in a way I never had before.

When I was in prison, Shane had moved to Seattle and married. He learned of Emma's death from my youngest son. He called my parents to ask for permission to come to Emma's memorial. We had not had contact since he left; I still hated him. But I did not have the energy to hold on to hate anymore. I was completely drained of emotion, only focused on losing my only daughter.

On the drive home, my stomach was in knots. I was nervous about seeing him after so long. We arrived in Missoula at five in the evening. When I walked in and saw my family, we all fell apart. Emotions about Emma were all around me, and our lives would never be the same. Our family was incomplete. Soon after, my oldest son arrived with Shane, who just held me. Everything from the past—all the hurt, betrayal and anger—was set aside to honor Emma. It was almost like we had never been apart.

We rekindled our friendship after that. We had to work through some hard stuff, but today I respect him. He comes and sees me from Seattle, and we talk and text several times a week. We reach out to each other when we are struggling. The most important piece is that we have forgiven each other. I feel free from all those ugly feelings.

I still confront tremendous grief and loss. It owns you, and has a life of its own. I have learned to embrace my feelings for what they are and I allow myself to feel them. I started counseling. Not mandatory for my parole, but because I needed it. I wanted it. Emma's death did not feel real at all, and I still found myself waiting for her to come home.

I felt guilty that I was not crying all day, every day. I found myself going to his office and grieving the loss of Shane more than Emma. On some levels, they felt the same—the death of my beautiful marriage and the death of my beautiful daughter. Shane was very present in my everyday life; but Emma was gone. Eventually, bits of Emma began to flow in, and I was feeling it. I decided I never wanted her to be forgotten; I wanted her to have a legacy.

I became heavily involved in our local AIDS service organization, Open Aid Alliance. They were beginning to open an above ground syringe exchange when the Executive Director came to me. "Shelly, how do you feel about the exchange program being called Emma's Exchange?"

My jaw dropped and my heart stopped for a second. My stomach did somersaults. "Yes, yes!" I said. Then she told me something I did not know.

In June of 2013, Emma was the very first exchange client. She was instrumental in getting it going, bringing in new clients, taking supplies out into the community. I felt a big smile stretch across my face. I was so proud; my daughter cared enough about her fellow addicts to help where she could. My daughter's legacy is Emma's Exchange.

At a fundraiser, I talked about Emma and all the things she was: A gorgeous redhead, a gardener, a very talented musician and singer. A wonderful sister, daughter, and friend. A crass sense of humor. She could make anyone laugh in any situation. Most of all, she was loved. Loved by so many people who dearly miss her.

I do a lot of public speaking in high schools. I could not save my own daughter, but maybe I can help save someone else's daughter. Combining Emma's story with HIV, safe sex education, addiction, incarceration, and loss all help me grieve Emma's death. I can not talk to a room full of people without feeling it. Telling her story out loud and being accountable humble me.

I talk to health care workers, treatment facility coordinators, pharmacists, and university students. I spoke to the state house and the senate and played a big role in getting laws changed. I stood with the governor when he signed the bill that resulted in syringe exchanges all over the state. Emma would be proud of her mother today. I know my sons are proud, too.

I have been working on rebuilding relationships with my sons in other ways. Fifteen months after Emma died, my blond youngest son and his beautiful Latina wife gave birth to a baby girl with outrageously red hair and very light skin. I make amends to him by being the best grandmother I can be.

My granddaughter and I have an intensely close relationship. We adore each other. I watch her and relive Emma's childhood. She is so much like Emma—her mischievous humor, and her red hair. With my oldest son, I just try to lead by example. We are slowly mending fences.

Refusing HIV medications and cheating death for eighteen years became taxing on my body. My health started to fail. Two years ago, I had an opportunistic infection called Wasting Syndrome and weighed 85 pounds.

I started to feel like I had done enough. I had lived and I was weary. My doctor put me in hospice care. I was ready to go and started making plans. Most of the people in my life disappeared; I didn't understand. I laid in my dog's bed and cried for four solid months. Hospice was in and out all the time, but I was way too sick and weak to spend time with my granddaughter. I couldn't even pick her up.

They gave me about thirty days to live. My youngest son and his bride had a quick ceremony with family just to get my name on their marriage certificate as a witness.

A year later, I was still just surviving. Suffering, too. At some point, my granddaughter became my driving force to live. I revoked hospice, and resumed the HIV medications. I am her caregiver three to five days a week, sometimes ten hours a day.

My youngest son, his wife, and my granddaughter moved next door to me. I have lots of good time with his family, each day a process of learning to heal. My eldest son finally started reaching out; my relationship with him has been the hardest. He and his father blame me for the death of my only daughter, but I understand. If it wasn't for all the self-work through treatment and counseling, I would be defensive. We blame others when we are unwilling or too afraid to look into ourselves and confront what we may have contributed. We all played a role, but today I can only focus on mine.

My recovery has given me so many things. Today, I am six and a half years clean. I have been an addict for forty-five of my fifty-five years, twenty years spent in the correctional system. I will remain on parole until 2023. I'm doing what I can by sharing my story in the community.

Growing up, I did not have a good relationship with my mother. Blaming her for not being the mother I needed her to be. Through this grief process, I learned to forgive her, too. As parents, we do the best we can with what we have, even when it's not always good. I look at my mother today and she is a survivor. A strong, generous, beautiful woman. I look just like her, and we are similar in so many ways. I'm proud to be her daughter.

Alabama is now twelve years old, and still by my side through all of these hardships. Her health is deteriorating and she is not the dog she was two years ago. I believe there is a connection between her health and mine. I still make amends to my two sons; I won't let them down ever again. I'm not willing to risk my time with my beautiful granddaughter or destroy the relationships I have worked so hard to rebuild.

I honor Emma by staying clean and through Emma's Exchange. The gift that Emma has given me is the opportunity to forgive. Forgiving is a process of healing that allows me to live without blaming, without regret, but with the best gift of all.

Hope.

## Travels With Charlie
### Chelsia Rice

❋

Two lesbians walk into a bar.

Wait. Let me start again.

Two lesbians walk into a bar in Marion, Montana: Population 886.

But this isn't a joke.

We came out of the Kootenai Forest National Forest in the NW Corner on Montana early in the morning, after camping at the bottom of the Libby Dam for three nights. On the banks of the river, we watched a nesting pair of eagles fight mid-air with ospreys, and a fawn frolicking in the shallows by turning fast circles on an 80 degree day. A hero stealthily moved through the water and snatched a shiner every few minutes, and the dam loomed overhead, 422 feet tall. It was my first time camping since the surgery that saved my life from an aggressive bladder cancer, and being off the grid was a little precarious. I wasn't yet able to control my newly reconstructed bladder, and climbing down the aluminum stairs from the rooftop tent every night to pee in the dark wasn't pleasant. I was still weak, still small, about 130 pounds, 30 pounds less than my typical weight, and my hair was barely grown-in and still a little downy from the regrowth after chemotherapy.

Charlie and I met in college in 2005. We both had returned to school after a long-enough break. She pursued a degree in education and I was learning to write. By the time I moved to Helena in 2011, we had survived young infidelities, a couple of break-ups, and a long-distance relationship, during three years of graduate school. Statistics say that over 50% of marriages that go through a cancer diagnosis and treatment end in divorce, but we'd muscled through the hardest of times, determined to live as much of a normal life with the days we had ahead. Weeks after I left the oncology floor at St. Peter's Hospital as an inpatient for two weeks due to post-surgery complications, camping joined our list. We wanted to be away from the grind, in nature, and together.

\*\*\*

We were just 20 miles from the family cabin and wanted to stop for a Bloody Mary and breakfast. We stopped at the first highway dive bar we could: The Marion Grill. Marion appears to have a population of about 50, but the internet says otherwise, ten times that. There are no houses to see from the road, just a handful of dirt pads where RVs can stop over for the night, and the fixed-up greasy spoon/dive bar where we decided to stop. Charlie and I walked in, dirty from camping, and posted ourselves at the bar. A few folks sat at small tables in the darker half of the room while we sat

131

under the warm lights and glowing bottles of booze. The front door of the bar cracked open, and light shone in like a spotlight, just as the bartender had set down our meals.

Staggering, but still confident enough to strut, a man in his 50s with dirt-caked boots, blue jeans, and a Carhartt jacket took a stool at the end of the U-shaped bar. His eyes were glossy and red, and his gaze landed first on the bar and then on us. I turned back to my meal.

Before we go there, let me tell you about Charlie at age 40: never one to wear a swimsuit, always preferring a tight tank and swim shorts; hair cut above-the-shoulder since high school, boyish, looking ten years younger than she really was.

I was lean for now, stripped of all the accoutrements that might give away my gender—big earrings or a skirt; camping clothes that were more Patagucci than rugged; and flip-flops.

I had to pee. I got up and headed in that direction, past the obviously intoxicated man. I noticed he was packing a pistol under his jacket. I caught the sight of it, but as I walked past, I kept my eyes up and fixed on my destination.

"Hey, you," he said, and caught my attention.

I leaned in with my eyebrows raised.

"Which one are you, the top or the bottom?"

I can't tell you how much time moved between the question and the answer, but my brain processed the question, my safety, and which response was most suitable, as time slowed. I looked around for anyone else that may have heard, but no one was listening. I had three choices: act naive, be witty, or call him out.

I chose to respond. "I don't know what you are talking about."

There was a pause.

"It's better that way," he said.

Sitting in the stall of that women's bathroom, I thought of all of the ways this could turn out. His gun discharging, Charlie confronting him, running out of the bar, crying in the car. The stall was dark and I was scared enough to be lost in thought, and unaware of my surroundings. Fumbling in my pocket, I found enough cash to cover our meals.

I passed him again as I walked back to the bar, his legs spread wide, his eyes following me. After a moment at the bar, I told Charlie what he had said, what I had seen, and asked her to go out to the car and get it started while I paid. Though he had said it to me, I was more worried about her, about her boyishness becoming ignition for his anger. Gathering her keys, she headed out. A minute later, I put the cash on the bar and followed. We headed east towards Kalispell, but even Kalispell wasn't a place where we'd feel safe.

I was shaken. I'd never felt threatened quite like this before. Strangers had yelled "Dyke!" out the window when I was walking with my girlfriends, and men had told me that I was a waste of a woman. But being isolated from a community that would intervene shook me to my core.

*Did he think I was a man?*

*Was I just a dyke?*

*How dare he treat me like that - I'm just recovering from cancer!*

Anger, fear, sadness and questions, so many questions rolling through my brain as we drove and I talked. "I can't believe that happened!"

Charlie, having lived in her body for decades, replied. "For people like me, that happens often."

That stopped the questions, the whys, all the inquiry, and while the fear didn't subside I thought back to all the women with short hair, the women who didn't conform in a style or a look that coincided with their sex, ex-girl-friends confronted in bathrooms when other women asked if she was in the right one, the police officer who pulled us over and said "sir" until she spoke and he stumbled on his words: "Um, ma'am." I thought about the women as far back as my mother, a young bisexual woman in the 80s, and how one of her friends lost her life in front of a gay bar because she was all of these things. I thought about our close call. I though of women who responded wrong, didn't leave, and what happened when they stood up for themselves. Honestly, I never realized until then. There was no poignant moment of realization, only a growing sensation, a widening of my throat. I thought I might cry as the wheels crackled on the chip seal.

*Feeding The Foxtongue*
Jenn Grunigen

❋

She never goes to her storage unit without bear mace. The man who lives a couple units down from hers has been insisting on giving her something to drink (a milk jug of water, a two-liter bottle of flat root beer); either he doesn't know how to be nice without being creepy, or he is creepy and dead-set on poisoning her. The bear mace (a leaky can her father found on a backpacking trip and brought back for her as a gift) is a precaution.

She does not live in the storage unit, but she spends enough time there that it is a home away from home, of sorts. She is in Missoula with her then-husband while he goes to grad school, and their small university apartment isn't exactly an appropriate rehearsal space for a black metal drummer who likes to keep the peace with her neighbors (and the housing authorities). The unit is uncomfortable; drumming in an uninsulated steel box is freezing in the winter and sweltering in the summer. Still, it is a hermitage, a place where she can safely home her foxtongue, which hungers for a den of story and rhythm. (Later, when she has been single for two-and-a-half years, she dreams of a tiny house just big enough for her and her dog. It will have birch walls and a fridge full of figs, kelp, and pickled plums.)

It is seven days before the summer solstice, but the storage unit feels like peak fire season. The box is dim, the door shut and locked in case the potentially-creepy-neighbor decides to show up with another liquid lure. The only light is a livewire blaze at the door's gapped bottom, as lancing and confounding as the downed powerline she will see sixty-nine months later at a dog park in Oregon, while wandering the unbroken white of the early morning aftermath of a snowstorm with her heeler-mix, Vixa.

In the summerbox, she is getting ready to leave her drums and meet C (then-husband) at the grocery store. Drum sticks down, helmet on, thirsty. She reaches for her water bottle. It catches on a strap, the strap catches on the bear mace, on the safety, on the trigger.

\*\*\*

The fox is unknowable to all but other foxes.

\*\*\*

She works at the Good Food Store, making juice for famous people she doesn't know, crying over onions, sneaking spoonfuls of leftover peanut butter in the walk-in. She dodges into the back when she doesn't feel like talking to the friendly, lonely, old man who always wonders why she's covering her beautiful hair whenever she wears a hat. It's winter. I'm cold.

Another man calls her Galadriel, Guinevere, and orders his PBF smoothie T-H-I-C-K—spells it out, as if she cared about his girth.

A woman with hair short and pale like a tow-headed baby calls her eyes stinkin' beautiful and that is okay.

And then there is Th. He comes in every few mornings for coffee (she tries to memorize his routine, but he seems a little feral and she can only ever catch the time—the day changes, changes, changes), sits in a corner and writes. Her obsessive foxtongue stirs, and not just because he has a foxjaw.

She paces every morning that she works in the beverage bar, skin buzzing, her vixenlick mind turning away from her apron full of story ideas scribbled on paper scraps, and focuses on Th coming in and ordering coffee. Her pockets spill over with giant robot reality TV shows, erotic snails, mythopoeic magpies, but she is tasting the air for something mundane to fill the hollow of all the times she said yes when she should have said maybe, or maybe even no.

Because she is curious and better at creeping than her storage-unit neighbor, she memorizes the name of the business on the side of Th's truck. Through the business, she finds his name, an unused Instagram, a couple videos on YouTube, and a Facebook profile overspilling with inspirational memes, pictures of dogs (she hopes they are all his), and poetry that teeters on the verge between decent and embarrassing.

One day, Th tells her he likes her shirt. It is her foxiest shirt, the one that looks like it was sewn out of a black fishing net, so she thinks maybe what he says means something. It doesn't. She thanks him and that exchange is the most they ever say to one another.

***

Grad school, halfway done, vulpine brain. She is half-asleep in the back of the car, sweaty, dusty, after a twelve-mile hike. C is driving, M is shot-gunning. Both are guitarists in her band. Both she fell in love with, though at different times. C she loved, M she will love. She will stay with neither.

C thinks she is sleeping. "She's always writing. Or working out. Or working on something."

He's right. She doesn't give him time.

Foxtongue.

***

She has only seen a fox in the flesh twice—strange, considering her veins are slick with the blue down of a summer Vulpes lagopus.

Nearly every year of her childhood, her family makes a pilgrimage to Montana. Her grandma on her mom's side grew up on a ranch in Roundup, and that side of the family are all geologists. She wades through streams on the hunt for garnets, paws through the soil for quartz, sucking on the crystals to clean off the dirt. She picks her way down a beach covered in tiny dead dragonflies, hackles up for rutting moose. And once, while en route to their campsite, the family van keeps pace with a scrubby crossfox, yellow as sulphur. Her dad stops the van, and the fox eyes them, trots into the woods. She thinks it had a mouthful of rabbit but maybe not.

135

Early morning, another fox, this one standing at the edge of her uncle's property on the Snake River. Her family watches through the kitchen windows. She creeps out the back door, thinking she is sneaky enough to get closest. The fox sees her and runs off.

\*\*\*

Once in the name of research, she burns a small handful of ghost peppers to inhale the fumes. When she maces herself in the face, it is like that, except there are a hundred ghost peppers on fire in her mouth and one eye. She spits curses, a deluge of phlegm running like twin magma fox tails from her nose, scumming down her throat. She empties her water bottle on her face, almost reaches for the jug of water her neighbor gave her, but doesn't want to add boiled-face-off-with-poison to her list of injuries.

The curses subside, the pain subsides... a little. A mouthful of tiny vixens gnawing, a socket of bees. She keeps her eye squeezed shut and swathed in a bandana as she rides to the grocery store, locks up her bike, and strides past C, straight into the produce section.

"Hey, are you just gonna ignore me?"

She turns and catches sight of him. "Oh! Sorry, I didn't see you, I just..." She pauses. "I bear maced myself in the face."

## The Nazi Next Door
### Cynthia Aten

❊

We park on a side street in Missoula, a block from our daughter's house. Hearts pounding, Ray and I look cautiously around as we take plastic shopping bags with toothbrush, toothpaste, and pajamas out of the car. Trying to appear nonchalant, we walk quickly to an alley and slip down it, still scanning as we go. We open the gate from the alley and cross the small yard past the children's wading pool to the back door. We knock and our daughter opens the door—she is expecting us. We enter quickly. The children are ready for bed. We kiss their little faces, their dear puzzled faces, goodnight. They've spent the night at our house before—they can't imagine why we'd spend the night at theirs. Not wanting to frighten them, we haven't said much about why we plan to sleep on a futon in their basement for awhile.

We worry that we might have been seen, that we are putting all five of those precious lives at risk.

We never expected to spend part of our third summer in Missoula as fugitives from our own home.

\*\*\*

In Christmas 2006, we held a holiday open house, like the ones we always held back in New Haven, which we had left eighteen months earlier. We invited new friends and neighbors. The granddaughter of Fran, who lived next door, was among those who came. Gaitane—in her mid-thirties, large, round-faced, with dark eyes and hair—hurried into our kitchen carrying a plateful of over-baked cookies.

"I just made these," she announced, as she placed them on the refreshment table. I thanked her, said I was glad to meet her. We didn't have a chance to talk, with the comings and goings of neighbors and friends, and I don't think she stayed long.

A few days later, late in the evening, our doorbell rang again and again. I looked out to see a wild-eyed Gaitane. Alarmed, I opened the door, and she stumbled in. Clearly intoxicated, she told us that her partner, who also lived next door with Fran, was drunk and threatening to kill her with his gun. She appeared genuinely terrified, and at the same time repeatedly asked if we had anything to drink. "Water," I said, "Orange juice." But that was not what she meant, and I knew it.

I talked with her for some time, urging her to call the police, saying I would help her to get whatever help she needed to be safe, but she wouldn't place the call. Gradually she calmed down and said that, truthfully, before

she left, her partner, Yates, had passed out and she was no longer afraid. Over my protests she returned home. I felt strongly that for Fran's and Gaitane's safety, with a drunk man and his gun next door, we needed to call the police. And so I did. Two officers soon arrived at our house to confirm what had happened, and then went next door. After a time, we saw them leave. Though I didn't know it then, the police arrested Gaitane that night. She was on probation for forging several checks on Fran's account, and one of the conditions of her probation was that she remain sober.

That was not the only thing we did not know. Neighbors on the other side told us about Gaitane's 2002 arrest in their backyard for drunkenness and resisting arrest, after which she had been sent to Montana's only long-term psychiatric hospital in Warm Springs for treatment. Those neighbors and others told us of hearing loud fighting and coarse, hate-filled talk on the conservation easement downhill from our houses, and of observing Yates's speeding and erratic driving on our quiet street. From time to time he had loudly broadcast Hitler speeches from the deck of Fran's house out across our backyards and the conservation easement. They knew that he periodically went off his meds and devolved into crazy behavior, exacerbated by alcohol and drugs. They had all been cautiously aware of him for years, but no one thought to tell us about this.

Soon after Gaitane's arrest, Yates, not a big man, but an aggressive scowler, showed up at our door holding a piece of our mail that had been delivered to him by mistake. It was from the Unitarian Universalist Association in Boston. "What is this?" he demanded. "Some kind of communist Jewish organization?"

"No," I replied, briefly explaining that UUA was a religious organization welcoming those of many different religious backgrounds and beliefs.

He stomped back to Fran's, a disbelieving look on his face.

At 2 a.m. on February 8, 2007, we startled awake to the sounds of at least five shots. Our lower level bedroom opens directly onto our backyard via a large glass sliding door, and the shots seemed to come from just outside.

Hearts pounding from the suddenness, without turning on any lights, we crept to the phone upstairs and called the police. We observed the patrol car's arrival and watched flashlights move around our backyard and the backyard of the house next door. The police found bullet casings from a semiautomatic pistol under their deck but no bullet holes. Yates was arrested and pled guilty to discharging a firearm within city limits, and his firearms—at least those he told the police about—were confiscated.

We put a stout closet rod in the sliding doors in our bedroom and on the main floor. We installed motion-sensitive lights in our backyard, and put in an alarm system. We'd had an alarm system in New Haven, where there had been break-ins in our neighborhood, and my beloved white Toyota Corolla had been stolen from in front of our house. But we had felt blessedly safe in our neighborhood in Missoula, where people never locked their cars or their houses. Illusions shattered, sturdy bars and alarm system in place, we did our best to return to peaceful sleeping in our bedroom.

In May, as we all finally emerged from our dens after the long winter, Ray and I set to work clearing winter debris from the little waterfall in our front yard, trimming back dead iris and grasses. One day, as I worked near his house, Yates was outside talking to Fran. Fran, tiny, white-haired, sat in a chair not far from him, but he spoke in a voice that was easy for me, some twenty feet away, to hear. At one point he said something like, "I think she's a Jew." Then: "I would never hurt their grandchildren—they're very cute, and they're white."

Suddenly, I knew he was talking about me.

The next day Yates was up on a stepladder at the corner of Fran's house with a spray can, talking loudly, ostensibly to himself. As I again worked in the front yard, I could clearly hear him say in a singsong voice, "Wasps are useless, just like Jews. They all need to be exterminated," as he sprayed into the eaves. "This will be the last thing you'll ever hear."

I stared defiantly at him. When our eyes met, he spit, and went back to spraying.

Ray was working in our driveway on the fuselage of a small two-seat single-engine airplane he was building in our garage, and he heard Yates yelling: "Jews. Stupid Jews. You all belong in a crematorium!" Then he drove off, shouting at Ray. "I hope you die in that plane."

Because of the clear biased hatred expressed by our neighbor, we contacted the Montana Human Rights Network, and found that Yates was on their radar. He was the contact person in Montana for a hate group, an offshoot of the American Nazi Party. The young man we spoke with advised us that there was strength in numbers, and suggested we get our neighbors to join us in petitioning for a protective order. We found an excellent lawyer, who cringed as she heard our stories. Eight of our neighbors chipped in with us to pay her fee.

We told our neighbors about our findings, and our concerns for the safety of all of us. They told us of past incidents—backyard drunkenness, hate-filled speech, erratic driving, Hitler speeches from Fran's back deck—and they all felt that Yates had escalated beyond anything they'd seen before. Individually, and in groups, we tried to talk with Fran, begging her to get Yates to move out of the house for her sake and ours, even making impassioned pleas for her to get her own protective order.

Fran was not worried at all about being harmed by "the kids," as she called Yates and her granddaughter. She said she needed Yates for transportation to drive her to a card group at The Village, the grocery store and doctor appointments. We offered to be her chauffeurs, to bring her meals, to help her sell the house and move to the senior housing where her friends lived. But she was adamant. She was not asking Yates to move out and she was not going anywhere.

Our fear and alarm turned to determination. We needed to get Yates out of the neighborhood and into treatment before tragedy. The family who lived across the street from Fran heard shots from inside her garage after Yates's firearms had been confiscated, so we knew he was still armed.

After the incident in our front-yard, I was reading in my third-floor workspace when the phone rang. It was Irv across the street.

"Where are you guys?" he inquired urgently. I told him I was upstairs and Ray was working in the garage.

"Good!" he barked. "Make sure you're not visible. Yates is marching up and down the street in his camo jacket carrying an AK47 and yelling stuff about Jews and the Torah and extermination. I'm calling the cops."

I ducked and crept downstairs, invisible to the outside, to warn Ray in the garage. The police, by now known to us by their first names, came in force and arrested Yates for carrying an assault rifle, obtained after his other weapons were confiscated. As a result of this incident, he was committed to Warm Springs for 90 days.

Twenty five days later, he was released with no warning to the neighborhood.

That's when Ray and I stopped sleeping at home. We did not feel safe in the house after dark.

Three evenings after his unexpected release, our neighbors to the west observed him surveying their house and ours with binoculars from his back deck, and they heard a litany of drunken racial slurs and references to exterminating the lost tribes of Israel. Chris called the police. Alan, the neighbor to the east of Fran's house, heard the noise coming from the back deck next door and left his house to speak with Yates, who then ran at Alan and attempted to tackle him. Big mistake—Alan was an elite wrestler in college and took Yates down easily. Chris, coming to see what was happening, called the police from Alan's driveway, and two units arrived. Yates was so out of control that he had to be strapped to a gurney and removed by ambulance, and he was off to Warm Springs yet again. All of this, and it was not yet fully dark.

The next night we slept at home.

Granting of our protective order became more urgent for all of us. We did not know how soon they would let Yates out this time, and he was clearly a danger to all of us, now that he knew that we were all in this together. On July 12, we were granted a Temporary Order of Protection. Yates was served in Warm Springs. On July 30, with our capable lawyer, eight of us appeared before Judge Karen Orzech to testify about the long neighborhood reign of terror. Our request for a Permanent Order of Protection was granted. Judge Orzech even added her own proviso, extending the area covered to the entire hill.

We neighbors celebrated with a big cookout on our deck. Day faded into night, and no longer fearing what might be aimed at us from the next-door deck, we remained outside, talking and laughing well into the night. Bob, the neighbor across from Fran and a well-known writer and singer/songwriter, sang some of his outrageous and delightful songs—though some had to be censored because of the children celebrating with us—and we all slept better that night.

Fran stayed in the house, Yates was eventually released, and I went out for a walk in the neighborhood one bright, warm October day. Suddenly

I saw a familiar beat-up blue Jeep Cherokee driving toward me. I abruptly ducked into the shadow of a large evergreen, hoping it would hide me, and the Jeep went past, Yates at the wheel, his eyes locked on the road. A few minutes later, the Jeep came back down the hill, now with Fran in the passenger seat. I had my cell phone with me—I hadn't gone anywhere without it for months—and at my first sighting, I called the police. Yates was in violation of our protective order. The police didn't arrive in time to catch him in violation. I went to the Sheriff's office the next day to sign an affidavit.

Eventually, Fran moved to The Village and joined her card-playing buddies. To our profound relief, Fran decided not to give the house to "the kids," and put it up for sale. A young couple bought it. We heard they were coming to Missoula to teach at the university.

One day, their car pulled into their driveway just as we were pulling out of ours. We rolled down our windows.

"Welcome to the neighborhood!" we called. "So glad you're here! As soon as you can, change the locks," we added, before driving away.

The next day we met their adopted son. He is African-American. And he has a beautiful Jewish name.

From a drug-addled, heavily armed Jew-hater to these open-minded and gentle folks.

"Yes!" we said to each other, "Yes!"

***

For me, this story demonstrates both the power and the limitations of memory, and how trauma lives on in one's body. As I started to write, I felt my muscles tighten, my heart rate increase and my breathing become shallow. I felt the way I had when we lived through all of it: tense, afraid, angry. As I wrote, I found myself inadvertently slipping into present tense as my tension mounted in recall—it was all happening again for me NOW. I realized that I had no clear sense of the order of events, the amount of time that elapsed. But I was perfectly clear about how I had felt.

The neighbors had to tolerate Yates's and Gaitane's annoying and threatening behavior for years before the final escalation. I think they were grateful that we took the lead to get him out of our neighborhood, and it certainly created a sense of solidarity among us.

But it was not the perfect solution. We knew Yates would eventually return to Missoula. Then what? We knew he had obtained a gun illegally before, and could likely do it again. After Fran moved off the street, there was no reason for him to come to our neighborhood anymore, and we didn't see him and the blue Jeep. But we knew it would be simple for Yates to return under cover of darkness, and we don't have bullet-proof glass.

In the way of a small town, we heard the news. A year later, the man who cuts Ray's hair warned that another client lived in the neighborhood to which Yates had moved. This person called the police after Yates brandished a sword and threatened children in the neighborhood. I was sad that another group of people just trying to live their lives were being intimidated by this man. The neighbors who moved into Fran's house eventually heard

the whole story. They tell us they still keep up with Yates's whereabouts. I don't ask.

My unease returns only rarely, but I do think back to those days in 2007, when the first mild nights of a new summer begged us to open our bedroom door. I have to remind myself to just breathe.

Yates may still be out there, but I won't let him deprive me of that sweet air.

*Teacups*
Jain Walsh

My mother put chopped raisins in the pancakes so we wouldn't notice the weevils. We did, but we pretended not to. She wasted nothing, especially not food. Practical and resourceful, she made clever use of what little we had.

My mother was a collector. She prized most her set of teapots, teacups and saucers, carefully stored in my Grandmother Vivian's china hutch. The ornately carved dark wood cabinet had fragile glass doors and drawers stuffed full of hand embroidered linens from Norway. The hutch straddled creaky boards in our old farmhouse. Every time I ran down the stairs, the cups and saucers rattled, chirping like a hundred tiny birds. My little earthquakes caused my mother no alarm. I knew the china was extremely precious to her, yet she never scolded me. Even though she was no stranger to punishment. She inherited quite a few of the china pieces from the mother of a dear friend back east. She acquired others from loved ones here and there, but most came from my grandmother.

"Your grandmother would clip the coupons off laundry soap boxes, save them up and mail them in to get these. She got one cup or saucer at a time. It took her years to make this set." She told me this on the one rare occasion we used the china for tea. I never knew my grandmother Vivian, who passed away before I was two years old. Still, I could picture her carefully collecting coupons, just the way my mother clipped out cardboard rebates on cereal boxes.

My mother collected the broken, the undesirable, things others had cast aside. She found beauty in the tarnished and stained, utility in the shattered and outdated.

My mother also collected people. Just as broken and undesirable. She had a gift for finding the beauty in them, too. All those teacups rattled, chipped and cracked, but still full of love.

She taught me to be kind, generous, and nonjudgmental. She always engaged in conversation and tipped Francis, a homeless man who sold newspapers outside the Fred Meyer. "No matter how poor you are, there is always someone worse off than you."

She taught me to be inclusive and welcoming: "I bet that person can teach you how to do something you can't, but you won't know if you're not friends." And most importantly, she taught me to forgive, even though she struggled to forgive herself.

143

Home with a stomachache, I miss yet another day of my fifth-grade year. I hate staying home, but I am perpetually sick, plagued with constant abdominal pain and nausea. Sometimes I say nothing and endure the dull achy pain throughout the school day. Often, it feels I have eaten shards of glass and I can't keep my pain to myself. Continually constipated, sometimes to the point of sepsis, I have been to the doctor for an exhausting amount of testing. The doctors offer no diagnosis, but I know demons live in my bowels: the sinful product of the pleasure of sex, slowly clawing and gnawing at my insides.

Al is my stepfather, and we climb into his junky brown Chevy truck. I must see the doctor again. The heavy door slams loudly and I crank the window down. The warm spring air makes me restless for summer. I scoot to the middle of the bench seat and fasten the lap belt. Al presses me to him briefly. He smells like Old Spice and cigarettes. The motor makes the truck shake slightly side to side, like an old dog getting up off the floor. As we leave the house, headed down our single lane dirt backroad, I can hear the grasshoppers chirping. We pass the solitary white mare who lives in the adjacent pasture. My bottom momentarily leaves the seat and slams down when we clear the kelly hump. Sloshing around in the clumsy pick-up only adds to the discomfort in my stomach. I wish we would have taken the Buick. As we drive towards the swamp, the grasshoppers jump through the golden rod and yarrow. I can see the trails that shoot straight down the hill and others that bisect the switchback. This network of trails serves as a playground for the neighborhood kids. I follow them to and from school.

Al stops the truck near the wooded confluence of the trails. He parks on the abandoned road that follows the base of the hills from the swamp over to the city park. The "No Motor Vehicles" sign stands, dimpled from years of sling shots and pellet guns. Near the entrance to the trail looms a large grey metal structure that once served as water distribution, surrounded by a 10-foot-tall chain link fence. "Do Not Enter—No Trespassing." Regardless, kids burrow paths under the fence to catch frogs. We sit in silence for a minute, the musty smell of the swamp water becoming more pungent.

"There." Al points at the structure. "If the doctor tells you you're pregnant, tell him a man grabbed you when you were walking home from school, and that he raped you behind there."

We rarely speak about what happens between us. It occurs without words. Al developed a language of looks and gestures years ago. I can't remember a time it was any other way. I did not need to be reminded of the consequences for speaking about it. His warnings constantly occupied my mind: Al would go to jail, and we would lose the farmhouse. We would lose each other.

"A doctor?" The words come out in a whimper. I try to process this, but Al offers no guidance. He closes his eyes for a few seconds, and finally nods. He starts the truck and continues driving the dirt road, up the steep and rutted hill to the paved street on the eastern boundary of the city.

I try to create a scene in my head. What did the man look like? When did it happen? Why didn't I tell someone? Al expects me to come up with these details. As I conjure up what the imaginary man was wearing, it hits me. I could be pregnant. I put my hands on my aching stomach. Horrified, I feel something growing inside me. Al pats my thigh three times. "You can do this. Be strong, be grown up."

At the doctor's office, I immediately go to the ladies' room. When I throw up, hot vile acid spews out of my mouth. I begin to cry, and I can't stop. I am certain this is morning sickness. I choke down my tears. Be strong, be grown up. I cup my hands and fill them with water from the sink. It spills down my shirt when I bring my hands to my mouth. Swishing the water in my mouth just makes the bile resurface. I spit into the sink and leave the water running to wash it out. A wet paper towel cools my red face. Muttering the lie underneath my breath, I try to convince the child staring back in the mirror.

In the waiting room, Al pretends to read a National Geographic magazine. At home, Al reads technical manuals for HAM radios and not much else. He is large, with a bit of a belly, well groomed, neatly combed dark brown hair and a thick, trimmed beard. He wears aviator glasses and the casual mismatched suit of his profession: car salesman. I am repelled. I am attracted. I am confused. I sit next to him. I desperately want to nestle into his lap, have him wrap his arms around me and gently hold me. He looks around the room, and quietly pushes me away as we wait for the doctor.

On the examination table, the doctor explains how the ultrasound machine will look inside my abdomen. He can tell I am afraid. He assures me that it will not hurt, but I hold my breath as the cold jelly that covers the instrument slides over my skin.

"Is there anything in there?" I ask a few minutes later, as he puts the wand of the machine away.

"Nothing to worry about." He reports with a convincing smile. He schedules another test and sends us on our way with a familiar set of recommendations. Eat more greens. Take laxatives and Tums for your upset stomach.

When we leave the doctor's office, Al drives me to my mother's work. The slippery green leather coach in the basement conference room typically serves as my sick bed. The room is empty today, but I can't be alone right now. I follow my mother to her office and curl up under the warmth of the Xerox machine, finding comfort in the consistent whirring and inky smell. I close my eyes to sleep, safe, five feet from my mother. I am not pregnant. I did not have to speak the unspeakable.

Three years later, I tell my mother about the abuse. Al convinces her that I am lying. The next day, I tell the police. The series of events begins, the warnings I always dreaded. Al goes to jail, but only for a few days. I am placed in foster care. Our family is broken.

On my 16th birthday, Al finally tells my mother the truth. She divorces him, but when I finally can return home, my mother is absent. Emotionally, and then physically. She had to dig herself out from the heavy burden.

Twenty-five years later, it still feels hypothetical when I discuss my childhood with my mother, as if it happened to someone else. And in a way it's true. I am not the girl I once was, nor is she the same women. Our relationship, complicated but close, survived many trials. For years, I despised her, resented her. Perhaps becoming a mother myself brought me around. I forgave her years ago, but she still holds on to the pain and the guilt.

The act of collecting dovetails with having nothing. When you are poor, you hold on to anything, in the hope of future utility.

We were always poor, and she was always a collector, but when I left home, something broke in her for good.

She began to collect more things. Every few months, I visited, and helped in the garden and with canning. I noticed the change in my mother. First, it was plants. Her flower beds erupted, and she collected tubers and starts of all kinds. The sun porch filled up with urns full of Easter lilies. In every window, ferns and spider plants hung from macramé yokes. The rose brushes were meticulously pruned, every inch of soil in the vegetable garden incubated tiny seeds. She doted over the plants, watered them, freed them from insects, and kept them blooming.

In 1996, she began to collect objects. Filling the places where I had been. Collectibles from yard sales, trinkets from the thrift shop, useless baubles from the dollar store.

Within a year, my mother was crawling into dumpsters, retrieving the treasures the world no longer wanted.

The week after Mother's Day, I stay with her and her new husband, Pat, in their single wide trailer. Her cluttered home is tidy, but stained yellow from two people who collectively smoke three packs of cigarettes a day. Every horizontal surface in the house is occupied. The cabinets and shelves overflow with tchotchkes. Priceless antiques Pat had collected on his world travels intermingle with plastic toys from Happy Meals and ceramic frogs. Boxes teeter everywhere, and piles must be shuffled to make room to sit down. The shower stall in her front bathroom is filled with cans of paint, stacked tall enough to touch the ceiling. I am confident those cans of paint have been there for over a decade.

Something is changing in her again. The landlord intends to put up a fence around the mobile home park. She must move her flower beds. "These pink daisies came from the house on Poplar," she reminisces. "I moved them from the farmhouse to here." We lived on Poplar Street more than thirty years ago.

"Should I try to save them?" I ask, sweaty, dirt on my face, shovel in my hand.

"No," she says. "I am ready to let them go."

At two o'clock in the afternoon, we take a break from the hot sun. We sit in peeling wooden lawn chairs that are falling apart, splintered and cracked, but she doesn't apologize. "We used to stain them every year, but at some point, it's not worth it."

She sits and lights a cigarette. I crack open a beer, and she slugs a rum and diet soda. "I am ready to let it all go." She is not talking about flowers and knick-knacks, but all the things and all the hurt that weighs her down.

She smiles, and I believe her.

## Please Do Not Be Bitter
### Tamara Love

The general manager of the store where I work in Missoula tells me that one of the store's white male customers, with whom I've talked a few times, called to ask questions about my department. During their conversation, the customer kept referring to me as "the colored girl." The general manager kept asking: "You mean Tamara?"

"Yes," he said. But despite her repeating my name several times, he still will not use it. Instead, I remain "the colored girl."

\*\*\*

I received an email this afternoon from a close friend. The email was a link to an article from the September 5, 2014 issue of the New York Times: "Settlement Is Approved in Central Park Jogger Case, but New York Deflects Blame." The friend who emailed the link is white. She didn't comment on the piece, just sent the link.

A year prior, at the Crystal movie theater, we'd watched the Ken Burns documentary "The Central Park Five." It was about a 1989 case in which five Black and Latino teens, aged 14 to 16, were charged with the rape and beating of a white female jogger in Central Park. The police forced false confessions out of two of the boys and used weak circumstantial evidence to convict all five of them. Reading the New York Times article, I learned that each of the five men were awarded $1 million dollars for each year of their imprisonment. I also learned that neither the city nor law enforcement conceded any wrongdoing. The rape occurred on April 19, 1989. The teenagers were convicted in December of 1990. Twelve years later, the Central Park 5 were exonerated using DNA. And after the actual perpetrator confessed.

After reading the article, I replied to my friend. I don't remember my exact response, but I remember being angry. I was angry about the time that the teens, now men, had lost with their families and friends. I was angry because they'd had to begin life over, attempting to secure transportation, housing, jobs, money. The men were exonerated in 2002, but the settlement wasn't finalized until 2014. I was angry because I knew that despite the overturning of their convictions, they will always carry with them the stigma of imprisonment. They will forever be known as the Central Park Five—not the individuals they are. Kevin Richardson, Antron McCray, Raymond Santana, Korey Wise, and Yusef Salaam. They will carry scars—of prison, funerals they couldn't attend, careers they couldn't build. Money is a poor substitute for time, love, and life lost. Surprised by my response, my friend could only offer: "I thought you'd be happy."

I couldn't figure out how to respond without sounding like the angry Black woman I am. So I said nothing. Inside, I thought f*ck white people, and their thoughts on what should make a Black person "happy" after a life altering injustice.

***

The Black Lives Matter t-shirt fit my white girlfriend comfortably. We discussed whether or not she should wear it around me. I was surprised when she asked me, because she normally didn't consult me on her clothing choices. "You should wear what you want to wear," I said. "As long as it's not offensive, I'll probably be okay." She'd purchased the t-shirt when Patrisse Cullors, a co-founder of Black Lives Matter, spoke at the University of Montana in November 2016. The Black Lives Matter movement spawned four years earlier, after Trayvon Martin, a 17-year old African American visiting his father in Sanford, Florida, was killed by a white male, George Zimmerman, a neighborhood watch captain.

We'd been dating for just a few weeks and still wanted to be sensitive to each other's needs. She spoke of her white privilege, and her desire to be sensitive to issues of race.

"How would you feel if I wore a White Lives Matter t-shirt?" I asked.

"I'd be horrified," she said.

Moments later, we both laughed uncontrollably, imagining walking hand in hand in our respective t-shirts as we ventured around the city.

***

The Wailin' Jennys are performing at Benaroya Hall in Seattle. I arrive at the venue early and take a seat at a table in the lobby until the main hall opens. At first, I hear the faint sound of chanting, but it builds very quickly as the voices approach and the people draw closer.

"Black lives matter!"

"Black lives matter!"

The cry punctuates the air as several hundred marchers walk past the windows that extend from floor to ceiling. Some of the marchers have signs: "Black Lives Matter." "Racism, Not In My Name." "Love." Inside, the Hall is almost cathedral-like in its grandeur, and you can't help but feel both small and important. The space has a low hum as concert attendees order coffee and cocktails, salads garnished with artisan cheese and light vinaigrettes. I watch the marchers as I drink sparkling water, acutely aware that I'm the only African American in eyesight.

I should be out there with them, I think.

I do not want to be out there with them. I want the marchers to go away. I want to be invisible. I want to blend in. Hot tears pool in my eyes.

Why are they marching?

Of course, they are marching for me. Black women. Black men. Native Americans. White women. White men. Other people of color. Solidarity, but I wanted no part of it.

James Weldon Johnson, an early 20th century African American writer, was once asked: "What wouldn't you give to be a white man?" In that

149

moment, as the Black Lives Matter marchers passed me, I considered my own response to the same question. Nothing. There's nothing I wouldn't give to be a white man. Name your price.

***

It's a comfortably warm and sunny evening in mid-April, and I'm walking my dogs in my Missoula neighborhood. I had an all-day event at my job and am grateful to be done. The dogs sniff the blades of grass and raise their legs to leave their mark. Two blocks from home, a Dodge Charger police vehicle pulls up beside me. The officer rolls down the window and stops. There's no one else around. Only neat brick-sided buildings, trees, well mowed lawns and a clean street. I keep moving at the dogs' pace, attempting to act casual, but I feel my heartbeat quicken and the familiar beginnings of an anxiety attack. I hear the muffled sounds of the police radio and I realize that I have no identification on my person, nor do I have my house keys. I have my iPhone in the side pocket of my khakis, but I know better than to reach for it. The officer is checking me out, and I know he is not interested in how I'm enjoying the walk or the weather or the welfare of my dogs. I'm aware that any move I make could be perceived as a threat.

How can I prove to the police officer that I belong here? I focus on my breath. I take in the magenta color of my dog's leash. I turn my head slowly to get a glimpse of the car.

Eventually, the window of the police car rolls up and the car moves on. I am grateful. I am angry. I am alive. When I get home, I post about this incident on my Facebook page. I need my friends to tell me I'm okay. I need them to assure me that incident was not. In responses, one gentleman encourages me not to "make any assumptions" because "who knows why the police car paused." My Facebook friend further posits that it could have been because I matched the appearance of a suspect or the officer may have "had a pebble stuck under his foot." Later when I meet with a group of friends, I'm again encouraged to give the officer the benefit of the doubt. I get the message. It's not the police. It's you, Tamara. You are being paranoid. Paranoid or not, I am scared. For the next several months, I ensure that I have my ID with me for every walk around my neighborhood.

***

I'm participating in a wilderness photography workshop in Glacier National Park. Around the campfire, one of the participants raises the question of who was camping for the first time. No one raises their hand.

"I came late to camping," I offer.

It's true. I'd camped once when I was in middle school and I didn't do it again until moving to Montana in my 30s.

"That's why I want to work with inner city youth," responds one of the participants.

It is quiet for a moment. My heart races. The words "inner city," code for "black and poor," triggers instant anger. I'd just shared with the group that I grew up in Flint, Michigan, a city now known for tainted drinking water,

150

that poisoned thousands of residents, mostly black, with high levels of lead and other toxins.

"I didn't grow up in the inner city," I say. I try not to sound angry, but my whole body shakes. I feel the need to offer many reasons why a person may have had limited exposure to camping. "My parents, like many Blacks, were not campers. Their parents were not campers. Some kids in my schools did camp. Maybe more than I knew or realized, but it didn't seem to be something that the friends I hung out with did. They did music camps, soccer camps, trips abroad and road trips. Not camping."

The woman who made the comment looks down at the fire. After a moment of silence, another white woman admits that she began camping later in life. She acknowledges that it hadn't been a family affair for her, either.

My response is not completely accurate. It obscures a certain truth. The first five and a half years of my life were spent in Flint's inner city. During this time, I had one of my first encounters with police. A policeman escorted me from my school to my home for a period of time because, unknown to me, I was in danger. My family moved from our inner city neighborhood after our home was burned down by one of our Black neighbors—a fact that is painful to acknowledge.

***

My father worked for GM, and my mother was a nurse. With their jobs and help from my grandmother, in first grade they purchased the nicest home they could—complete with a white picket fence. It was a neighborhood of business executives, school teachers, college professors, factory workers, small business owners, and nurses. We were the second Black family in our neighborhood. The schools my brother and I attended were 93% white. My mother had moved us from the inner city into suburbia after determining that where the white children were going offered her children any sort of guarantee of a way out of poverty.

Now, I live in Missoula. A city approximately 89% Caucasian. Hispanics comprise the next largest population with 3.5%. Native Americans make up 2.4%, and African Americans fewer than 1%.

White people have surrounded me since I was six years old. It began in primary school, continued through graduate school and in to my work and where I've chosen to live. White people surround me, and often I feel like an intruder. I'm the person perceived as a threat. What will the brown skinned person (who also has a haircut usually worn by Black men) do? It seems subconscious. It also seems conscious. They weren't exposed to enough Black people so they are afraid. It is my job to make them feel safe.

***

The car slowed to a stop beside me. The driver leaned in my direction. "Are you a professional dog walker?" I want to look around, confused as to why she would be asking me. But she wasn't the first person. A year before, two older white women walking on the same block also asked if I was a professional dog walker. Apparently, it seemed like I might be there to help take care of the dogs of white families.

151

I wanted to ask: "Are you a professional car driver?" Instead, I told them that I was not.

"Do you know how I might find a professional dog walker?" She asked.

"No," I replied.

***

In June of 2017, an impromptu Black Lives Matter rally is happening today. My girlfriend told me about it and I felt that I needed to participate. I needed to confront the part of me that has feared being visible, the potentially negative consequences of speaking up and speaking out. A small group, approximately 15 people, have shown up on the Higgins Street Bridge near Caras Park. My girlfriend is there, and so is my good friend, J. The organizer, a young white woman, begins a tearful explanation of why we are marching. I don't connect to her tears, because I get a sense that the brutality Blacks have suffered at the hands of the police is not something she connects to. Instead, it seems like just another peace march that she organizes and that Black Lives Matter is a theme that fits the moment. Protest signs display the names of some of the Black people who've died as a result of police violence. My friend J notices that the name of Eric Garner is spelled incorrectly. He informs the organizer. He repeats this a couple of times before she finally responds.

"Is it?" she asks.

Eventually, she looks up the spelling of Garner's name using her smartphone. A new sign is made.

Our group of 15 people march from the Higgins Bridge to the sculpture of red XXXs at the north end of Higgins Avenue. During the half mile walk, a chant is attempted, but then it falls quiet. This is not the Seattle march I had witnessed.

***

I am delighted to have dinner with another close friend, a friendship I cherish. During the dinner conversation, my friend recounts a Chris Rock special, in which he proclaimed that some Black people are niggers. My friend, who is not Black, repeats this again. "It's true, right? Some Black people are niggers." She laughs, and looks to me for agreement. No. No. No, I say on the inside. On the outside, I force a smile.

***

A couple of months later, on a hazy Sunday afternoon, I arrive downtown at the XXXs at Circle Square once again. There's already more than 100 people gathered, and the crowd swells to more than 200. The event is billed as a "Solidarity March with Charlottesville, Virginia." 32-year-old Heather Heyer, was killed while she participated in a protest against a white supremacist rally. The white supremacists were rallying against the removal of a statue of confederate general, Robert Edward Lee.

At this Missoula rally, there's a palpable buzz in the air. I'm aware that this event is much larger than the last. I feel a mix of disappointment and shame—disappointment that the Black Lives Matter march wasn't better attended and shame for comparing the Black Live Matter March to this

152

Solidarity March. I can't help but think that just marching for Black lives is not enough to draw a crowd. In the Solidarity March, we honor Heather Heyer, a white woman, and Native Americans. I understand the inclusion of Native Americans, because they are often silenced. I am also aware that there is a history of prejudice between Blacks and Native Americans that complicates things. But what right do I have to feel anything? Say anything?

The march organizer is the founder of Missoula Rises, an activist group. Her smile is warm, if not overly effusive. Shortly after I arrive, she walks over to me to introduce herself. We shake hands.

The rally begins as the Missoula Rises founder recounts the events in Charlottesville, thanking all of us for being present. She speaks about the white majority, of which she is a part, and their responsibility to speak up. Eventually, two Native Americans, Lauren Small-Rodriguez and her partner, Dustin Monroe, speak about the racism that their family and many Native Americans experience in Montana.

Finally, we march.

The march organizer addresses me: "What do we want to chant?"

"Black lives matter," I say. My stomach tightens as I hear myself say this.

"That goes without saying," she replies, as if my response was silly.

I want to tell her that those words were not chanted at the last event I attended—an actual Black Lives Matter rally. But I remain silent.

"Who wants to be at the front? Who wants to lead the chants?" She looks directly at me.

I feel too visible. I shake my head, uncomfortable, vulnerable. She asks the question again. I glance at my girlfriend, standing beside me, and drift back to the middle of the marchers.

A few days later, my girlfriend tells me that my picture is in the Missoula Independent. They've done an article on the march. In the picture, I'm punching the air. My eyes are closed, my face is tilted downward, and my mouth is open. I'm in the middle of chanting something I know to be true.

"Black lives matter."

*Making the Men*
Leisa Greene

After the turn of the Millennium, during the inhospitable part of winter when snow blows sideways and the ground is frozen, we moved to Grass Valley Drive.

Earlier that fall, Wayne enters our trailer park doublewide with an excitement in his eyes I've seen only once before—when we traveled all the way to Seattle's Safeco field to watch the Mariners play. This time, however, it is at the prospect of buying land. Our friend bought ten acres of prime Montana land, dividing it up into two five-acre plots. One is for our family if we want it.

"We can do this, Leisa. It's beautiful out there," Wayne gushes. "Let's go check it out."

I glance down at our year and a half old daughter, Jalynn, as I consider it. She has been spending her day making a Lego cake in my oven while our sons, Dustin and Michael, are in school. It's a typical fall day in Missoula; chilly and filled with the smell of dead leaves, cut grass, and burning slash piles. I squeeze snugly into my XXXL pullover jacket and put Jalynn in a thick, pink zip-up fleece. Sweat beads down the back of my winter coat while I wrangle her into the car seat.

The rough dirt road to Grass Valley makes the car ride slow and laborious. Wayne drives carefully in order to avoid pothole damage to a tire or the underside of the car. Our active daughter falls asleep and I lean back to enjoy the peace.

Wayne crosses a section of railroad tracks and heads up a steep bluff. We reach the top and are greeted by flatland filled with knapweed. He makes a left turn on to Grass Valley Drive, close to the site of the old drive-in theatre. I spy a hay field with a rusted, singlewide metal trailer parked in front. I'm relieved when we don't head up the tire-trenched driveway. Outside of Wayne's window is a newer, forest-green doublewide, shrubs around the base and a built-on porch. As the road curves, we drive towards the railroad tracks again. Reluctance starts to build in my mind at the sight of it. We slow at a metal trailer missing a section of siding, rotting two by fours on display. Wayne grins and cranes his head toward the land.

"This is it!" he chirps as we get out of the car. This is so unlike him that I find myself scrutinizing his face while he points out the distant city and our five-acre boundaries.

"The old trailer can be removed. I know it's by the railroad tracks, but we'll get used to that. We can buy a new trailer, or move the old one. Doesn't matter."

The wind is blowing hard where we stand. Our plot perches on top of a bluff, no trees or mountains to block the wind or even slow it down. Breathing deeply, Wayne faces the gale and hovers one foot over the wild grass, pushing the tall tips aside with his boot. "It's beautiful, isn't it?"

I stare at the side of his face incredulously. He's taking in what he thinks is beauty. "Are you serious?" I can't help but laugh.

He gazes at the tall, dry grasses as if they are lush and green, and the knapweed as if it is wild lupine. Wayne squeezes my arm, "Come on, honey, you'll get used to it. Just think- no neighbors right outside our door." He lifts his arms. His flannel shirt strains at the shoulders. "Look at all this space."

Space? I already feel like I take up so much of it, isolated in my large body. I feel outcast. I'm used to living in our little trailer park with close neighbors. The only solace I find in my isolation is being around people. I crave the sharing of days, babysitting each other's children, or catching a moment of easy connection, even the bad jokes. The ability to give a nod across the driveway to another human being, to help them unload their car of groceries.

Not only that, but I have a strong urge to be liked and accepted in my large body. Loved. I want to be adored, and I can't have that if people aren't around. Space away from people is what Wayne wants.

\*\*\*

To Wayne, home was a potato farming and ranching community in Shelley, Idaho. His father rented land to run the potato farm and worked it for twenty years, until it finally broke him. After that, his father took a job with the county, doing weed control. Wayne's Popeye muscles appeared after he landed his first job, milking cows at a local dairy farm twice a day. He learned how to move pipe and drive a tractor before he was ten, and his family raised enough of their own chickens to feed the family. After purchasing and caring for the chicks, they were butchered and frozen, as soon as they were full grown.

Four months after our wedding, the family expected me to help butcher and clean the chickens, their version of a family activity. I stood at the sink, stripping off what remained of the feathers and pulling the skin off the meat. The meat was strangely warm. I watched out the window with a growing unease while I worked, gazing towards the coop where his family grabbed the birds and chopped their throats.

\*\*\*

We close the sale on the property in January of 2000, in the midst of the Y2K scare. People think computers will crash, electronic transfers of money will be lost, and the economy might collapse. We're required to wait a week for everything to die down before signing the official closing documents.

We can't upgrade to the lumber house I wanted, but we do go from a tin trailer to a manufactured home. Picking out my own decor alleviates some of my disappointment. I choose all the carpet colors and cabinet styles. Curtains and a sunken tub become discussions around the dinner table. The boys and I decide that a blue semi-shag carpet is clearly Montana Vogue.

We spend that first winter of the millennium on our purchased five acres in a new manufactured home set on a cement foundation. Even though it is a trailer, it's much larger than our precious home, and all three children have their own bedroom. Our new home has a family room and best of all, two bathrooms. It's a good size for a growing Mormon family.

*** 

It's an April weekend morning, and we've lived in the home four months. Early spring has rolled out a long, wet, and muddy welcome mat. The soil is sticky clay, rocks seem to grow out of the ground. Our master bedroom window faces the desolation, as well as a large power pole facing east. My new habit is to sleep as much as possible, whenever possible. I doze blissfully until 8 A.M., until Wayne enters the bedroom and opens the window. A cold breeze falls on my face, and I roll aside to avoid it. Wayne is insistent.

"Leisa, wake up. Listen."

I rub my eyes blearily and then push myself up with both hands. "What are you—"

"Shhh, just listen." Wayne displays a half smile when mischievous, and he pulls me toward the window, throwing his arm around me. "It's the first meadowlark song of the season."

It's the first time I've ever heard a meadowlark sing. The clear, melodic, quick notes are the kind I wish I had learned to play on my flute when I was eight. I feel each note serenading me. Songs emerge from his round, yellow belly, hovering in the air, as he perches on top of the power pole. Singing.

*** 

The grasslands blossom with a vibrant green after the spring rains, filled with wild hyacinth, wild bergamot, and heartleaf arnica. One afternoon in early June, Wayne sends the boys outside to pick rocks to pile them on our parking area. Our swiftly growing rock pile is directly below the meadowlark's perch. Wayne and the boys slam rocks into the wagon, one by one, and pull the wagon to empty it. By the time they drag the wagon back, it seems as if more rocks have already appeared. This is their project that first spring, laboring day after day on the rock harvest.

In the living room with Jalynn, I fold laundry, and hear the boys bickering outside. I turn my eyes out the front room window.

Dustin is working hard, his lips pinched. I pause and wonder if it's sweat or tears that bleed down his cheeks. My eldest son has the wheelbarrow, yet won't move it. He prefers to stroll to the rocks and carry them back to the barrel. Sometimes, Dustin walks a long distance each way only to gather dust on his knee-high socks.

Michael, on the other hand, works smart. The scar above his eyebrow disappears in the creases on his forehead, as he sizes up the task. Short-statured, he decides to take the blue iron wagon with him everywhere he goes, picks up all the rocks in the immediate vicinity, and tosses them straight into the wagon.

Wayne stops to supervise their work.

"Come on Dustin! Work faster! At your pace, we'll never finish," Wayne

156

hollers and wipes his forehead with his sleeve. He walks back to the shed, leaving the boys to their work.

Through the window, I hear Dustin's voice growing angrier, and then murmuring as he walks back to the wagon. Michael feeds off this, and huffs as he throws another rock in the wagon, so hard it nearly cracks.

***

The weather turns torrid too early in the season. The wild grasses grow dry and brittle as fast as the heat comes. I head outside to meet Wayne, his face pinched, upset and dwelling.

The well isn't pumping enough water to keep the grass seed wet. The well pumps at six gallons a minute, but Wayne needs ten times that. The first sign of the water table rests 240 feet below us. Wayne's vision of green, lush grass now seems impossible. The soil is mostly clay, the topsoil inadequate, and won't produce without water.

My husband pulls the round cement top off the cistern and climbs in, but is quickly distracted by a small frog. He calls to the kids to come take a look. As they pass it back and forth, I wonder how it can survive here.

"I guess the frog knows where to go when things are dry," Wayne explains as he takes the creature from Dustin's hand. "He's a smart one. Let's put him back in, he'll live."

That little frog renews Wayne's hope to make something green and lush out of the land. However, my own hopes evaporate in the arid heat.

***

My fears encompass more than our lack of water. Leah, my best Mormon friend, makes her daily call to me. She is gossipy, but I admire her athletic ability and smarts. After we discuss the church gossip of the Frenchtown Ward, she changes subjects to our sons and their Boy Scouts troop. I lean against the window, eating a chocolate chip cookie. I brush the dust off the sill until she launches in. "Leisa, Dustin's different from the other boys."

"Oh?"

"Um, you know. He acts... girly. Some of the other women brought it up in Relief Society."

I pause, mid-bite, staring down at my dusty fingers. Leah fumbles over her words, to trying to find a way to make it easy on me. "What if he's... gay?"

I don't answer her. My heart wants to defend him, but I don't.

I've known for years that Dustin is gay. I knew before the day he came through the door in a blue flowered blanket tied like a dress, donning my high-heeled shoes. He twirled a wand in his hand, singing, "I'm a fairy!"

My brother Brett, visiting at the time, agreed. "Yes, you are!"

I felt shame that day, too.

I glance at the chocolate chip melting onto my finger, my attention drawn back to tense reality. Leah breaks the silence. "We're all wondering— what's in the water to make him so different? I would dig another well."

When he's home, Wayne spends every moment outside. When I'm not busy with the children or church service, I spend my time reading and sleeping.

157

Wayne puts the water on a timer, moving the hose every twenty minutes from spot to spot. He knows exactly when the well shuts down and how long it takes to refill the cistern. Wanting to be involved, I work on a flowerbed by the back door. He sprays knapweed, spreads grass seed, and adds topsoil and fertilizer whenever he can. He moves the rocks that grow out of the ground from watering, and repeats the process, always dragging the boys along. He purchases a riding lawn mower to cut down the wild grass, but the land has become so terribly dry, dust follows him as a chaperone. As soon as he finishes mowing, he resumes dragging hoses, reeking of sweat, gasoline and wild grass.

*** 

Wayne surprises us by building a lifted playhouse from abandoned wood and tin. It's mounted up high, designed as a miniature version of our own home. He attaches a nine-slot ladder that rest on a porch deck protruding out from the front of the playhouse by two feet. He painstakingly constructs railing around the deck. Jalynn, now two, takes great glee in climbing up and down the ladder and playing in the little house. Michael and Dustin concoct make believe games inside, and fill the four walls with their Pokémon fantasies.

Wayne also builds me a raised garden bed; the only way things will grow on our tough land. Raspberry bushes and apple trees, transplanted from his parent's home in Idaho, begin to flourish. He plants seeds: spinach, beans, peas, radishes, and beets. Wayne puts in large tomato plants and more trees.

Before he leaves for work, I'm assigned precise instructions for watering. Soak the trees and the garden early in the morning. Water the back section for twenty-minute intervals, always sure to shut off the water. As soon as he gets home, he waters the front yard. At the close of the day, we water the garden and the trees.

Wayne is persistent and patient. Someday, this land will be what he envisions. If he works painstakingly, it will be what he wants it to be. I question if it's what I want it to be, or if it ever has been.

*** 

Five years later, we argue viciously in the living room. I know what to say that will get to him the most. I know it like an old friend, who stayed with me throughout in this desolate journey to a place I never wanted.

"I can't live in this! I can't live in this goddamn desert!" I sputter, and jab a finger outside, towards withering blades of grass and our sacrificed good intentions.

*No Feet Touching the Floor:*
*The coals and gifts of a scrambled life growing up in Butte,*
*before I turned into a person.*
Claudia Brown

❊

The house that I grew up in still inhabits my dreams. It is the setting of my longest-lived feelings and the ground of my being. My neighborhood was my outer world, a secondary place to my inner world. Born in 1937, my childhood gave me freedom and isolation, loneliness and stories. It gave me compassion and the inclination to look for the long view of things.

Our parents were flapper-era rebels from respectable families, intent on being free from societal restrictions, but imprisoned by their own compulsions. My siblings had lots of personality. My sister, Robin, was the light of my father's life; they loved each other so very much. They had so much fun together. She was vivacious and confident, our Pollyanna. Her version of the truth was inspiring, affirming, disarming. Her truth didn't resemble my truth at all, but she was believed because my family needed it. She faced the difficulties in our family with a survival response that kept hurtful events from affecting her. She was a princess—and later a queen.

Unhappiness owned my mother. When I was nearly five, I went to her in the kitchen as she chopped food at the cutting board. I reached up for a hug. She told me, "Go away! Leave me alone!" The rejection pierced my young heart in a way that remained, convincing me of my unworthiness.

Aloofness was a dominant quality in my mother. She wasn't mean or cruel, but she worked to cover unhappiness. A toss of her head brought her back to the present. She had a pleasant, English-Scottish appearance like her father; glasses, brown eyes with a slant at the outside edges. She often seemed to look beyond the present. A hint of a dimple marked her chin; a smile might appear when inspired. She pretended to hide her unhappiness when she was called upon for a response, except at home with her family. She was book-smart, but daily life threw her for a loop.

My mother would get up at noon, sometimes coming downstairs screaming. We never knew what was the matter; our father took her to the doctor, where she was told to behave herself. Now, we wonder if she was bipolar. My mother and I shared a common escape: daydreaming. People even said I looked like her. I hated her because I thought I would turn out to be like her. Now I ache for my mother, and realize that she was in her own hell.

In the 1940s and 50s, our neighborhood framed a large vacant lot. Among the weeds, butter-and-eggs and foxtails grew, delights for my bouquets. That vacant lot was the gathering place of all the children, perfect for

playing hide-and-seek or kick the can. I can still hear our version of the all's-clear cry echoing in my memory: Allee-allee-olson free!

In the center of the lot was a large excavation covered with boards, the Fox-Hole, dug by the boys—and only for the boys. It housed their World War II fantasies. They shot imaginary German and Japanese soldiers with wooden guns and sticks, and blew up enemies with their explosive voices. I was there, watching, hiding at the edges.

Dust swirled among the weeds on the boulevard in front of our house. A great tree once grew there, gone by the time we reached school age. Several blocks away was our sledding hill, surrounded by little self-made houses and empty fields. Where the Civic Center now stands was an expanse of ground that the circus pitched its tent upon. Copper Creek—our name for Silver Bow Creek—was truly orange. We played on its toxic banks, unaware of potential harm.

We had no curfew except for darkness that got in the way of our play. Emptiness filtered in when other kids were called inside. When we needed a sibling at home, we exercised our lungs from the front door: "BILLYYY!"

Our house, the locus of my inner world, was a mix of old privilege and new poverty.

The front door opened to a strip of bare flooring, its varnish gone. The living room was on the left, dining room directly to the right. Our thread-bare rugs and worn furniture were once elegant, handed down from our parents' more prosperous family homes. The dignity was gone from an ornately carved and scrolled coffee table.

A weighty German stein with a porcelain castle atop its lid sat on a tall uniquely crafted scrapbook table, handed down from our father's father. The table was handmade from exotic Philippine wood with brass inscriptions. It housed museum-quality books of early American etchings and military albums belonging to our grandfather, Louis Peck Sanders, a Spanish-American War officer. Best of all, it contained a photograph album of Filipino torture devices. We poured over these, awe-struck and darkly thrilled. On the opposite wall was a scratched Victorian desk. A large crumbling fossil of a mastodon molar weighed down its corner.

There were secret places in our house. The closet of the downstairs bedroom was beneath the stairs. Christmas presents and undistributed campaign posters for my grandfather Morris and Uncle Ken were hidden within it. Our Grandfather Morris served two terms on the Montana Supreme Court; Uncle Ken ran unsuccessfully for the State Legislature. On the closet shelf above the coats was a book wrapped in brown paper. It was about alcoholism, and I presumed it was sent by my grandmother. When I asked my mother about it, she scolded me. "You are not supposed to be snooping around in this closet! Don't you say a word about it!"

Further along that bedroom wall, we discovered that we could crawl in the underside of the staircase, the framing for the stairs pressing upon us. The room with the closet was not used as a bedroom, but as a pass-through connecting other rooms. This created a circular runway for us when Billy

chased Robin and me around and around the house. The stairs were for play, too; we would bump down on our bottoms, and also use the stairs as grades in our pretend school. The first stair was first grade. When we answered a question correctly from whomever got to be the 'teacher,' we were allowed to move up a grade.

In our glassed-in back porch was an old steamer trunk, left over from our grandparents' travels and our parents' honeymoon. So many intriguing drawers with curious leftovers, including little white boxes of petrified wedding cake, without question, we ate every piece.

Robin and I did our own screaming and cat-fighting. We were the cats, with scratches on our arms from fighting over whose turn it was to hold our baby sister, Lydia. Billy was the dog-fighter, energy run amok. He wrestled me to the floor, straddled me and drummed his fingers into my chest. I was serious and sensitive, fun to torment: "Claudie Bejeanie the Big Fat Weenie!"

One of the games Billy invented was Around-The-House-With-No-Feet-Touching-The-Floor. Starting on top of the kitchen table, we leapt to the door frame and swung around to the stairs. After that, a careening leap across the banister and a jump to the dresser. One long stretch to pounce one foot on a doorknob, the other foot reaching for the opposite doorknob, followed by a final swing into the living room. We leapt from one piece of furniture to the next, shimmying around the archway frame and rappelling from the open front door to the dining table.

Robin tried leaping and swinging from the chandelier, but dropped when the ceiling plaster cracked. The challenge was to make that final leap to the kitchen door and swing as it closed, leaping onto the stove. It was usually on a Saturday, while our parents were still in bed.

At night, we put on a variety show for Mother and Daddy, to prolong the evening, so we could get out of going to bed. Billy and Robin were naturally boisterous cut-ups. Robin made up a dance, as would I, awkwardly. Billy recited Robert Service poems:
"...The Northern Lights have seen queer sights,
But the queerest they ever did see
Was that night on the marge of Lake Lebarge
I cremated Sam McGee."
Mother and Daddy's amusement encouraged encores. When television began to pop up into people's lives, our father made it a priority to purchase one. It dominated our evenings.

My mother loved to recite poetry. When we came home from school, she would often be leaning against the stove, smoking, and singing:
"A capital ship on an ocean trip
Was the Walloping Window Blind...
And also reciting,
Abu Ben Adem, may his tribe increase
Awoke one night from a deep dream of peace...."
At night, she took us into her bed and read to us. The book Christopher Robin belonged to us exclusively, because the sign on the tree where Winnie

161

the Pooh lived had our last name, Sanders. My sister's name was Robin, and we called our baby sister Pooh.

Evenings were a satisfying time for our mother. Once when there was no food for dinner, she created a party with delicious, cinnamon-sugar 'pie crust cookies.' She was a skilled oral reader, and passed that on to us. Before Lydia was born, Mother tucked us in and plumped the pillows around our heads. To me, she whispered, "You're my lady-baby."

The Presbyterian minister, Reverend Logee, came to visit one day. He told us that God Is Love. I considered his message, but everyday life did not fit with his pronouncement. Where was God's love for me? It felt like a betrayal, a promise unmet. I considered myself to be a Martha, someone who washed pots and pans in the kitchen and complained. Robin was like a Mary. I loved the Sunday school singing. In my heart lived a melody, but my experiences did not fit Presbyterian Sunday School theology. Later, I came to realize that my faith is in forgiveness. For my parents, for my family—and for myself.

What I did know to be true was an ineffable experience in my backyard. When I was five years old, I made mud pies decorated with dandelion suns and asparagus seeds. It was a warm summer day, sunlight enveloping me with the aroma of mud and green, satisfying muddy slickness squishing in my hands.

Suddenly, in that one moment, all boundaries melted away. All existence was the light, no girl form, no edges, all inhabited by the cosmos. Anointed. The universe cracked open and gave me a gift. No words or human thought, simply an existential luminous moment.

I went inside in a daze and told no one. There were no words to say.

Throughout my life, I have gone back to that moment. It left me wondering, unwilling to give it a limit of human definition. With time, I've come to relate that moment with what I am called to do; to face what is happening to the earth: glaciers disappearing, oceans polluted and rising. The air we breathe becoming polluted and heating. Animals, plants, and insects disappearing. I accept that luminous gift by believing in mystery beyond our limited minds, believing now in love, respecting Creation by acting to heal the earth.

## She Went Up In Flames
### Lisa Hunt

My husband staggered into bed, awakening me. Sour breath reeked in my face. His naked body crawled over mine, hands groping. He yanked down my pants.

"Get the hell away from me!" I shoved him off and shot out of bed. To avoid the usual drunken confrontation, I stormed down the hallway to our apartment-sized kitchen. Slamming cupboards open and closed, I fixed a bowl of cereal. Like a robot, I sat down at the table to eat. Milk sloshed from my spoon with every bite.

Hoping Mike had passed out on our bed, my thoughts raced to our 18-month-old son, Zac, asleep in his own room. I must keep him safe.

Suddenly, my husband appeared in the kitchen. He stumbled across the room, rummaging through the cabinets. He grabbed a saucepan from the cupboard as if to cook an early morning breakfast.

Instead, he turned and slammed it into the back of my head.

I opened my eyes, flat on the floor. Mike stood above me, the saucepan still in his raised hand. Instinctively, I kicked, and he toppled over. I pinned his neck to the washing machine with my foot. Adrenaline pumped through my veins. Blood gushed from my wound.

"I'm so sorry," Mike slobbered. His voice gasped. Reluctantly, I removed my foot from his neck, releasing him. "Here, take this." He offered a dirty towel from the laundry basket, shoved it towards me. I slapped his hand away, dismissing him in silent disgust.

I forced myself up and rushed to the bathroom. Standing in the shower, the water flowed red down my body. Blood pooled in the drain. Steam filled the room. I trembled as terrible thoughts tripped through my head.

When I emerged from the bathroom, Mike had cleaned up the mess in the kitchen. He also had cut the phone cord.

With a calmness I didn't recognize, I handed him four sleeping pills.

"Take these, and we'll talk in the morning," I said, as gently as I could, and then waited for him to pass out.

\*\*\*

My seven year-old son Zac and I drive north on Highway 93. We are traveling from our home in Missoula, to visit family in Troy. As we approach the town of Arlee on the Flathead Indian Reservation, cars and trucks litter the powwow grounds. Being of Native American descent, and feeling summoned by a force greater than myself, I pull in.

Zac and I meander towards the pavilion. Beautiful harmonies wash over us like spiritual rain. Inside the earthen floor arena, hundreds of Native people sway rhythmically to the music. Sweet vocals and acoustic guitar accompany the pulsing beat of the drums. I squeeze my son's hand. He appears equally mesmerized.

A friend in the crowd recognizes us. "Lisa! Zac!" She shouts. and maneuvers her way towards us, embracing my son. "I can't believe you're here." She looks at me, surprised. I am the last person she would expect to see at a Native American revival. I have never believed in Christianity.

Today, I feel an uplifting presence I didn't know I was missing.

A tall Native American man welcomes us. He speaks of the peace available from a loving God. He speaks of redemption—of finding the ability to leave behind a life of pain and uncertainty. He speaks of unconditional love - we do not need to feel lost and alone. He welcomes us into a relationship with the Creator and His son, Jesus.

Weeping, I fall to my knees in surrender. I realize I am still living a life constantly searching for a means of escape. For the first time, a deliverance is being offered.

The pastor invites all who feel weary or empty to come forward and receive the love of Christ in our hearts. A hand touches my shoulder. I look up and see Zac, with tears in his eyes.

"Mom, let's go up there."

*Luck*
Jaimie Alexis Stathis

The first time I visited Missoula, I arrived at night and woke up in the morning to find my car missing. I'd spent the summer in Oregon and was heading back to college in upstate New York. My high school buddy, Eddie, needed a lift back to Missoula and I welcomed a reliable co-pilot. On my westbound trip at the beginning of the summer, two armed men had rushed into my motel room on the outskirts of Chicago. One held a gun to my head while the other ransacked the room, looking for cash or anything that could be sold in a hurry. They took nothing, and I was physically unharmed. I was lucky.

I thought I'd already paid my dues, and couldn't believe my stupidity in leaving my car—loaded up with most of what I owned, and two bikes strapped to the hatchback—overnight on a city street. The scenario was typical for college kids: we arrived late, went to a party, had more than a few drinks, and left the car for the night. The university neighborhood seemed a safe enough place to leave a car, but when Eddie and I biked back in the morning, lattes balanced in our other hands, the car was clearly not where I'd left it.

Growing up in and around New York City, I was taught to take certain precautions.

At the top of the list was to never keep anything of value visible in a car. New York was more dangerous and crime riddled in the 1980s and 90s than it is now; most of the cars that were parked on the street had "the club" or a similar anti-theft device. Some people taped handwritten signs in their car windows: "Nothing to take. Everything already stolen" or "Car unlocked. Please don't break window." Glove boxes and center consoles were left open, just to prove there was nothing of value inside the vehicle. It wasn't uncommon to see a guy on the street corner hawking a car stereo with a cluster of wires dangling out the back along with an umbrella, a half-used liter of motor oil, and a box of Kleenex. Folks carried pullout stereos around like purses and wouldn't dare leave so much as an exposed shopping bag in the backseat, even if it held nothing more than old newspaper. New Yorkers don't leave much to chance.

But this was Montana. It was safe, right? Eddie saw the dread on my face, the escalating panic that moved in on me like a hot date. He lit a Marlboro and casually glanced up and down the block.

"Welcome to Missoula," Eddie said through a laugh. "They probably just towed it around the corner."

It was hard not to be smitten on the spot with a town that gives "courtesy tows" on street-sweeping days, but I also fell in love with the way that Missoula introduced me to all the possibilities of life, manners of being I hadn't even known were options.

We walked all over town and never looked over our shoulders. We ate huckleberry pancakes by day and drank whiskey by night. We spent hours in bookstores and left with arms piled clear to our chins. We stopped at every playground. After finding the delicate balance on the teeter totters or spinning each other silly on the merry-go-round, we pumped our legs on the swings to see who could fly higher, though the best was when we fell into sync.

We hiked up a craggy trail named Sleeping Woman to a peak with 360-degree views and a Salish name that translates into "shining." We ran whitewater, fished poorly, skinny dipped and re-created a few unfortunate scenes from *A River Runs Through It*. We softened into the ancient hot springs that nestle into a ridge a steep, 1,000-foot climb from the parking area. The springs are just above the site of an old gold mine and not far from where Meriwether Lewis became the first white man to cross the Continental Divide. There is a history of prospecting and exploring on that ridge. There is life and death in that canyon.

The pools cascaded from a notch that felt both haunted and blessed, and the waterfall inside the cave felt like a 100-handed massage. The sound of the pounding water in that cave was loud enough to drown out even the loudest existential questions: Where is home? Where do I belong? Why am I here?

*** 

I was supposed to stay a night or two in Missoula, but our first date lasted almost a week. Staying longer than intended—the sign of most successful first dates—meant I had only two days to drive across the country in order to make it back to New York in time for my classes. I'd also fallen back in love. On the final morning, I slinked away before dawn from both Eddie and Missoula. The sun came up as I crested Homestake Pass and blinded my teary eyes that didn't quit overflowing until I hit Billings.

I slid cassette tapes into my car's stereo and listened to Wallace Stegner's voice tell me about western landscapes and belonging—to them, for them, with them. I come from a long line of deeply rooted New Yorkers, and Stegner's collection of essays on place sounded revolutionary to my ears, as I didn't know if I was running away or running toward. As a self-described tumbleweed, it turns out I felt more at home among western prairies and mountains than the well-worn hills of my childhood, though I occasionally longed for those softer lines and return to them only to find myself bouncing back to the West. After a few more decades of circling about, I accumulated enough experiences in order to comprehend that Stegner's collection of essays is transcendent and timeless because it evokes everything we were and will always be. It speaks to our senses, honors generational memory, and encourages tribal connection.

For the next five years, I visited Missoula regularly. I didn't think of it as a place to live until I'd moved back and forth across the country a couple more times and realized there aren't many places that could top the quality of life. Missoula had been so good to me on vacations, yet I wasn't sure how we'd fare in a long-term relationship, the one that eventually becomes mundane. The kind that wants to know what's for dinner and if anyone paid the car insurance and why it's still snowing in June.

When I started to consider Missoula as home, I was newly-divorced, directionless, and exhausted. I was only 26, but felt ancient. I narrowed it down to two options:

1) Move to Manhattan, continue working in finance.
2) Move to Missoula, see what happens.

I'm a fourth generation New Yorker and worried that if I grew my own, adult-sized roots in the city, I might never leave. I feared being stuck more than I feared actual fear. Missoula seemed like a good place to reclaim my youth, live closer to the bone, explore my limits. I told Eddie that I was ready to consider the possibility of our dreams coming true, together.

I felt prepared for life in Montana. I'd read my Annick Smith, my Gretel Ehrlich, my Terry Tempest Williams. I knew how women in the west survived and I wanted to be among them. On New Year's Eve 2000, I left New York in the rearview mirror and showed up in Missoula with two duffel bags and a round-trip plane ticket. I considered the return ticket like a ripcord only to be used in the case of an extreme emergency. I had a high tolerance for emergency, a resilience waiting to bloom.

From the start, life in Missoula wasn't how I'd pictured. More often than not, Eddie felt like a stranger to me. I kept a picture of us from boarding school on our refrigerator as a reminder of who we'd been. Most people didn't recognize him and asked, "Is that your brother?" In the photo we're walking across the quad right after graduation. I'm in a white dress and he's wearing a tie but removed his dark green blazer. We have our arms around each other's waists and I'm somehow both falling away from and turning toward him.

I'd imagined our life would be more wholesome, more Montana. I pictured it like the scenes in the books I'd read, that we'd be like the couple who rescues a cabin trapped behind vinyl siding for 40 years. We'd restore the cabin and then raise kids and vegetables and occasionally the roof. Sometimes, we'd drive scary stretches of black ice, but together we'd be safe. Maybe we'd be like the monkey-wrenchers or Earth Firsters—we'd be stewards of the land and advocates for the animals. We were both raised in the suburbs, but I thought maybe we'd become the folks who whipstitch journals for Christmas presents from hides they tanned themselves, from elk they walked through thigh-deep snow to hunt. Maybe.

At the very least, I envisioned Eddie and I doing the things we'd done on our trips to Alaska or Oregon and during my visits to Montana. I saw us curled up on a couch, passing a book back and forth as we read chapters

aloud to each other, underlining our favorite parts. We'd drink cocoa, sometimes spike it, stay in bed all day on a Sunday. I imagined us summiting peaks, soaking in hot springs, laughing our asses off.

I thought we'd do the simple things—the aspects of life so guaranteed they don't require promises—planning meals, gathering ingredients at farmers' markets, sharing a single bottle of wine as we prepared and ate dinner over candlelight with cloth napkins. Sometimes steak, sometimes rice and beans.

He'd teach me to kayak. We'd cross country ski into Forest Service cabins or fire lookouts. I'd write our beautiful love story. We did some of it. Then Ed told me that most of that stuff was for chumps. Life was stressful and our ends were frayed.

Eddie went to jail for 45 days over a petty weed crime. It wasn't a long sentence, but it might have been life changing. He was stressed. I climbed thousands of feet to the top of Mount Sentinel every morning in semi-successful efforts to restore my sanity. I felt a little like a woman struck by lightning alone in her pasture, crawling her way to safety. Our life in Missoula turned out to be more about loud diesel pickups, velour sweatsuits, and popping bottles of Cristal at noon on a Tuesday.

At the turn of the last century, Missoula still had a punk club over a laundromat. Eddie had a fun habit of chucking himself over the bar, though his signature move was technically more of a pole-vault. One minute he'd be standing there aggrandizing one story or another, and the next he'd be flying over the bar with a flat back, taking out customers' drinks while burning flesh and fabric with the cigarette that perpetually dangled out of his mouth. He was fun, funny, and exhausting.

Most nights we went out together, though I frequently woke up alone because Eddie had passed out on the couch on his way to bed or because he hadn't come home at all. I'd wanted to reclaim my youth when I moved to Missoula—giving up spreadsheets and shiny pamphlets, Jackie O. sheath dresses with vice-like jackets, weekly mani pedis—but all-night parties every night of the week were more of a throwback than I'd expected. Some would say the move was a mistake. That would be putting it politely.

The first year or so in Missoula, I cycled through jobs because I found it challenging to keep one among all the chaos around me, but in September, 2001, I started teaching in a Montessori school. I felt grounded and happy as I regained my independence.

One morning, I woke up early and turned on the television. This was how lonely people kept themselves company before smart phones. We lived in a railroad-style apartment, and as I made my way back to the living room with coffee and an English muffin, I had a view of the TV screen. I've never been a fan of films with car chases, shootouts, or violence, and I cringed at the sight of the stupid movie trailer that played during the Today Show's commercial break. What kind of barbarian would make a film where planes fly into the Twin Towers? It took a minute to recognize it as news.

On the morning of September 11th, I'd lived in Missoula for 36 weeks, not quite the gestation period for a human, but long enough inside the womb

for life to be viable. Even before the attacks, I felt myself becoming whole in ways I couldn't have anticipated, in part because my first nine months in Missoula had been anything but easy. I felt I was being broken down, not building strength. While I was living it, I saw no correlation between the books I'd read about women thriving in the west and what I was actually experiencing. 20 years later, I can see that the path to self-actualization is not separate from the path that tests our edges, and stresses our seams.

I sat on the living room floor that morning, trying to call my family in New York, but the lines were overloaded. My coffee and muffin became cold and hard. As I sat there, alone on the splintery wood floors, something shifted. I wondered if my bad decision had in fact saved my life. If I'd chosen Manhattan over Missoula, there's a decent chance I wouldn't have been alive that morning.

In that moment, it became clear to me that home is less a point on a map and more of a deep sensation of belonging. Home is not an address, not a point on a map. Home is something that exists inside of me.

Eventually, I got a call through to my mother. It might have been hours. It might have been well into the afternoon. The sun might have moved behind the apartment. It was the kind of day where time suspends and the ways we usually measure our days lose meaning.

## Menacing Rack
### Kelley Provost

I was walking into *The Lion King* on London's West End when I found out that I had cancer.

***

We planned our trip to Europe for months. Me and my family were going to be gone exactly thirty days and had plans to hit London, Paris and then Spain. My cousin had a house on the Mediterranean, so he and his family had invited us to spend time with them in their beautiful villa. I had a to-do list a mile long:
—Manicure/pedicure
—Call post office to hold mail
—Groom Lola
—Earplugs
—Buy trashy magazines
—Earplugs
—Get mole on upper thigh checked
—Get armpits waxed
—Lose 20 lbs
—Mammogram
—Earplugs
When I had that mammogram, I had just turned 40. I had not quite made it halfway home from the imaging facility when I was phoned back. They wanted to look closer.

I returned to the office visibly shaken, but oddly interested. I liked attention. I was excited, yet mildly terrified—and honestly, that's how I lived my life. The radiologist did his magic, showed me the clear image of a lump and sent me over to a surgeon.

At this point, the thrill was gone. The very real fact that I had two little boys was starting to make me perspire. Which I hate, because it messes with my hair. I met with Dr J, who was adorable and kind, petite with warm features. She knew her business.

"I don't like the looks of this mass," she said. "It's too far down in the breast to biopsy, so I'm going to take it out." This suspicious lump's eviction leads to a lumpectomy. I recall having that plummeting boulder hit my stomach; who else do I tell?

I told my husband, my sister and my mom right away. I needed support. I was going to go under general anesthesia for this procedure, which excited me. As a recovering drug addict, I took what I could get. An added "perk"

was that the darned lump was located near the chest wall; in order to locate it precisely, they were going to have to stick a needle through the breast. They offered me Valium for this portion of the fun, but I foolishly turned it down. Cute little Dr. J sliced into my right breast, located the mass, took it out and sent it to a lab who the hell knows where. Relief came when she called me on a Saturday morning to tell me it was benign.

I'm going to fill you in on a little secret—my boobs have been trying to kill me for years. In the 7th grade, I was starting to looked less like Opie from The Andy Griffith Show and more like Molly Ringwald. I got my braces off. The only thing missing was something to fill the bra I was wearing purely for a hidden decoration. I got my wish seemingly overnight, as I grew from an A to a D cup, which left deep, purple stretch marks. I started high school stacked. I never felt comfortable at how large they were for my little frame.

This began the years of thick bra straps. They left me with huge, deep grooves at the top of my shoulders. I hid my bra from my dates and even my girlfriends. I always had five hooks. I dreamed of a tiny, cute cotton bra with flowers on it. Maybe a front closure, or even just two hooks.

There were no trips to Victoria's Secret. There were no sassy, colorful straps. I was forced to wear a bikini because I needed an extra-extra large top even though I wore an extra-small bottom. Many people piped up when I'd lament.

"I'd take some!"

"I'd kill for your chest!"

They had no idea that when I unfurled those bad boys that they would graze my navel. I looked at least twenty pounds heavier in clothes because of my ample chest. I am very aware of how vain all of this sounds and it is: I was five foot five, weighed one hundred and five pounds, but, ten of those were fatty, flabby breast tissue. It's a wonder I never tipped over.

During and after pregnancy, my breasts were a sheer horror. They swelled to a size K. You can't buy that in stores. In Dillard's, I tried on bras and wept in the dressing room.

"Can I help you, ma'am?" the nice lady with the normal sized breasts queried.

"No!" I sobbed in return. You could have fit a bowling ball in my bra cup. I was hormonal, and deeply concerned that my tits were going to be bigger than my baby. Eventually, that fetus finally grew and protruded past my engorged breasts. I was so relieved when people noticed my baby bump rather than my lady lumps.

I hounded my insurance company for a breast reduction. They required me to do nine months of physical therapy instead. I jumped through all the hoops, but still they kept turning me down. I even started running. Let me tell you something. Running with a large chest is not only uncomfortable— it's dangerous and painful.

I bled. A lot. My skin was raw under my breasts, at my shoulders where the straps laid, and under my armpits. It stung when I'd get in the shower. In 2015, I trained for the whole 26.2 miles of the Missoula Marathon. I had

done a half-marathon the summer before and lived to tell about it, so I genuinely wanted to push myself and my hefty chesty to the finish line.

On our 18 mile training run, I was absolutely battered. Walking and beaten. I could see my friend's husband sweetly waving me in. Almost there. A bee flew down my shirt, and I ripped it off so violently and quickly that I pulled a muscle in my neck.

"You're bleeding," someone announced. I hadn't noticed the man fiddling with his sprinkler right near my traumatic battle with the bee. He pointed to my upper midsection. Blood trickled down my chest. I had ran so far in the heat that my scabbed, raw skin was bleeding.

I went straight to my doctor's office and had him take pictures of everything: The stooped shoulders, the bloodied armpits, the carnage of my torso and under-boobs. It looked particularly infected that day, which was perfect. For the first time in a long time, I felt hope. My husband's insurance company had just paid for his coworkers second full knee replacement.

But those bastards denied me again. Even my doctor could believe it. This wasn't about looking cute in a bathing suit. This wasn't about spaghetti-strapped tank tops. This wasn't about strapless prom dresses or never being able to wear a button down shirt. This was about the health of a 42 year-old woman who desperately wanted to run a marathon, realizing that her menacing rack was making that damned near impossible.

They say God has a funny way of doing things, and I suppose that's true. I finally surrendered. Three days later, I got a letter from my insurance company. My case had been reviewed by a third party, and the denial had been overturned.

Surgery went great. I was swollen for a few weeks, with drain tubes snaking out of me and a lot of ace bandages. I knew instantly that it was a vast improvement. A million times smaller. A million times more likely I could finally wear a cute little two hooked bra.

***

Our flight to London left on July 2nd. Five days before we flew out, I walked into Advanced Imaging and had my routine mammogram. I've never had a normal mammogram; the two years previous both were imaged further because of suspicious scar tissue, but I never raised a brow. I was not afraid or concerned or worried in the least. I even had my two little boys and my mom with me. I had my precious bandeau bikini top on under my clothes, since we'd planned a trip to Splash Montana after this quick ultrasound.

Due to my experience with abnormal mammograms, I didn't bat an eye when he said I'd need to return Monday to get a biopsy for a suspicious mass on my right breast.

"I'm flying out of the country for a month on Sunday, I'll have to do it when I get back in August," I replied. The doctor cast a slow look at his assisting tech. "Cancel the rest of my day."

There was a cosmic shift in the atmosphere. I asked him how long it would take, because I had my family in the waiting room. He suggested they

go on without me. My mom doesn't drive with the kids, so I had to call my sister. She did not like the tone in my voice, but the doctor's tone was no better when he returned.

"When are you coming home from your Europe trip? You might have to either stay behind and join your family later or come home early for treatment," he murmured.

He couldn't tell me anything definitive, but nurses suddenly appeared from out of nowhere and ushered me into a hidden waiting area. I had never seen such fluffy couches, cozy lighting, cookies and soda. What the actual hell? They told me they were sending the samples of my unidentified yet increasingly ominous mass to the lab for biopsy. I slid a small ice pack into my bikini top to replace the sample they'd taken.

I went to the water park anyway, stunned.

That night, my dear husband came up with a plan, for the worst case scenario.

I would go and enjoy as much of our vacation as possible. If I needed to come home immediately for cancer treatment, I could fly out of either Madrid or Paris. I gave my family the luxury of not freaking out, but certainly a part of me did exactly that. I let myself surrender the uncertainty and helplessness. I continued to be open with the people I was closest to and took to heart their sincere well-wishes. I resisted the urge to be resentful at their reactions. "I'm sure it's nothing."

\*\*\*

We flew out July 2nd. My dear friend Anna shuttled our circus to the airport. We were excited and prepared as we could be; the boys oblivious to my personal plight, the cursed tits. At our first layover in Minneapolis, I fought the very real and serious urge to buy a pair of bedazzled Balenciaga sunglasses for $500. "I'm probably dying of cancer" let me feel pretty entitled.

After a long flight, we arrived in London. Jet-lagged, but still jazzed from the excitement, we set off to enjoy our first night on this uncertain vacation. We wouldn't find anything out for a few days, because of the 4th of July holiday. I found myself able to find a rickety balance, somewhere between relaxed and highly anxious.

London was bloody awesome! We took the tube everywhere, minding the gap, visiting the queen at both her "office" (Buckingham Palace) and "the cottage" (Windsor Castle). I had all the fun, ate all the food, and enjoyed each day as if it was my last—while forcing myself to believe it wouldn't be. I ordered tiramisu at every place we dined.

\*\*\*

On July 5th, we are supposed to find out the official news. We keep busy with a full day at the wax museum and head back to our flat to freshen up before the performance of *The Lion King*.

As we primp ourselves, I notice the time. It's 4 o'clock; and I watch as 5 ticks by. We silently sweat bullets, waiting for my phone to ring. It doesn't.

I'm anxious, and I call them instead of waiting. The sweet receptionist is

painfully aware of the news I'm waiting for, and promises she'll call me the second the results come in.

Running late, we eat at McDonald's instead of a fabulous restaurant. After shoveling a sub-par Quarter Pounder down the hatch, we rush to the subway, only to become instantly lost when we exit. All of us adults are stressed, but try to check ourselves for the sake of our little boys, who definitely don't know the gravity of mommy's news. They just want something sweet and a souvenir.

Finally, we ask someone where the theater is. We're just around the corner. As we hurry, the phone rings. We are silent, despite the insane amount of noise on the street. I keep one hand clutching my son while the other puts the phone to my ear. Dr. Frederick Tai, my general practitioner, breaks the news. "You have breast cancer."

I'm sure he was weirded out by my chipper and downright cheerful response.

"Thank you. I suspected so. Listen, we're headed into the theatre now, so thank you again."

Hell, I thought. At least I can sob in the goddamned dark for a few hours.

***

As the first act ended, and the lights went up, I sent for everyone to go potty and get treats. I knew the nurse navigator had the real information I sought: What is the actual diagnosis? How serious and dire was my current situation? While I listened to the message she'd left and memorized the number she'd told me to call, I realized that making it to Spain was my top priority. I was truly grateful at that moment that it was me who had cancer and not someone I love.

I sat outside that majestic theatre in the heart of London, among the chaos of five languages being spoken. I called home to Missoula to speak with her. I hoped to get some good news: Thankfully, I did.

"It's the best kind of breast cancer. It's slow moving, and you wouldn't do any good rushing home. Enjoy your family and vacation. I'll set up appointments for your return."

I returned to my family with the good news, beaming from ear-to-ear. Carrie and Scott had tears in their eyes. We could breathe; we could relax. We finished the evening with a celebratory dessert at the fanciest restaurant we could find. Never before had I looked forward to living so much. What I would find out in the next few days was that I had been diagnosed with Invasive Ductal Carcinoma. They assessed the tumor to be just over one centimeter.

We finished off London with a sushi dinner and the London Eye. We used our passports a second time when we boarded the chunnel for Paris. My husband and I were certain we would be seeing marine life while we were submerged in the tunnel, but seamlessly arrived to our apartment for the week. On the other side of the steel door was a huge courtyard, the lawn and shrubbery beautifully manicured. An oasis hidden in the heart of Paris.

Back to reality, I was able to really see my kids' faces, join in their

experience, and finally participate. I was living in full color with surround sound.

We had a much more relaxed schedule for this leg of the trip, and leisurely found a restaurant where there was not a lick of English spoken. With our limited French (I'm being kind here; I know how to say "eat feces" and "thank you") we ordered dinner, excited and anxious to see what we were actually served. We had steak tartare, tuna tartare, quinoa mint salad. The boys ate bread and french fries.

During the next several days, we hit the Eiffel Tower, The Louvre, and Notre Dame. My sister kneeled at every altar, lit every candle and prayed unabashedly for my health. With my senses heightened and my spirit awakened, we continued to explore and fall deeper in love with the city. Having the stress lifted from my shoulders, I began to truly sink into our vacation just as we headed to our 3rd destination.

In Spain, I truly unwound. My cousin's villa was beautiful, and that was an understatement. Casa De Erika was named for Urs Keller's mother Erika, who had passed away in 2005 from cancer, ironically. Urs's legacy was an amazing home tucked away on a hillside in the vacation community of Moraira. In the wake of my recent shift of perception on life, this was the perfect place to truly unwind.

In the three weeks we stayed in Spain, I never wore a bra.

I went topless on every beach.

*Plentywood*
Pam Truman

After a 12 hour day in the field surveying for oil and gas, I usually spend my evenings alone in my sleazy motel room, lifting weights and working out to the soundtrack from "Flashdance." A collapsible weight bench and barbell always travel with me from town to town. I lug around a mini-fridge, too, so my eating options aren't limited to gas stations.

After my work-out, I guzzle a tall glass of orange juice and slap together a sandwich or toss a quick salad. I dine in my room at a tiny table for one. Then, munching on a stash of chocolate-chip cookies, or indulging in a precious slice of left-over pie (if the motel has an early morning café), I watch *Dallas* or a rerun of *MASH*. Within minutes, I'm asleep.

Eat, work, sleep, repeat, the lifestyle suits me—no cooking, cleaning, or domestic duties. For the first time in my life, I am completely independent. Almost everything I own fits under the topper in the bed of my little brown Nissan pick-up. My home is the wide-open sky and ever-changing landscape.

I hike for miles in a slow, cold drizzle, searching for an elusive control point. I am disheartened when I finally discover it, right in a heap of scrap metal in some old farmer's dilapidated barn. When I climb to the highest peak, I am elated when it reveals an intact U.S.G.S. marker, and unobstructed views for miles.

Rivers and streams, even a murky green cattle trough on occasion, quench my thirst during unbearably scorching summer treks. In a moment of respite, my arms pillow my head under a lonely shade tree. I watch wispy-white clouds drift across a cerulean sky. I relish these moments. In the winter, stalactites of snot dangle from my nose. In between shots, I pull elbow-length mittens over my fingerless wool gloves to prevent frostbite. Arctic Sorrels, silk long-johns, and insulated Carhartt coveralls ward off hypothermia. It is hell to pee.

In 1986, the oil exploration boom is ending. When my crew, 1741, shuts down, my survey partner, B.C., and I are transferred to seismograph crew 1750, currently stationed in Plentywood, Montana.

***

B.C., a grizzled, gray-haired ex-hippie, leans against our company pick-up truck. Emblazoned on the door is a map of the world, and our logo, G.S.I., a subsidiary of Texas Instruments. Taking a nervous swig from his constant companion—a thermos of strong, black coffee, B.C. scans the quickly darkening horizon. His brows furrow in concern. Ominous black

clouds churn overhead. They threaten the late afternoon sun hanging low over the desolate, wide-open plains of northeastern Montana.

We race the impending early spring storm, and I hurry to set up over my final turn-point. I stomp one leg of the weathered yellow tripod firmly into the rock-strewn pasture, then fasten my instrument securely to the plate. I dance with the other two legs until the theodolite is positioned over the point. Stepping on the legs, I push the tips into the ground and adjust their lengths until I gain purchase. I rotate the outer two dials of the instrument with my thumbs, and the third dial with my forefinger. I center the bubble. The T2 is level.

A gust of wind whips my short, sun-streaked hair. Widening my stance for stability, I peer through the optics. Nearly 2 miles away, fluorescent green flagging flaps in the wind. I zero in the back-sight just as fat drops of rain splash my face. Impervious to the escalating weather, I swivel the instrument in the direction of my foresight, and scan for my target. Darkness looms as cold beads of water pelt the back of my neck. I finally spot color and finesse the dials, precisely focusing the crosshairs on my target. The wind screams across the prairie. I shout the angle, my voice nearly swallowed by the gale. B.C. records the degrees, minutes, and seconds in a soggy survey notebook. The last lingering glimmer of daylight fades while I repeat the turn two more times. My partner checks my numbers for accuracy. In the twilight, he shoots me a thumbs up.

I carefully unscrew the expensive instrument, latch it inside its padded hard-shell case, and place it safely on the floorboard of our crew-cab. Favoring his bad leg, B.C. yanks the tripod out of the ground, straps it shut, and slides it into the bed of the truck. While my partner knocks a wooden lath into the ground to designate our turn, I quickly unfurl a few arm-lengths of pink flagging. Battling the wind, I loop them around the lath and pull the knot tight. We dash for the truck just as the heavens truly let loose. With a lop-sided hop, B.C. hoists himself into the driver's seat. I ride shotgun to man the gates on our way out.

Our survey truck bounces through the muddy pasture, cutting wide ruts in our wake. The sudden storm put us in a precarious position—either we accomplish our mission or we wait days for the pasture to dry and risk losing the contract. We did our job, but our Permit Agent will probably hear from an irate rancher, after he inspects the muddy ruts left in our wake.

B.C. slows the truck and I hop out to close the last gate. Leaning my shoulder into the post, my boots search for traction in the slippery sludge. Lunging forward, I squeeze the fenceposts together and tug the wire loop over the top. The gate is secure. Before climbing back inside the cab, I rub my sloppy palms down the front of my mud-splattered jeans.

Reaching the deserted highway, we turn south towards town. The steady rain intensifies to a solid curtain of water. Even with wipers at full speed, we can barely see. B.C. drives blindly for several miles, until he gives up and pulls over at a remote, roadside dive. The neon lights flash: Raymond Bar And Grill.

Loaded with seismic cable and racks of geophones, other white G.S.I. jug trucks fill the parking lot. A few unfamiliar other rigs litter the spaces between, the crew is here. As usual, they shut down at the first smell of rain and head straight to the nearest bar.

We pull into an empty slot where B.C. parks our truck. My stomach rumbles at the smell of greasy food, reminding me that I haven't eaten since my bowl of Cheerios early this morning. We slam our cab doors simultaneously and duck, scurrying for cover. I race to the front door and wait for my partner. He hobbles behind me, dragging his bad leg. My eyes light up when I notice the red Ford truck parked in the lot. I bite my lower lip and smother a smile. He's here.

B.C. and I find a secluded corner and order burgers and fries. Smoke hovers below the dim lights, and Bob Seger blasts from the jukebox. The entire jug line crowds around the bar, all male, geophone placement technicians. Glass bottles bang. Crude jokes bounce around the room, chased by raucous laughter. By the looks of some of the juggies, the crew has been here awhile.

I immediately spot him—smooth tan skin, feathered blonde hair layered to his shoulders, and cool blue eyes. His buddies are a tall, scruffy redhead, and a curly-haired teddy bear of a man, and they straddle bar stools on either side.

My partner and I inhale our meals in comfortable silence. I wipe a trail of grease from my chin with a napkin and swipe my last fry through a puddle of ketchup. If the rain continues, tomorrow will be a rare day off. Our crew works 7 days a week, so rain days are highly coveted. We can do laundry. My mud-caked clothes certainly need it.

As I walk towards the cashier to pay my bill, I notice the blue-eyed blonde still at the bar with his buddies. I pause to pull a wad of cash out of the front pocket of my button-fly 501 Levi's. I live strictly off my weekly cash per diem, known as a hotshot. My paychecks go straight to the bank for deposit in my hometown, Hays, Kansas. The only withdrawals that come out of the account are for my truck payment and mortgage.

A year ago, I purchased a cozy one-bedroom fixer-upper farmhouse with an attic and a few out-buildings on a couple of acres. It sits on a quiet, tree-lined hill a few miles south of Hays. When I'm home on break, I have my own private retreat where I can hang out and tinker with home-improvement projects. It is my someday place. Someday, I will be ready to give up this nomadic, seismic lifestyle. Someday, I will be ready to grow up and settle down. Not yet.

Tonight, the rain patters on the metal roof. The possibility of a day off, and the tan, quiet towhead remind me of those somedays.

I turn to B.C. "You go on ahead. I think I'll stay for a bit." I nod towards the jug crew milling around the bar. "I'll catch a ride into town later."

B.C. raises his eyebrows, then cracks a smile. He offers a wink.

"Don't worry, I'll be fine," I assure him. "I'll see you in the morning. Unless it rains," I add, returning the smile.

B.C. limps to the survey truck. I mount the lone empty stool at the end

of the bar, hooking the heels of my muddy work boots over the bottom rung. My nose flares at the sharp tang of testosterone mingled with crusty clothes, sloshing beer, and second hand smoke. Although I blend in seamlessly with my fellow workers in the room, I am the only woman. I run my fingers through my short, damp hair and tuck a few loose strands behind my ears. The burly bartender moseys over and I order a Coke.

"She needs a fuzzy navel!" Someone hollers from the crowd, and laughter ensues. I smirk, accustomed to the crude humor of the seismic crew. I assume it is just another sexual innuendo.

Instead of the soda, a tall fruity concoction slides my way. It takes me a moment to realize that my drink is the fuzzy navel they referred to. It smells like orange juice, so I tentatively take a taste. Across the hazy room, I watch the sun-tanned blonde maneuver to the jukebox, faded blue jeans tight across his narrow hips. I see him punch in a selection, and Stevie Nicks and Don Henley croon "Leather and Lace." Nursing my drink, I pay attention to the lyrics for the very first time.

The next time I dare look, the blue-eyed blonde has disappeared. Cigarette smoke burns my throat. My eyes water. The surging bass beat of the next song pounds in my ears. What was I thinking? I'll always be just one of the guys. Slipping off my stool, I quietly escape out the door to the covered patio. Surrounded by a waterfall of rain, I inhale a deep lungful of clean, cool fresh air.

A gunshot of thunder cracks, nearly sending my fuzzy navel crashing to the floor. As a child in Kansas, I had witnessed plenty of thunderstorms, but never a crash like this. Reverberations shake the building. A flash of lightning ignites the night sky. For an instant, darkness bursts into daylight. A second gunshot booms. Fireworks explode across the horizon. Illuminated webs weave heaven with Earth. Mesmerized, I shiver in the damp, chilly air.

A warm jacket slides across my shoulders. I turn away from the spectacle, and into eyes the color of a clear blue mountain lake. Goosebumps ripple through me.

The blonde hairs on our arms stand erect, but we are barely touching. We are electrified.

The Storytellers

Marylor Wilson is 84 years old, and currently lives in Missoula. Born in Billings, she also lived in Helena, Bozeman, and spent a year in Paris. She received a bachelor's degree in French from the University of Montana. She is inclined to be writing whenever she has a pencil and a piece of paper handy. She has two darling daughters, and three darling granddaughters.

Dolly Browder retired from her practice as a Licensed Midwife after attending home births for 37 years in western Montana. She resides with her husband in Missoula. Their two daughters live and work in New York City. Dolly occasionally works as an expert witness in midwifery cases, is a docent for a local museum, practices yoga five days a week, rides her bike whenever possible, and travels the world.

Elke Govertsen was born in Missoula, Montana, raised in Alaska, zinged around the world and has come full circle back to Missoula. She founded Mamalode magazine because she believes story is everything. She unabashedly loves her teenagers. And Keith Richards.

Jenn Ewan co-founded the law firm Sova, PLLC, which works with startups, entrepreneurs, and innovative companies of all shapes and sizes on corporate and employment law matters. Born in Bozeman, she spent her early childhood on a ranch near Three Forks, and graduated high school from Troy, Montana. She lives in Missoula with her two kids, and until taking the memoir class that inspired her piece, thought law school had beat the creativity out of her writing.

Mara Panich is a writer, artist, and bookseller in Missoula, Montana. She holds a BA in Creative Writing and English from Purdue University and completed post-graduate studies at the University of Montana. Her work has been published in *CutBank Online*, *The Missoulian*, *The B'K*, and is forthcoming in several anthologies.

Jessica Bruinsma is originally from Colorado, and moved to Missoula in 2003. She has lived in Montana for the better part of the last sixteen years, and now resides in Columbia Falls. She fell in love with the mountains and people here early on, and has no intention of leaving anytime soon.

Former healthcare administrator Victoria Emmons relocated to Missoula from the San Francisco Bay Area in 2015 to be near family. Then the family moved to Arizona; but Victoria was hooked on Montana, where she continues to find inner peace writing poetry, short stories and a novel. Her work appears in several anthologies and at www.rueSleidan.com.

Julie Janj lives in a crumbling hotel and works in a crumbling building in

Missoula. She volunteers for people who don't care for her, which is just the way she likes it. She also likes being on time, being polite, and following through, three things she demands of all her consorts.

Originally from New Mexico, Emily Withnall now teaches and writes in Missoula, Montana. Her work has appeared in *GAY Magazine*, *Tin House*, *The Kenyon Review*, *Greetings from Janeland* (Cleis Press, 2017), *The Rumpus*, *Orion*, *Indiana Review*, and *Ms. Magazine*, among others. She is the recipient of the Kurt Brown AWP Award and the Barbara Deming Memorial Fund and she is a writing fellow with Center for Community Change. Her work can be read at emilywithnall.com.

Hannah Bourke is an artist and songwriter living in Northern California. She lives with her white rabbit, Villanelle, whom she found wild on the streets of East Missoula. She still yells "Gospe!" whenever it feels right.

Jessica Fuller resides on her 20 acre homestead north of Eureka, Montana, with her mother, daughter, son-in-law, and various pets. She started writing her memoir in the winter of 2018 with encouragement from Richard Fifield and fellow writers in the Eureka area. In addition, she enjoys going for nature walks, making beaded jewelry, camping, hiking and spending time with family.

Aimee McQuilkin lives in Missoula with her cats and dogs and teenage daughters. Exploring gravel roads in the saddle of her bike or the wheel house of her land cruiser are her favorites. Old men and Korean food aren't so bad, either. Aimee learned the definition of irony in her sophomore English class and never looked back.

Robin O'Day studied Creative Writing at the Davidson Honors College at the University of Montana, before completing her degree at San Francisco State University. She is an alum of the Michael Chekhov Theatre Company in New York City and was an anchor and journalist at the CBS affiliate station, KPAX. She lives in Missoula with her husband and two daughters.

Kirsten Holland is a nonprofit development manager. She's currently writing the story of a remarkable dog named Bug. Kirsten and her husband live in Eureka with their pack of rescued dogs and cats, horses, and a mule named Clarence.

Ame Boyce is a true Montana badass. As far as she knows, she comes from a long line of heretics, comedians and cowpokes. When she isn't spending time with one small boy, two large dogs, and one gorgeous husband, she is teaching boxing or drinking wine.

Sharma Shields is the author of a short story collection, *Favorite Monster*, and two novels, *The Sasquatch Hunter's Almanac* and *The Cassandra*. She graduated from the University of Montana's MFA program in 2004. She lives in Spokane, Washington.

Jaime Alexis Stathis was born on the east coast, but grew up in Montana where she was raised by a human in a dog suit. She now lives in the Sierra Nevada foothills of Northern California with her partner, Martin, a dog in a human suit, if there ever was one. She is currently working on a memoir about her grandmother, a love story titled *Don't Tell Me What To Do*.

Joyce Hocker loves her life in Missoula where she mentors younger therapists, teaches life writing in the Montana Osher Lifelong Learning Program, volunteers at the progressive and inclusive University Congregational Church, and reads late into the night, her cat Lonestar on her lap. She is the author of *The Trail To Tincup: Love Stories At Life's End*, and *Interpersonal Conflict*, now in its tenth edition.

Alena Gostnell was born in Conrad, Montana, but raised between Shelby and Libby. She currently lives in Missoula.

After spending her early childhood in Oregon, Teresa Lundy's parents moved her and her siblings to northwest Montana in the early 1980s, where her father worked as a logger. She stayed in Montana for more than twenty years before moving back home to Oregon to become an Industrial Safety Consultant, working mainly with loggers. A member of the Confederated Tribes of Siletz Indians, Teresa resides in Corvallis, Oregon, where she enjoys her life with her friends, family, and especially her dogs, Bean and Otis.

Gleaning lessons from a long life of community activism and teaching, Gladys Considine writes of real people, family, work, play, love, life and death. Starting on a remote sheep ranch in Powder River County, then to Washington, DC, and back to Missoula, the journey has brought her to a good life mentored and guided by ordinary, everyday women. Having time to write is only one privilege of becoming an older woman.

Audrey Koehler Peterson has lived in Missoula for 69 of her 74 years, with time out to be born in Helena, to work briefly at the Pillsbury Company in Minneapolis, Minnesota, and to complete a graduate degree at Pennsylvania State University. As an alumnus and a Professor Emeritus of the University of Montana, most of her waking hours for 42 of those Missoula years have been spent at the foot of Mount Sentinel on the UM campus. Adding to that good fortune, she married Lorin Peterson, a home-town boy, and her children Ross and Amy also live in Missoula with their families.

Ashley Rhian is a fifth-generation Montanan, born in Billings, and raised in Missoula, where she resides with her husband, son, and dog. The titles she holds closest to her heart are photographer, author, wife, mother, daughter, athlete, and survivor. She loves to eat trashy food, be outside in the summer, spend time with her family, and travel.

Jane Peterson currently lives outside Missoula. A Montana native, she was born in Helena and lived in Great Falls and Fort Benton before going to college in New Orleans to pursue her dream of teaching in higher education. In 2014, she retired from a university in suburban New Jersey and returned to her home state after 49 years to build three connected yurts in the woods with her partner, Eileen.

Beth Cogswell grew up in Great Falls, Montana and Boise, Idaho, and has lived in Missoula for over 30 years. She holds degrees in English Literature and Journalism. Beth has served in leadership roles for several non-profit organizations, in the fields of women's health, the environment, and child welfare. She and her husband Rick have two teenaged sons, Finn and Sam.

Jessica Spears earned a Master's Degree in Education from Montana State University in Billings. She has served as a stay at home mom for children with special needs for the past thirteen years, and is the author of the blog www.spearsfamily-project.blogspot.com. She lives in Missoula, with her husband and three children, two of whom have Autism diagnoses.

Sav Shopay was born and raised in Utah, but a heart for adventure has taken her all over the country. In addition to writing, she is also an avid hiker, horsewoman, and disability advocate. She currently lives in Phoenix, Arizona with her dog, Ethel.

Sarah Aronson is a Montanan by way of Alaska. Her debut collection of poems, *And Other Bodiless Powers*, won the 2018 New American Poetry Prize. She is also the host of the Montana Public Radio literary program and podcast, *The Write Question*.

Emily Johnson grew up in Los Angeles, and moved to Missoula, Montana when she was eighteen, to study creative writing at the University of Montana. In her downtime, if she's not writing screenplays, doing stand-up comedy, or hosting a garden party, she's probably hiking a mountain (very slowly). She's still learning how to move through this difficult and unforgiving world, but she has great friends to navigate it with.

Shelly Carney is the mother of two sons (ages 33 and 23), one deceased daughter (who would be 29 today) and grandmother to one granddaughter, age 4. She volunteers with Missoula's Open Aid Alliance and Emma's Exchange. Open Aid Alliance coordinates and schedules Shelly's public speaking events.

Chelsia Rice lives in Helena, Montana with Charlie Crawford, her partner of 15 years. Together, they own and operate Montana Book Company in downtown Helena, and strive to provide a safe space in the bookstore for all, but especially at-risk teens.

Jenn Grunigen currently lives in Eugene, Oregon, with her dog Vixa and two fig trees. She is a writer, drummer, and comic book editor. Vixa enjoys grass and would like to be a cow when she grows up; the fig trees have yet to decide on a career path.

Cynthia Aten is a retired pediatrician and former Chief of Undergraduate Medicine at Yale University Health Services. She grew up in North Carolina, started her family in Cincinnati, lived for 34 years in New Haven, and chose Missoula while listening to Kim Williams on NPR in the 1980s. Though it took more than 20 years to make it happen, she has been a Montanan since 2004.

Jain Walsh works as a crime victim's rights attorney serving clients all over rural Montana. She is passionate about providing underserved and marginalized people with access to justice. In her free time, Jain enjoys traveling, dancing, hands-on projects, and making mixed tapes.

Tamara Love is a writer, teacher and lover of the arts. She's a fan of rivers, lakes and oceans. She has an MFA in creative writing from the University of Montana and lives in Missoula, Montana.

Leisa Greene is currently on a fourth edit of her memoir, *Early Out*—a story of a mother's coming-of-age as her two gay sons come out in a conservative Mormon community. Her other writing consists of: "Windshield," featured in *Bright Bones: Contemporary Montana Writing*; the short online essays "Brother Townsend" and "A Jamboree Family;" and playwrighting "The Beckett Syndrome." Leisa was born in Butte, lives in Missoula, and holds a BA in creative writing from the University of Montana.

Claudia Sanders Brown, from Butte, has lived around western Montana and mostly in Missoula with her forester husband, who is now in the Great Beyond, and three children, who are now in their fifties. She has four grandchildren. She has been a preschool teacher, hiker, photographer, gardener, and is now a busy environmentalist.

Lisa Hunt currently resides in Missoula, and holds a BA in Native American Studies from the University of Montana. She volunteers for domestic abuse programs, as well as her local church, and advocates for the empowerment of people in need and environmental issues. She enjoys traveling to visit family and friends, and exploring nature with her three children.

Kelley Provost is a proud native Missoulian. By occupation, she calls herself a homemaker, stand-up comic, Dragon Boat racer, and survivor. She loves love, and her life's greatest joy is seeing humans being kind to one another.

Pam Truman earned degrees in Science and Music Education from Fort Hays State University in Kansas. She lives in Eureka, Montana, with her husband Lyle, a native Montanan. Their three grown children—Amanda, Luke, and Laura encouraged her to share her stories.

# Acknowledgments

✳

We leave the flowers where they are. This anthology is a collection of stories from women across Big Sky Country, and like those wildflowers in the title poem, they have bloomed into beautiful, unforgettable things. My hope is that they will be allowed to spread. My hope is that they will be passed on, seeds scattered, and allowed to take root in the lives of any woman seeking solace, joy, or inspiration. Every woman has a story of their own, and may this book offer hope and strength to anyone willing to share their particular truth.

This book would not be possible without Amber Boyce, my partner in all things. Thank you to the male students in our memoir classes; I appreciate your support and your kindness, and most of all, your words. David Queen and Word West were incredibly patient and made this book absolutely gorgeous. I'm also indebted to the sensational women who helped edit these submissions—Sav, Beth, Pam, Victoria and Sarah. Thank you to the places that hosted our memoir classes: Sunburst Arts in Eureka, The Osher Lifelong Learning Institute at the University of Montana, the Zootown Arts Community Center, and every woman who offered up her living room. Personal thanks to Kathy Springmeyer, John Rimel, Aaron Parrett, Mary Baker-Johnson, Mike Young, Lucy Hansen, Frank Casciato, Nina Alviar, Tess and Sam from the Montana Book Festival, Kim Anderson, Kia Liszak, Heather Stockton, Cassandra Sevigny, Sally Thompson, Rita Collins (And St. Rita's Amazing Traveling Bookstore and Texual Apothecary), and the nurses and doctors at Cabinet Peaks Medical Center in Libby, Montana.

I'd also like to thank the non-profit organizations that have partnered with us at our events in public libraries: Women's Opportunity And Resource Development in Missoula, Safe Space in Butte, The Friendship Center and the YWCA in Helena, the YWCA in Great Falls, and Haven in Bozeman. It is my hope that this book and these writers may travel to every public library in Montana, in conjunction with the women's advocacy groups in each and every town. Knowledge is power, and local resources are invaluable.

This anthology emerged from five years of teaching memoir classes. My own life has been forever changed by witnessing the bravery of these writers, and I did my best to get out of the way and offer up a safe space. It has been the biggest honor of my life to be entrusted with these stories, and I hope readers everywhere will find themselves in these pages, and not feel alone or ashamed. You are seen, and you are heard. May these stories bring you hope and strength and courage.

Thank you for supporting these authors, and Humanities Montana and the Zootown Arts Community Center. I am so very proud of these women, and it has been my privilege to unleash their voices into the universe. May this be the beginning of a revolution, of wildflowers popping up in the most unlikely of places. May every woman be allowed to grow and bloom and inspire, and most of all, realize that their story matters.

Yours,
Richard Fifield